Lost Love

Book Seven in The Redstone Chronicles
J. T. Bishop

Eudoran Press LLC

Eudoran Press LLC.

6009 W. Parker Rd. #149-913

Plano, TX 75093

Book Cover by J. T. Bishop

Cover photos by dundanim, Dmitri bakulov, svetograph

Lost Love/First Edition 2024

ISBN eBook 978-1-955370-58-5

ISBN Paperback 978-1-955370-63-9

ISBN Hardback 978-1-955370-69-1

To the future. May there be lots to be thankful for.

Other Books by J. T. Bishop

Chapter One

Esmerelda knocked on the door to room 520. "Housekeeping." She listened for a response but didn't hear one. She knocked again and spoke a little louder. "Housekeeping." She pulled her universal key card on the lanyard around her neck, swiped it across the reader, and opened the door. She poked her head in. "Housekeeping."

Seeing the unmade bed and used towels on the floor of the bathroom, but no one in the room, she pushed the door open and walked inside. The floor was littered with dirty clothes and the small table in the room was covered with fast-food bags and wrappers. She'd seen much worse, though, and picked up the towels and tossed them outside the bathroom. After grabbing her cleaning tools from her cart in the hallway, she wiped down and disinfected the bathroom counters and shower and mopped the floor. Once the bathroom was clean, she moved into the bedroom. Picking up the clothes from the floor and the bed, she tossed them into a chair beside the table with the fast-food trash.

Stripping the sheets from the bed, she thought of the resident occupying room 518, which she'd just cleaned. Smiling to herself, she recalled bumping into him two days ago, and her heart thumped. He was a handsome man, who was about twenty years younger than her, had a wicked smile and magnetic charm. He'd been wearing a cowboy hat and boots, and a long-sleeved shirt tucked into jeans that emphasized his firm butt. Esmerelda blushed just thinking about him. She had seen him before, but yesterday had been her first chance to talk to him.

He'd been friendly and flirty, as if he knew how to speak to women, especially those who were older than him and who tended to get less male attention, particularly if they worked in the hospitality industry. He'd asked for her name, and he had given his. Trick Monroe, he'd told her, and he'd shaken her hand and thanked her for her hard work. Customers rarely acknowledged housekeeping staff, so Mr. Monroe's kindness remained with her throughout her shift, and she'd hoped to see him again, but so far, she hadn't. Not that she expected anything from him, but just the thought of a brief flirtation excited her. She hoped he wasn't checking out anytime soon.

She remade the beds with clean sheets and dropped the dirty ones into the pile of towels on the floor. Being in Vegas, to preserve the valuable but diminishing resource of water, the hotel towels and sheets were no longer washed each night, but when guests requested fresh linens, which this one had, Housekeeping complied.

After finishing with the beds, she collected the trash, dumped it into the can beside the table, and pulled the bag from the can to throw it away when she heard a knock. Holding the trash bag, she turned and saw a man standing just at the threshold of the door. For a moment, she thought it was Mr. Monroe, but hid her disappointment when she saw it wasn't. The man was tall and well-built like Trick, but had darker hair, a narrower face, and he didn't exude the same charm and charisma.

"Excuse me," he said. "I'm sorry to bother you."

Smiling as she'd been taught to do when interacting with a customer, she stepped toward the door. "Yes?" She knotted the bag of trash.

He shook his head and offered her a sheepish look. "I'm afraid I've gone and locked myself out of my room. I thought I had my keycard, but I guess I don't. Could you open my door by chance? All I need to do is grab my card. It won't take but a sec." He pointed. "I'm just down the hall. Do you mind? I'd go to reception downstairs, but I'm in a hurry." He pursed his lips when she hesitated. "Please?"

Esmerelda's training included not opening doors for anyone, no matter how desperate a guest may appear. There'd been too many thefts and complaints when unsuspecting staff had opened up rooms for people who'd lied about why they were there. As much as she wanted to help, she couldn't. "I'm sorry. We're not allowed to. I can call reception, though, and let them know. Maybe they can send someone up." She reached for the phone attached to a belt on her hip. "It shouldn't take long."

He glanced at her nametag. "Esmerelda, is it?" He took a step toward her. "Pretty name."

Holding the phone, a sliver of concern made her stomach tighten. It didn't escape her that she was in a room by herself with a strange man at the door. Her friend Suni was cleaning down the hall. One good scream would alert her that Esmerelda needed help.

He stopped and held up his hands. "Sorry. I hope I'm not scaring you. I completely understand why you can't open my door." He paused but made no effort to back away. "There's no need to call reception. I'll just head out and stop at the front desk on my way back in. Thank you for your help."

Esmerelda released a relieved breath when it seemed he was about to leave. "Thanks for understanding."

He smiled and nodded, but then narrowed his eyes and stared at her. "Is that onyx?"

Esmerelda touched the stone hanging from her neck. It had been a birthday gift from a good friend, and Esmerelda wore it frequently. "Yes. It is."

"It's beautiful." He leaned closer and took another step. "I hope you don't mind. I'm a fan of jewelry, especially unique gemstones. Where did you get it?"

Esmerelda glanced down at the stone, surprised he thought it was anything special. It was only a small stone wrapped in sterling silver. "My friend gave it to—"

He reached and took her wrist, and before she could react, or even attempt to scream, a strange fluidity rushed through her. Her heart rate soared, her limbs became heavy, and her mind went blank. She blinked and tried to speak, but couldn't. Her knees buckled and he took her in his arms before she could fall to the floor.

"I'm sorry, Esmerelda," he said, lowering her to the ground, "but I need your help. I promise it's for a good cause."

Terrified, but unable to move, Esmerelda fought to struggle or yell, but all she could do was blink. She prayed that once he let go of her, he would take her money or jewelry and leave, but when he straightened, his features blurred and changed shape. She blinked again several times, unsure of what she was seeing. The man slowly transformed in front of her. The contours of his face softened and changed. His torso and legs became shorter, and his clothes morphed into a beige skirt and shirt similar to her own, including her nametag. His short hair grew longer and darker and, shocked, she realized she was looking back at herself. Esmerelda didn't understand. The man had turned into her. Was she looking into a mirror? Had whatever he'd done caused her to hallucinate? It had to be, because there was no other explanation.

The man, who was now her, smoothed his hair and the pockets of his uniform and smiled. He unclipped Esmerelda's keycard from her lanyard and held it up. "Exactly what I needed. Thank you." He even sounded like her. Looking satisfied, he stepped away. "You don't mind if I borrow your cart, do you? I just need to check the room next door. It won't take long." Moving around the trash and pile of linens, he walked out the door. Before closing it, he leaned in. "You rest well now."

Seeing him shut the door, Esmerelda swallowed. She tried again to move, but that same heavy fluidity traveled to her face and eyelids, and closing her eyes, she lost consciousness.

Chapter Two

Trick Monroe nursed a beer at the hotel bar. It was still early, and he rarely drank at this time of the day, but after his frustrating week, he felt the need to indulge. Wiping some beer from his lip, he reviewed his actions since he'd arrived in Vegas, wondering what he'd missed.

While still in Texas, and just before returning to San Diego, Trick had received a call from Lindsey's father, Ben, telling him Lindsey was in trouble. After hearing the details and the fear in Ben's voice, Trick had changed his flight out to San Diego to the first flight to Vegas. All he knew was what Ben had told him—that an enemy of the Cryptid Unit, or the CU, the secret organization Ben and his family were members of, was on the loose, and he'd set his sights on Lindsey, who'd left San Diego abruptly and disappeared to Vegas.

She'd called Trick in Texas before Trick had spoken to Ben. She'd been barely coherent. Her call had surprised Trick because she'd never been the type to get drunk and reveal her vulnerable side. She'd always been a brash, tough and confident woman who didn't take shit from anyone, least of all Trick. And despite their obvious attraction to each other, and Trick's attempts to get to know her better, Lindsey had refused any suggestion that they become romantically involved.

Before talking to Ben, Trick had figured out enough to assume a troubled previous relationship was the reason for her inebriated state, but after her unexpected phone call, it became clear there was more to it than just a broken heart. And whatever had happened, it was messing with Lindsey's head. Enough that she'd disappeared to Vegas without telling anyone. She didn't have her phone, and she wouldn't talk to her family. And now she was somewhere in the city, drowning her sorrows in copious amounts of booze, unaware of the danger she was in.

Taking another sip of his beer, Trick sighed. The moment after he'd landed, he'd grabbed his bag, found a reasonably priced motel off the strip, and had started looking. He'd flashed Lindsey's photo everywhere, but no one recognized her, and it didn't take long to realize his problem. Trying to find an attractive woman who was hitting the bars in Vegas was like trying to find a piece of straw in a bale of hay. There were too many to count.

After talking to Ben again, who still hadn't heard from Lindsey and who'd sent his son Garret to Vegas to help with the search, Trick realized he was going to have to take a different approach. Garret, who Trick assumed was already in Vegas and also searching, had not reached out to Trick, which didn't surprise him. After meeting Garret and Lindsey's family and learning who they were and what they did, Garret had shown Trick nothing but hostility. Trick guessed why. He didn't want his sister to get hurt again. It was an understandable concern. Trick's ladies' man image had done him no favors.

After Trick's first few days of failing to find Lindsey, his new tactic took him to the Vegas police department, where he'd filed a missing person's report. He wondered why nobody had done it sooner but realized that none of them had guessed Lindsey would stay gone this long, and even if she had, that either Trick or Garret would find her. Apparently, though, when Lindsey didn't want to be found, she knew how to hide. Rubbing his face, Trick didn't want to think of the alternative—that the enemy had already found Lindsey, and she might be dead.

Trick took comfort that his friend Mason, who'd gone home to San Diego with his sister Mikey after leaving Texas, had told him he didn't sense Lindsey had joined the spirit world. And being the reliable medium and paranormal investigator that Trick knew Mason Redstone to be, Trick believed him.

Filing the police report had helped little, but according to the friendly rookie officer named Samantha Novak, who Trick had given his report to, things like this usually resolved themselves. Missing people, especially those who came to Vegas to drown their sorrows, eventually went home. Trick couldn't tell Sam Novak that Lindsey and her family were part of a clandestine group that sought and studied cryptids and hunted those that endangered humans. Trick had encountered a couple of nasty ones, and he shuddered at the memories. If it hadn't been for Lindsey's fighting skills, her mental toughness, and unwavering courage and duty, Trick would've been in a grave and not drinking his current beer.

Taking the last gulp, he set his glass down and ate a few nuts from a bowl on the bar. That morning, he'd gone to a different section of the strip, but had no luck finding Lindsey or anyone who'd seen her. He'd given up and had headed back to the police station, where he'd found and spoken to Sam Novak again. She'd told him that there had been no updates on Lindsey, but the report had gone out to their officers in the field, and she'd be in touch with Trick if she heard anything.

Trick had to wonder how seriously Sam Novak had taken him. When he'd made the report, Trick had used his customary charm as he often did when talking with women, and Sam Novak was no exception. If he hadn't been so worried about Lindsey, he might have made more of an effort with Novak. Her round green eyes, full eyebrows and lips, and long auburn hair she'd pulled back into a tight bun, which only accentuated the curve of her cheekbones, would normally send him into full flirt mode. But he got the sense she'd experienced plenty of men's overly friendly behavior in the past and wouldn't tolerate more. Trick was sure she suspected he was either a lovesick boyfriend looking for a girlfriend who'd left him, or worse, an abusive lover who planned to bring the woman who'd scorned him back home. Trick didn't care what Novak thought as long as she and her colleagues searched for Lindsey.

After his visit with Novak, and deciding he needed to think, Trick returned to his hotel room to splash some water on his face and get some lunch. When he'd arrived at his room, he'd bumped into the friendly housekeeper, Esmerelda, again. Her cart had been in the hall, and he'd greeted her as she'd left his room, but she'd been more subdued today, and had acted surprised that he'd spoken to her. Guessing she was having a rough day, he'd gone into his room and hadn't thought more about it.

After getting cleaned up and feeling a little fresher, he'd returned to the lobby, planning to eat, but seeing the bar, he detoured, and ended up ordering his beer instead. Now staring at the bowl of peanuts, he wondered again what to do. Searching the various hotels and bars was getting him nowhere. There had to be a better way. He picked up his phone and willed Lindsey to call him again. If he could talk to her, he could tell her the danger she was in, and then, logically, she would come out of hiding. She'd made one phone call to Trick since the one in Texas, but he'd been in the shower, and she'd left a message, telling him not to worry, that she was still in Vegas, and to tell her family she'd return when she was ready.

When Trick heard it, he'd almost thrown his cell out the window in frustration. He'd tried to call her back, but a fast-food restaurant had answered, and Trick had hung up. No matter where he was now, he kept his phone close by. He'd gone to the fast-food place, though, to check it out, but no one there could help him locate Lindsey.

Setting his phone down, Trick groaned and wondered again what had sent Lindsey into a spiral. Ben wouldn't tell him the details, insisting it was Lindsey's story to tell. But he told Trick that he suspected Lindsey would return after the next three days, assuming no one had found her before then.

Trick wondered about the significance of the three days and assumed that whatever haunted Lindsey had occurred around this time, and as the anniversary of that unknown event neared, Lindsey had gone into her tail-spin. Ben hadn't admitted that, but hadn't denied it either. Ben also hadn't denied that the closer they came to the anniversary, the more dangerous it became. Did this enemy plan to take his revenge on the same day that Lindsey dreaded? Had he found her and was just biding his time? Had Trick already failed? Discouraged by his lack of information and progress, Trick ran his hands through his hair and groaned.

A snort beside him made him straighten, and he glanced over when a man slid onto the stool next to him. Trick widened his eyes when he recognized Lindsey's brother, Garret.

Tall, broad-shouldered, and handsome, like his dad, Garret glared at him. "I should have known I'd find you sitting at a bar, drinking." He snorted again. "I always knew you were a loser." He reached for the bowl of peanuts. "And when I find my sister, I'm going to make sure she knows it."

Chapter Three

Trick debated his responses. Several came to mind, but he chose the high road, since he guessed Garret had to be as worried about Lindsey as he was. "Nice to see you, Garret. How'd you know I was here?"

Garret's sneer remained. "We've known your location since you arrived."

Trick eyed his phone on the counter. "You're tracking me?"

"We're part of a covert operation looking for one of our own. Of course, we're tracking you. If you find her, we need to know where you are."

"If I found her, I'd tell you where we were."

"We don't assume anything, Monroe, and neither should you. You have no idea what you've gotten yourself into."

Trick picked up on Garret's anger. It was hard to miss. "You're mad your dad brought me in, aren't you?"

"None of this situation is your concern."

Trick swiveled to face Garret. "If it wasn't for Lindsey calling me, you wouldn't even know she was in Vegas. I'm the reason you're here."

"We'd have figured it out. And if it had been up to me, I'd have told you she was in Vegas for a Bachelorette party and left it at that."

"But it wasn't up to you. And Lindsey contacted me. Not you. Why do you think that is?"

Garret scowled.

"Maybe because she doesn't want to talk to her family?"

"Leave it alone, Monroe."

"Leave what alone? Your sister came here to get away from something, or at least try to. What is it none of you want to talk about, and she refuses to discuss?"

Garret's jaw tightened. "That's between our family." He narrowed his eyes at Trick. "Of which you are not."

"If it's between family, then why can't Lindsey talk to hers? Why did she call me?"

Garret's tone sharpened. "She called because she knew Dad would contact you, and he would trace the number she called you from to Vegas. It was her roundabout way of letting us know where she was without talking to us. You were a means to an end. That's it."

"Maybe, but I think it was more than that. She needed to talk and was drunk enough to call the person she wanted to speak with, which was me. Not you. And not your dad."

"Exactly. She was drunk. Everyone does stupid shit when they're drunk."

"What's your excuse then, because you look sober to me?" Taking the high road could only last so long.

Garret snorted. "Go home, Monroe. I'll take it from here."

"Have you found her?"

Garret scoffed. "Not yet. But I will."

Trick swiveled back toward the bar. "No, you won't. Lindsey knows you too well. She knows where you'll look."

"You think because you've been through a couple of near misses with her that you suddenly know her?" He snickered. "You don't know shit. Is she even aware you're in Vegas looking for her?"

Trick sighed with frustration. "Not that I'm aware."

"And you've still come up short." He made a sarcastic chuckle. "Guess you're not the hero you want her to think you are."

Trick's impatience flared. "Sounds to me like she needs a hero right now." The bartender asked Trick if he wanted another drink. Trick shook his head and asked for the bill. "And since she called me, and not you, I'm going to do what I can to help her out of whatever mess she's in." He pulled out his wallet. "And if she really is in the terrible trouble that Ben implies, I'd think you'd want as many people out here looking for her as you can get, Garret." He pulled out his credit card. "Unless, of course, you'd rather be the one to find her, which means assuming the risk that you'll be too late, and she'll end up dead." He dropped his card on the counter.

Garret's face twisted. "If you understood what the hell you were talking—"

Trick smacked his hand on the bar. "What I'm talking about? If you're so worried about Lindsey, then tell me what I'm missing. Who's after her? Why is she in danger? What should I be looking for?"

Garret looked away.

The bartender returned with the bill, and Trick gave him his card. "Exactly. You and your family are too busy keeping secrets. That's fine. But in the meantime, Lindsey needs help, and you're so caught up in your own ego, you can't accept the assistance that you and your sister need." He pointed at himself. "I'm not here for accolades or fist bumps, Garret. I want to find your sister and make sure she's safe, and I know you want the same. Once we do that, then you can hate me all you want. I don't care."

Garret didn't ease up on his hard stare. "You don't fool me for one second, Monroe. I know your type. If I thought you were here for the right reasons, I'd tell you everything. But I know what you want." His gaze traveled over Trick. "You're a player. And once you wear her down and get her into bed, you'll be gone. You don't care about Lindsey any more than you care about the last woman you slept with, whose name I suspect you don't even remember. And if that means I have to personally escort you out of Vegas, then I will. I'm not just here to protect her from the bad guy. I'm here to protect her from you, too."

Fed up, Trick slid off the stool. "What's between me and your sister is none of your concern, but I can assure you of one thing. Your sister can take care of herself and doesn't need you to protect her from anything, least of all me. And I am not here to make things worse for her. I'm here because Ben asked me to come. And until somebody can explain to me what the hell is going on, and can convince me I'm not needed, my butt's not leaving Vegas." The bartender returned and slid the credit card and receipt back to Trick. Trick leaned over to sign it. "And for the record, her name was Juliana." He put his credit card in his wallet and slid it into his pocket. "You take care, Garret. Good luck in your search."

Garret slid off the stool. "Where the hell do you think you're going?"

Trick headed for the exit, with Garret behind him. "I'm going back out to look for her. Did I not make that clear?"

"Did I not make it clear that we don't need you? I'll find Lindsey on my own."

Trick walked into the lobby and a sea of slot machines, hearing their bells and whistles, and smelling a whiff of cigarette smoke. "And how's that going for you?" He turned toward Garret. "According to your dad, these next three days are crucial. Lindsey needs to be found soon, or she may not be found at all. Is that true?"

Garret stopped, and his face furrowed.

Trick bit back a curse. "Is it true or not?"

"Maybe. Maybe not."

Trick did curse then. "I don't have time for games. If you love your sister, then tell me what I'm up against."

Garret shut his mouth.

"Fine, then I'm—" He turned and stopped when he saw Officer Novak walking down a carpeted path between various machines where patrons fed their coins. Assuming she was here to see him, he stepped toward her. "Officer Novak?"

Spotting him, she frowned. "What are you doing here?"

He frowned back at her. "This is my hotel." Flashing lights at the end of the lobby caught his eye, and he noticed two police cruisers in the front driveway at the hotel entrance. Distracted by Garret and the slot machines, he'd missed them. "What's going on?"

She stepped around him. "There's been a report of an assault on the fifth floor. They sent me over to help with the canvas."

"Assault?" asked Trick, confused. "But I was just up there. My room is on the fifth floor."

"It must have happened after you left." Novak headed toward the elevators.

"Assault?" asked Garret. "What kind of assault?" He walked beside Novak along with Trick.

Trick glanced at Garret, wondering why he cared.

Novak reached the elevators and hit the Up button. "Apparently, a member of Housekeeping was found unconscious in one of the rooms. I'll know more when I get up there."

Trick thought of Esmerelda, the friendly housekeeper who'd been cleaning his room earlier. "I'm going with you. I spoke with a staff member when I was upstairs. I want to be sure she's okay."

Novak shot a look at him. "Any luck finding your friend?"

"Not yet, no," said Trick. "Any updates on your end?"

"No. Not since this morning." The elevator opened and Novak stepped on, along with Trick and Garret. She glanced at both of them. "You two don't need to follow. This is a police investigation. You need to stay out of the way."

Trick noticed the way Novak gripped her belt buckle and the tension in her shoulders. He wondered if this was her first call out in the field. "We'll stay out of your hair." He spoke to Garret. "Although I'm not sure why you're sticking around."

Garret eyed the illuminated floor numbers as they ascended. "Call it curiosity."

Figuring there was more to it than that, Trick almost asked Garret to elaborate when the elevator arrived, and the doors opened. Trick dropped his jaw when he saw the activity on his floor. Officers walked through the hallway and there was a stretcher outside the door next to his room. A uniformed female member of Housekeeping stood beside it and spoke to another uniformed woman lying on the stretcher.

Trick stepped down the hall and recognized Esmerelda as the one on the stretcher.

"Mr. Monroe," said Novak. "Stay here."

Another officer approached and tried to stop Trick. "Excuse me, sir, but you need to stay back."

Trick moved around him and approached the stretcher. "Esmerelda? Are you all right?"

The housekeeper's face was pale, and her gaze darted around the hall. She held her friend's hand in a tight grip. "Where is he?" she asked, looking around. "Is he gone?"

"Esmerelda?" asked Trick. "It's Trick Monroe from room 518. Are you okay?"

Novak spoke to the officer in the hall and walked up beside Trick. "She's the one who was assaulted. She was found unconscious."

Esmerelda's friend, whose face was as pale as Esmerelda's, spoke to Novak. "I found her in there." She pointed at the room next door to Trick's. "She kept raving about a man who looked like her. He took her hand, and she couldn't stand up."

"He looked like her?" asked Novak. "What does that mean?"

Esmerelda waved her hands and tried to sit up. "He was me. He was me."

"Esmerelda," said Trick, settling her back down on the stretcher. "How long ago did this happen after you saw me?"

Esmerelda stared at him. "See you? No. I didn't see you."

"Yes, you did. When I came up about an hour ago."

She rocked her head back and forth. "No. No. No."

"She's hallucinating," said the officer next to Novak. "We need to get her to the hospital. Novak, help Farmerton canvass the floor. Find out if there were any other incidents or reports of strange men in the hall."

Trick put his hand on Esmerelda's wrist. "Esmerelda, can you describe this man? Have you seen him before?"

Esmerelda met his gaze. "He was me. I saw him."

"What did he want?" asked Trick.

"Sir," said the officer, "they need to take her. Please, step back."

Esmerelda sputtered. "He wanted my key. To see a room."

"What room?" asked Trick, guessing a robber had attacked the house-keeper to access her keycard. "Did he say?"

Two attendants secured Esmerelda on the stretcher and started to push her down the hall.

"Next door," she said, as Trick stepped back and they moved her down the hall. Her friend stayed with her. "He was me," Esmerelda repeated. "He was me."

"The perp must have drugged her," said the officer. He eyed Trick. "You on this floor?"

"I am," said Trick, wondering about his own room.

"You should check it. Make sure everything's where it should be."

Trick nodded. "I will."

Garret stood to the side of the hall, watching but saying nothing.

Trick, watching as Esmerelda, still raving, was wheeled onto the elevator, pulled out the keycard to his room. He stepped to his door, swiped it over the reader, and entered. The officer approached. "Anything?"

While the officer held Trick's door open, Trick looked around, but everything seemed in place. "Nothing. Looks okay to me."

The officer nodded. "Okay. If that changes, let me know."

"I will."

The officer walked away but as the door closed, Garret appeared and held it open.

Trick raised a brow at Lindsey's brother. "You want to look too?"

Garret's face clouded. "We need to talk."

"I thought that's the last thing you wanted to do." Garret didn't answer and Trick swept his arm out. "You want to talk, then talk."

"Not here. Somewhere else. Pack fast because you're checking out."

Confused, Trick pursed his lips. "I am? Why?"

"Because he's found you, you idiot." He crossed his arms and stood beside the door. "Move your ass, and I'll call Dad."

Trick almost argued, but seeing Garret pull out his phone, Trick sensed now was not the time to question anything. He grabbed his duffel bag and started packing.

Chapter Four

Trick sat in the diner not far from the hotel where he'd just checked out. He ordered a cheeseburger and fries from the menu and smiled at the waitress, whose gaze traveled over him and then Garret. Garret ordered a tuna melt and a soda.

She smiled at both of them. "Coming right up, gentlemen."

Garret watched her walk away.

Trick uncurled his napkin and set his silverware on the table. "I figured you'd prefer the ladies who dance on tables instead of the ones who serve food on them."

Garret's familiar sneer returned. "Shut up, Monroe."

"It's going to be hard for us to talk if I do that."

Garret ignored him and opened his own napkin. "I'll never understand what she sees in you."

"Lindsey?"

"No, Madonna."

Trick chuckled. "We met once backstage when she was on tour. Would you like to hear about our secret escapade?"

"Do you ever stop lying?"

"I never lie when it comes to women, Garret. Do you?"

Garret's frown deepened.

"I guess that would require you to actually come out of your secret cave to meet them, which I'm guessing you rarely do, since you're so busy trying to save the world."

"Somebody's got to do it."

"You don't have to dedicate your life to it."

Garret set his jaw. "You think you know everything, don't you? You just sit on your ass wearing your stupid cowboy hat and boots, while you charm women out of their clothes, having no idea what's really going on out there."

Trick rested an elbow on the table. "I was a Texas Ranger, I work with a paranormal investigator and medium, and I've seen Lindsey in action. Believe me. I know what's going on out there."

"You've barely touched the surface."

"Then why don't you explain it to me?" Trick studied Garret and wondered if whatever had messed with Lindsey's head was messing with Garret's, too. "What don't I know?"

Garret made another derisive snort and looked out the window of the diner.

"If you're not going to talk to me, then why am I here?" asked Trick. "Who followed me to my hotel and assaulted the woman who cleaned my room?"

Garret rapped his knuckles against the table with annoyance and looked back at Trick. "He's following you."

"Who's following me? And why?"

"He's hoping you'll lead him to her. Which means he's not as smart as I thought."

The waitress arrived and set their drinks in front of them and rested her palms on the table. "You two from out of town?" she asked with a flashy smile. She wore a tight T-shirt that revealed her midriff and jeans that left little to the imagination. Her curly blonde hair spilled over her shoulders and her long sparkling earrings swung from her ears. She eyed Garret. "I give great tours."

Garret scowled at her, too. "I'm familiar with Vegas. Thanks."

Her smile fell, and she glanced at Trick.

"Sorry," Trick glanced at her name tag, "Shanna. My friend isn't very good with women. I do much better. Unfortunately, we're here on business and our time is short, but thanks for your kind offer."

"Just bring the food when it's ready," Garret uttered.

She glared at him. "Sure thing."

Watching her walk away, Trick hoped she wouldn't spit in his food after she spit in Garret's. "You really need to work on your social skills."

"I'll worry about my social skills after we find Lindsey."

Trick raised his brow. "We?"

"You know what I mean."

"No. Actually, I don't. Are we working together now? Are you going to protect me from this unknown adversary?"

"If I was certain it wouldn't risk Lindsey, I'd have left you at the hotel."

Trick's patience snapped. "Listen, I came here because I expected to learn something about who's after your sister, but if you're going to waste my time, I can get a cheeseburger somewhere else."

Garret held Trick's gaze. "He's an assassin."

His stomach tightening, Trick straightened. "What's his name?"

"We don't know his name. Dad calls him Proteus. I've called him Morphman, but prefer the more elegant title, piece of shit."

"Catchy. Why Morphman? Why Proteus?"

"Proteus, because he's a Greek sea god who can change shape. Morphman, because that's what this guy does. Morph."

Trick narrowed his eyes. "You mean like a wolf or a bat?" He recalled his encounter with the shape-shifting cryptid in the mountains and the thought of facing that again almost made him lose his appetite.

"No. Much worse and more lethal. He morphs into other people."

Trick tried to take that in. "How does he do that?"

"If I understood it, I'd tell you. His type is rare and none of us knows how they came to be. All we know is that this one has it out for us."

"Why is that?"

Garret paused. "There was another like him that was captured and studied, and when he tried to escape, he was killed."

Trick rested his elbows on the table. "Something tells me there's more to that story."

"Regardless, the one that was killed had a son who has similar abilities, and when his father died, the son set his sights on my family."

"Why your family? Did one of you kill the father?"

"No. But we were instrumental in capturing him."

"How so?"

Garret picked up his soda. "That's all I can say." He sipped his drink.

Trick debated pushing to get more information but figured that was pointless. "Why is he after Lindsey?"

"Lindsey's vulnerable because she doesn't know he's out there. We know he's active, so our defenses are up. And if he kills her, he knows it will destroy us."

Trick shifted in his seat. "Why is he active now? Where's he been all this time?"

Garret set his soda down. "Imprisoned for the last five years."

"You mean like his father?" Trick wondered what was going on. "I'm guessing this is no ordinary prison?"

Garret took another sip of his drink. "It isn't."

Guessing that was all he was going to get, Trick moved on. "Who put him there?"

Garret paused. "My family."

Trick shook his head. "Wait a minute. Your family is responsible for capturing the father of Proteus and Proteus? How'd you manage that?"

"We were assigned to capture the father, which we did. He went to prison, where he died. His son blamed us, took his revenge on us, and that's when we captured him too, and he was sent to the same prison as his father, where he escaped three weeks ago."

Trick furrowed his brow. "What do you mean by revenge? What happened?"

Garret's grip on his glass tightened. "I can't say."

"Of course you can't." Trick sensed this revenge story would reveal a lot about why Lindsey had run off and Garret carried so much hostility and distrust. "And now he's targeting your family again by going after Lindsey."

"Which is why it's so important that we find her. We need to bring her in to keep her safe."

"And once you bring her in, what then?"

"We'll figure that out when the time comes."

"How do you catch a man who can change faces with someone?" He pointed. "Is that what Esmerelda meant when she said the man who assaulted her looked like her?"

"That's how I knew he'd found you. He took on Esmerelda's appearance to get into your room without alerting anyone."

"Why me, though? What was he looking for? And how did he know I was here looking for Lindsey?"

Garret leaned over the table. "I heard what you said to that Officer Novak. You filed a missing person's report?"

"I did. I was running out of options."

"That's how he found you."

Trick didn't understand. "How'd he do that?"

Garret pushed his drink back. "You don't think a man who can become anyone can impersonate an officer long enough to find out that Lindsey's been reported missing? And then get the personal information of the man who filed the report?" He cursed. "I can't believe you ever closed a case as a Texas Ranger."

Trick told himself to play it cool. "If I'd been told I was dealing with a shape-shifting assassin, I would probably have made different choices."

Garret set his jaw and looked away.

"What was he looking for in my room?"

Garret looked back. "Anything that might give him an advantage. Any information about you or Lindsey. Something that belonged to her." He aimed a sharp gaze at Trick. "Do you have anything like that?"

"Something that belonged to her? No. Why would that help him?"

Garret seemed to relax. "Because you are not immune. He can impersonate you too, and the more he knows about you, the better. Especially if he thinks Lindsey trusts you. And if he were to have something Lindsey knows belongs to you, it's that much easier to get close to her."

Trick's stomach curdled. "You mean he could become me? Just because he was in my room?"

"Not quite. It's more complicated than that."

"Then please, enlighten me." The thought of this assassin getting close to Lindsey because she believed he was Trick made him ill.

"He has to physically touch you long enough to morph. It's what he did with Esmerelda. He grabbed on and sucked the energy out of her long enough to morph. He can mimic clothing too, but the more he takes on, the more energy required. Objects like wallets, jewelry, a woman's purse or a gun require a lot more energy, so he typically won't create those, unless it serves his purpose. And if he creates those things, the shorter time period he can remain morphed. The more he creates, the harder it is to maintain."

"So, in order to become me, he would have to incapacitate me."

"Or kill you. They're both options."

Trick fell back against his seat. "That's comforting."

"That's why he wants to follow you. If you find Lindsey, all he has to do is become you, and Lindsey wouldn't be the wiser."

Trick ran a hand over his head. "Shit."

"No kidding."

Imagining Lindsey trusting a fake Trick scared the hell out of him. "There's got to be a way to get to him. He must have a weakness."

"He does. Just because he can become you doesn't mean he knows you, your thoughts, or your history with Lindsey. He might look like you, but he won't know what you know or act like you act."

"Will he sound like me?"

"Yes. He can mimic your voice."

"Shit."

"No kidding." Garret sat back as the waitress brought their food. She did not try to flirt.

"Thanks," said Trick, unsure if he could eat.

Shanna walked away, and Garret picked up a fry. "That's why I had to get you out of there. He's aware of you, and if he thinks you'll lead him to Lindsey, he won't stop. That's why you have to leave."

Trick paused before he picked up his burger. "Leave? Why am I leaving?"

"Because you're a threat to Lindsey, and the sooner you're out of here, the safer she is." Garret munched on a fry. "And if you really care about her the way you say you do, you'll be on the first plane out of Vegas without bitching about it, and you'll leave Lindsey to me and her family." Looking like he'd just hit the jackpot, Garret sat back and smiled.

Chapter Five

"How stupid do you think I am?" asked Trick, wondering why Garret would actually think that would work.

"I think you already know the answer to that question."

"You're just as vulnerable. If he knows I'm here, he sure as hell knows you are, too."

"But I know what I'm up against. I've dealt with him before."

"That's not the issue. The issue is that Lindsey doesn't know the danger. She doesn't know that you may not be you and I may not be me."

Garret lowered the french fry he was about to eat. "Lindsey knows me way better than she knows you. If I walk funny, she'll notice." He ate the fry.

"Not if she's three bottles in to whatever she's drinking."

Garret's face fell. "The same goes for you. If anything, she's more vulnerable to you."

"And why is that?"

"Because, no matter how much she tries to deny it, there's something between you two. And that puts her at risk, whether you want to admit or not."

Trick hesitated, wondering if Garret had a point. Was Lindsey in more danger if Trick found her? Would her guard be down, making her an easy target? He stared at his burger and debated his options. "I'm not leaving, Garret."

Garret glared. "Are you not listening to—"

Trick raised his hand. "I've heard every word, but nothing you've said convinces me she's safer if I'm gone." Garret opened his mouth to argue, but Trick wouldn't let him. "I get your logic. You think her feelings for me, if there actually are any, will cause her to let her guard down, but Lindsey's guard is never down, unless she's drinking, and then she's vulnerable with either of us. And let's face it. The reason she's here, which no one wants to reveal, is messing with her head, and this Proteus knows it." He paused. "And I think it's messing with your head, too, Garret, possibly making you just as vulnerable."

Garret tensed. "I've dealt with this monster before. I've seen him in action. I know what he can do, and if he comes near me, I'll know it."

"You're overconfident. If he became me, would you know? If he'd become Officer Novak, would you know?"

"I'd know because he has a tell."

Trick gaped at him. "Now you're telling me? Hell, if you can detect a tell, so can I. And how do you know he has a tell?"

"Because I've seen it. And it was confirmed while he was in captivity. His father had something similar."

"Tell me what it is."

Garret studied him as if questioning what to do. He picked up his tuna melt and took a bite.

Trick, trying to remain patient and not let Garret get to him, forced himself to take a bite of his burger and chew.

Garret swallowed and drank some of his soda. "If I tell you, will you leave?"

"No."

Garret glowered at him.

Trick set his burger down. "You haven't convinced me that Lindsey is safer if I'm gone." He sipped some of his coffee. "And if there is a tell, that gives me an advantage."

"Not if you miss it."

Trick leaned in. "Stop beating around the bush. Since he knows I exist, I need all the information I can get, not just for Lindsey's sake, but for mine, too."

Garret grunted his annoyance. "Fine. When he's about to morph, his skin ripples. We think it's his body preparing for the transition."

"That sounds pretty obvious."

"You'd think, but it's not. It's very subtle. And it's fast. If you blink, you could miss it."

"Then I'll keep my eyes open. But what good is this shimmer if he's already got a hold of you? Doesn't that mean you're already screwed?"

"I didn't say it was a great tell."

Trick slumped. "Perfect. This guy ripples in front of me, I'll know I'm toast."

"If you see it, and he touches you, move fast. You'll only have seconds to get away before you succumb."

"Great. Let's hope I'm as eagle-eyed and fast as the Six Million Dollar Man."

Garret's jaw clenched. "Damnit, Monroe. This isn't a joke. Stop being so damn cocky."

"I'm not being cocky. I'm being honest, and I'll be careful." He thought about it. "You say he does this when he's about to morph? What about once he's already morphed? Any way to know that I'm not talking to the Morphman right now, thinking it's you?"

"Only if he gives himself away with his lack of knowledge about his victim. So, if I tell you I think you're great for Lindsey, you'll know it's not me."

"I'll keep that in mind. Does Lindsey know about this tell, where he shimmers before he morphs?" He picked up his hamburger, although he had little appetite.

"She does now."

Trick wondered what that meant. "That just reiterates my point that she could easily miss it if she's not at a hundred percent. And right now, she isn't."

"Lindsey won't miss it."

Trick held his burger, but didn't take a bite. "How do you know?"

Garret didn't answer.

A thought occurred to Trick. "Did she miss it once before?"

Garret looked away.

"Is that what's got you both tied up in knots? This guy got to someone close to you and you all missed it? And you're blaming yourselves?"

Garret looked back at Trick. "My sister has been through hell and back these last five years. We all have. But she carries a guilt none of us can ease because we carry plenty of it on our own. It's been like a boulder on our shoulders none of us can shove off." He pushed his plate back and eyed Trick. "You want to know why you're a danger to Lindsey? Because out of all of us, she cares more deeply than anyone, but she hides behind a layer of bravado none of us can penetrate." He paused and interlaced his fingers. "When we were kids, and our dad was in the military and traveled a lot, we lived with our mom in a motorhome. It wasn't big, but it was mobile, so if we needed to leave fast, mom could get us on the road. At the time, we didn't know why, but we just accepted it as our way of life. Marcy and I were pretty comfortable making new friends, and Trey had his computers; all his friends were online. But Lindsey struggled the most. She's always been more introverted and didn't make friends easily. When she did get close, she'd go into a slump whenever we moved, and after a while, she stopped trying because she knew it wouldn't last. Even after Dad came home and revealed his work, and the moving slowed and then stopped, and we joined his cause, Lindsey remained reluctant to get close, until..."

Trick waited. "Until what?"

"She trusted someone and was betrayed."

Trick set his burger down. "If you live long enough, everyone gets their heart broken, Garret. It's called life. And what does that have to do with me?"

"I'm not talking about a broken heart. I'm talking about much worse. Lindsey is dealing with a broken soul. She lives with it every day and she's the strongest person I know and the bravest, but she's also vulnerable because of it. She's tough, but also emotional. She wants love but denies it and thinks she doesn't deserve it. And my biggest worry is that she'll use that as an excuse to destroy herself."

Trick frowned. "What does that mean?"

Pensive, Garret sat back. "Her feelings for you scare her, and if she thinks those feelings could...weaken her, or lead to another betrayal, she'll do whatever's required to protect her loved ones."

"What are you saying? I won't betray her."

"So you say, but that's not the betrayal I'm referring to. If she learns Morphman is back and thinks he'll use her to get to you, or us, she'll sacrifice herself to stop him." He paused. "And I'll be damned if that's going to happen."

Trick pushed his plate back. "That makes no sense. Her death would only hurt you and your family more." He didn't mention himself, although he knew losing her would devastate him.

"That's not the way she sees it. She sees herself as the problem, and if given the chance, especially in her current state, she'd let him have her if it meant protecting us." He took a breath. "She believes she deserves to die."

Trick clenched his napkin. "Are you saying she's suicidal?"

Garret paused. "Lindsey's loyalties are unbreakable and when those loyalties were betrayed and..." He paused and his jaw tightened. "She's never recovered, and she'll do whatever it takes to prevent that from happening again, which puts you right in the middle of it. Her feelings for you have confused her and the closer you get, the more confused she becomes. And when she learns Proteus is back, especially now, it's going to open old wounds that have barely closed and reignite the past. The last thing Lindsey needs right now is you, Monroe. So, if you care for her, set aside your ego, book the next flight out of Vegas, and go home."

Trick stared at Garret in stunned disbelief. Trying to understand, he tossed his napkin on the table. "You obviously love your sister very much."

"Of course I do. She's my sister."

"Ben loves her too."

"My dad loves her more than life itself. He'd die for all his kids."

"Then if what you say is true, why did he ask me to help? Why call me if he thought it would only hurt Lindsey?"

Garret's shoulders relaxed, but his face didn't. "My dad believes in true love, and because he's a dreamer, he mistakenly believes that's the only thing that can save Lindsey."

"You obviously disagree."

Garret set his hand on the table. "I'm not saying love can't save Lindsey. I question whether you're the man to do it." He pushed his own plate away. "My dad can see past certain flaws." Garret tensed again. "I can't."

Trick nodded. "I can understand that. If I had a sister, I can't say I wouldn't feel the same."

"Good. Then you'll leave."

"On the contrary. All the more reason to stay."

Garret cursed.

"I know you don't trust me, Garret. You have every reason not to. But what you think you know and what you know are two different things. If the only way I can prove I mean Lindsey no harm and that I...truly care for her is to protect her, then that's what I'll do."

"I don't want you to prove anything to me."

"Then I'll prove to Lindsey that I'm not going to hurt her and she can trust me. I think Ben's right. That's exactly what she needs." He pulled his plate back. "Now that we've cleared that up, eat your tuna melt."

Garret hardened his glare. "You asshole."

Unfazed, Trick heard his cell ring and hastily pulled it from his pocket. Seeing an unknown number on the display, his heart hammered. Hoping it was Lindsey, he answered. "This is Trick."

A male voice responded. "Trick Monroe?"

Trick didn't recognize the voice. "Who is this?"

There was a chuckle. "Your competition."

Trick's heart hammered harder. "For what?"

Another chuckle. "Lindsey, of course."

Trick stared at Garret. "Proteus?"

Garret's face fell.

"It's a good nickname," said Proteus. "Ben's a smart man. Too bad Garret didn't inherit his brains. Tell him to eat his lunch. He's going to need his strength."

Stunned, Trick looked around the diner. "Where are you?"

Garret swiveled and looked behind him and at the other diners. "That son-of-a-bitch."

"I've been watching," said Proteus, "and when I find what I'm looking for, old grievances will finally be settled. I'm sure Lindsey looks forward to that."

"Leave her alone."

Proteus sighed. "I would, but her family forced my hand. Now I look forward to picking them off, one by one. And I'll gladly start with Lindsey. She and I have a history. Did Garret tell you?"

Trick gripped the phone. "No, but I'm getting the picture."

"When you find her, have her fill you in. It's quite a story. One I've relived many times while sitting in my cell. Just like the story I'm living now."

"Which one is that?" Trick kept looking, but didn't see anyone watching them. Garret continued to listen and studied the patrons.

"The one where I seek my ultimate revenge. It took longer than I thought, but as it turns out, the timing is perfect."

Trick tried to breathe evenly. "I'm not going to make it easy for you. Neither is Garret."

"Garret's a fool. But you, you could be interesting. When you find her, tell her I still think of her, and look forward to seeing her again."

Trick's heart slammed against his ribs. "Listen, why—" The line went dead when Proteus hung up. Feeling a little shaky, Trick lowered his phone. "He's gone."

Garret pulled out his wallet and threw some money on the table. "We're getting out of here."

"Where are we going?"

"That asshole called you. I'm taking you to the airport. You can catch the next flight out."

Trick returned his phone to his pocket. His mind whirling and his adrenaline coursing through him, he recalled everything Garret had said about Lindsey and their family, and hearing Proteus' threatening voice in his head, chills raced down his spine. Then, most importantly, he thought of Lindsey and decided.

He slid out of the booth, grabbed his wallet, pulled out some cash, and tossed it on the table. "You win. Let's go."

Chapter Six

Holding his duffel bag in his lap, Trick watched as Garret pulled up to the curb at the departure section of a major airline at the airport. He put his hand on the door handle. "Thanks for the ride."

Garret looked over at him. "Thanks for leaving."

Trick hesitated. "You be careful and take care of Lindsey. Make sure she's safe."

"That's my priority. And keep your eyes and ears open. I don't trust this asshole. Once I get Lindsey out of here, Morph will search for another way in, and he could still use you to do it. Better to keep your distance until this business is settled."

Trick nodded. "Tell Lindsey..." He sighed. "Hell. Tell her to be careful, and not to do anything stupid, and that I left to keep her safe."

"I'll tell her." He gripped the steering wheel. "You take care, Monroe. And I'll call dad and explain why you left."

Trick nodded. "Thanks." He opened the door, stepped out, and closed the door. After Garret pulled away, Trick adjusted his hat, threw his duffel bag over his shoulder, and entered the airport. He walked up to the first available ticket agent. "I need the first ticket out of here going to San Diego. The cheaper, the better."

The agent typed on her keyboard, studied her monitor and gave Trick his options. Trick chose a flight that thankfully departed in two hours. He paid for it and took his boarding pass. He headed to security, where he waited in line, showed his ticket and ID, sent his duffel bag and boots through, and headed toward his gate to wait. His gun had traveled home with Mason in Mason's checked luggage, since Trick couldn't bring it in his duffel bag.

Finding a seat, he eyed the gate and the people around him. Restless, he leaned his head back, closed his eyes and set his mental alarm for one hour. An hour later, he opened his eyes, pulled out his cell, and called Mason.

Mason answered on the second ring. "Hey, Trick. How's it going? Any luck finding Lindsey?"

"Hey, Red. Not yet. She's not making it easy, but that doesn't surprise me. Her brother Garret found me just fine, though."

"I wondered when he'd show. How'd that go?"

"About as well as expected. He doesn't want me here. Thinks I'm a threat to his sister."

"He's a protective brother."

"I know he means well, but he could use a little work on his social graces."

"Sounds like someone I know."

Trick adjusted his hat. "At least I'm charming and look good in my hat and boots."

"If Garret lightened up and smiled more, he could be just as charming."

"And you could return to Texas and move in with your dad."

Mason chuckled. "I see your point. What's your next move?"

"That's why I'm calling. I've had some updates you should know about."

Mason's tone turned serious. "What is it?"

"The man who is looking for Lindsey broke into my hotel room. According to Garret, this man could use me to find Lindsey."

"How so?"

"Garret informed me he's an assassin and a shapeshifter. And not your run-of-the-mill bat or wolf. He morphs into humans and imitates other people, including their clothing and voice."

Mason didn't say anything.

"You still there?"

"I'm absorbing this. He can change into another person?"

Trick recalled a popular TV show. "You ever watch *Game of Thrones*?"

"No."

"Ask Mikey. There's a character that does something similar. She'll fill you in, but it will give you an idea of how dangerous this man is."

"And he's after Lindsey? Why?"

"He's after Ben's entire clan, but this man and Lindsey have a history that no one wants to discuss. Ben calls this guy Proteus."

"A god who can change shapes. Makes sense."

"Figures you'd know that and not *Game of Thrones*."

"I take pride in that."

"Anyway, apparently Proteus' father was captured by Ben but died in prison. Proteus didn't like that and came after Ben, and my guess is he used Lindsey to do it. He got far enough to do some damage, but not before he got captured himself. He's been in captivity the last five years until he escaped three weeks ago."

"And he's coming after Lindsay again?"

"She doesn't know he's out, which makes her vulnerable. Plus, the mental shitshow she's dealing with that he caused isn't helping. Garret didn't escape unscathed either, which explains a lot."

"So, what are you going to do?"

Trick heard the agent over the loudspeaker announce the pre-boarding for his flight.

"Are you at the airport?" asked Mason.

"I am."

"Why?"

Trick paused. "I wanted to call and tell you I'm going to be flying under the radar for the next few days. You won't be able to reach me."

"What are you up to?"

"You know me, Red. Nothing good."

"Do I need to join you?"

Trick considered that. "Not yet. Let me work on a few things. Once I know, I'll get in touch."

"I don't like this. How will I know you're alive?"

"You're the medium. You tell me."

Mason paused. "I swear, if you come to me in spirit form, I'll kill you twice."

"Consider me warned."

"Why the secrecy?"

"Proteus is aware of me and my connection to Lindsey, and, for some reason, I think I make him nervous. I need him to think I'm out of his hair. I can't find Lindsey with him on my back. It's too risky."

"But how are you going to find her without coming out into the open?"

Trick recalled his meal with Garret. "Garret told me a few things during a scintillating lunch, and I think I may have an idea where she is. But I can't approach until I know it's safe for her and for me, and this is the best way to do it."

"You sure about this?"

"I am."

"Then be careful. And call me as soon as you can. I'll give you forty-eight hours. I don't hear from you, I'm coming in."

"Forty-eight should be plenty."

"So you say. If needed, though, where should I look?"

Trick watched as passengers stood from their seats to stand in line as another round of boarding was called. "You remember where my mother lived for a short time, when we were first partnered up?"

"Vividly."

"Start there and the seedier the better."

"Will do."

A woman on the phone with a backpack slung over her shoulder and carrying a big purse passed him on her way to stand in line to board. "I've got to go."

"You be careful, partner. Don't let Proteus steal your decent looking face."

"I'll do my best, and I'll call as soon as I can. Tell Mikey not to worry, either."

"You know she will regardless, and so will I until I hear from you. Don't make me tell Aunt Ray news she doesn't want to hear."

Trick thought of Mason's Aunt Ray from Texas, who hadn't hidden her crush on Trick. "God forbid."

Mason paused. "Talk soon, partner."

"Talk soon." Trick reluctantly hung up, knowing his friend was concerned but unable to do anything about it. Focusing on Lindsey, he stood and approached the line of passengers at the gate. Holding his phone in front of him and studying it, he bumped into the woman with the backpack.

"Hey," she said. "Watch where you're going."

He lowered his phone. "I'm so sorry, ma'am. I apologize. I got distracted. It's been a day." He flashed a smile at her. "And I get nervous when I travel."

She yanked her backpack higher on her shoulder and her purse bounced against her hip. "No big deal." Her face softened. "I get nervous too."

"I'll just get out of your way." He brushed past her and dropped his phone into her purse. "You have a pleasant flight."

"You too."

Trick went to the back of the line, but instead of stopping, he walked past it and kept going. He left the secured area, found the taxis, waited for one and got in. After telling them his destination, he sat back and, hoping Lindsey was okay, debated what to do once he arrived.

• • • • • • • • • •

Lindsey cracked an eyelid open and stared at the sun brightening the sides of the closed blinds. The dim light gave her little trailer a sad and lonely look, but that's the way she preferred it. It suited her mood. Wondering what time it was, she decided she didn't care. The hours, minutes and days had all rolled into one. Her head pounding, she closed her eyes to block the sun and her bladder protesting, she forced herself up with a groan. She scratched her head, ran her hands through her disheveled hair, and reached for the glass by the side of the bed. Seeing it was empty, she pushed up and stood with another groan, and headed into the tiny kitchen, where she poured herself some more tequila, took a swig, and put the glass down. Grimacing, she eyed the messy kitchen. She'd eaten little since arriving, but whatever plates and utensils she'd used were piled in the sink and scattered across the counter. Liquor bottles, some empty and some half-full, sat among the dirty plates and dishes. She turned away from the mess and entered the small bathroom, where she avoided the mirror. Looking at herself only depressed her. The last time she'd done it, her reflection had shocked her. Her eyes had gone dull, her hair and clothes were a mess, and her cheeks were sunken.

After using the bathroom, she returned to the kitchen and grabbed her glass. She took another swig of the alcohol, added more tequila, and recapped the bottle. Her stomach rumbled, and she debated going out for some food. She couldn't remember when she'd last had a decent meal. The thought of eating, though, made her feel ill, and she left the kitchen and sat at the small rickety table beside her bed. She sat her glass down and stared at her small space. The bed sheets were rumpled, the lumpy couch had what few clothes she'd brought strewn over it, and the tiny TV that sat on a small stand pushed against the wall stared back at her as if tempting her to turn it on, but she didn't. She preferred silence. It forced her to sit in her pain without distraction, which is what she deserved.

Holding her head in her hands, she allowed herself to reconsider her options. Was it time to go home? Had she punished herself enough? Should she call her father and tell him she was okay? Should she call Trick again?

The only one that sounded appealing was calling Trick. He was the only one she could talk to who didn't know what she'd done, who wouldn't speak or look at her with pity or judgement. He could see her as she once was—honorable, good, and worthy. But calling him only made her angry at herself for giving in to her need for absolution. She didn't deserve it, and she didn't deserve anyone good in her life. It was her punishment for her failure, and she would force herself to live with it.

Seeing the small black-and-white photo she'd set on the table, she picked it up and stared at it. Five years, she said to herself. Five years since that brutal day when she'd lost the most important person in her life, and it had been her fault. All of it. No matter what her family did or said to prove otherwise, it didn't matter. Over the years, Lindsey had reached a point where she could function in the world as long as she could focus on her work in the CU, but when this time of year came around, she needed to disappear. Usually, it was only for a few days, and her father's pleas for her to return would bring her home. But this year was different. Something about the five-year mark had triggered something dark and ugly, and she'd left without telling anyone. She told herself it was just a difficult anniversary, but it was more than that. In her heart, she knew this year was different because of Trick Monroe.

She'd thought she could handle him and his rugged good looks, piercing eyes and charming humor, and she'd done pretty well until their trip to the mountains where he'd almost died at the hands of a violent cryptid. Their fight for survival had stirred emotions in Lindsey she'd sought to keep buried, but his charisma and smile didn't make it easy, and when she found herself falling for him mere weeks before the painful anniversary, she chastised herself for being so weak and stupid. Never again could she allow herself to be vulnerable and manipulated. Never again could she allow herself even the smallest attraction to another man. The cost was too high, the pain was too great, and the risk was too unimaginable to consider. Her family would never allow it, and neither would she. Lindsey's mistake had been allowing someone in who'd taken everything from her, and she'd never do it again, no matter how sexy, sweet, and smooth talking he might be.

Besides, she told herself, Trick had no interest in her other than as a conquest. Once he'd bedded her, he'd move on, and Lindsey had no plans to be another notch on his belt. That bored and diminished her, and if she had to deny herself, then so would Trick. He could move on to the next woman and leave Lindsey alone.

Satisfied that she'd handled her feelings for Trick, she smiled to herself, confident that he would no longer be an issue in her life. Her smile dropped, though, when she considered calling him again. Her last call had gone to voicemail, and she'd been disappointed not to hear his voice, but after leaving her message, she'd been glad he hadn't picked up. It would have only weakened her. He would have asked again where she was, and she might have told him. She'd certainly been drunk enough.

Eyeing the tequila, she took another drink, and feeling the alcohol hit her stomach and her head go foggy again, she stood and returned to her bedside, where she set her glass down on the nightstand. She lay down, pulled the covers over her, and ignoring her growling stomach, closed her eyes and tried again to forget long enough to allow herself to sleep.

· · • • • • • • • ·

The cab pulled up to the fast-food restaurant that Lindsey had called Trick from two days earlier. It was two blocks off the strip and in a seedier area. Trick paid the cabbie, got out, grabbed his hat, and tossed his duffel bag over his shoulder. Not looking around, he entered the small restaurant and approached the counter. Since he'd barely touched his cheeseburger from the diner, he ordered another one, along with some fries and a drink. After getting his food, he went to a table near the window where he put his burger and fries down and sat. Looking out the window, he could see the cars driving by on the busy street and the dingy hotel opposite the fast-food restaurant. He'd gone in there on his previous trip, where he'd shown Lindsey's photo around after her phone call, but no one had recognized her.

Eating his burger, he ignored the dingy hotel and studied the area just down the street. A rickety fence and overgrown trees almost obscured the mobile home park that would have been hard to see if not for a sign at the front of a driveway leading into the park. It had block letters that read *For R nt. Dai y and onthly*. It had seen better days and letters were missing, but its meaning was clear. When Garret had told Trick about him and his siblings living in a motorhome in their youth, Trick had immediately thought of the park near the fast-food restaurant. Was this where Lindsey had been staying? It would suit her needs. It was cheap, provided shelter, could barely be seen from the road, and there was a liquor store and a small grocery nearby. And it wasn't far from the strip, where she could go to make her occasional phone call to Trick or anyone else and not be traced back to the mobile home park.

Trick ate his burger and fries and watched the driveway to the park. No one came or went, so it was obviously quiet. He knew it was possible she wasn't there, but his gut was telling him he was on the right track, and he always followed his gut.

After he ate, he stood and tossed out his trash, used the facilities and headed outside. He took a few minutes to study his surroundings, but saw no one suspicious, so he headed across the street toward the park, walked up the driveway and onto the property, where he saw another dirty sign that said *Office* with an arrow on it. He followed the arrow to a rundown recreational vehicle that probably hadn't been on the road in years, put his hat on, adjusted his duffel bag, and knocked on the dirt-encrusted door.

"Yeah," said a male voice. "Come on in."

Trick opened the door and took a step into a cloud of cigarette smoke. He waved his hand and tried not to cough and heard the soft sound of a TV playing. A man stood from a small couch, put out his cigarette in an ashtray, and walked over to a waist-high counter with a grimy laptop on it. He wore ripped jeans, and a worn Mickey Mouse T-shirt, and his stubbled jaw and unkempt long hair told Trick the man hadn't seen a shower recently.

"What can I do for you?" The man glanced at the TV where a baseball game was playing.

Trick smiled and eyed the game. "Who's playing?"

"Yankees and Orioles."

"Who you rooting for?"

"I got money on New York."

"Sounds like a good bet. I've always been a Texas Ranger fan myself."

The man scratched his stomach. "They made me a lot of money when they won the pennant."

Trick looked around, wondering where that money had been spent, because it hadn't been on housing. "I wish I'd bet on them, but I've never been much of a gambling man."

"Then why are you in Vegas?"

Trick smiled. "Good question. I'm actually looking for someone." He pulled his picture of Lindsey out of his pocket. "She would have checked in about a week ago." He held it out. "Have you seen her? Her name's Lindsey, but she may have registered with a different name."

The man eyed the photo and then Trick. "Who's asking?"

Trick held out his hand. "Name's Trick. And you are?"

The man hesitated, but then shook hands with Trick. "Danny."

"Hey, Danny. Nice to meet you." Trick shifted the weight of his duffel bag and kept his tone casual. "I bet she told you to keep her presence secret, didn't she? And offered you extra money for it?"

Danny didn't respond.

"I figured." He thought fast. "I'm actually her brother, and our father passed two weeks ago. Lindsey didn't handle it well, and we stupidly argued about some things, namely the inheritance, and after the funeral, she took off. I knew she'd come to Vegas, because Dad used to bring us here when we were kids, and it's a connection to something familiar."

"How do you know she's not at some hotel? There are way nicer places than here."

"Lindsey doesn't like hotels much. Not since that story about the woman who drowned in a hotel's water tank and wasn't discovered for days. You can imagine what those guests were drinking and bathing in." He made a face. "Plus, Lindsey loves motorhomes since we used to travel in one as kids. And she called me from that restaurant on the corner," he pointed toward the fast-food place, "just two days ago."

Danny studied him with a look of distrust.

"I know this is unusual, but I suspect she's also here because it's cheap, and she's never been one to hold on to money for long. That's one thing we argued about." He leaned closer. "How much did she give you to stay quiet if anyone came asking?"

Danny frowned, and Trick admired the man's loyalty. A roar came from the TV and Trick and Danny swiveled toward it. "Damn it," said Danny when he saw the Orioles had scored.

Trick decided to see how much of a betting man Danny was. "How about I make you a wager?"

"What's that?" asked Danny.

"If I'm right and she's here, and you tell me what room she's in, I'll pay you a hundred dollars."

"And if you're wrong and she's not here?"

"I'll still pay you a hundred dollars for your time." He raised his finger. "But there's a caveat."

"What's that?"

"You lie to me, and you owe me two hundred bucks."

"How will you know if I'm lying?"

Trick turned serious and leaned even closer. "You heard of the Texas Rangers, the lawmen?"

Danny nodded. "Sure."

"I used to be one of them."

Danny arched an eyebrow.

"And we can read liars from a mile away." He held Danny's gaze and narrowed his eyes.

Danny paused. "I don't have to take the bet."

Trick leaned back. "No, you don't, but you didn't even ask why I was here, looking for Lindsey."

"Why's that?"

"Because Dad left her, and me, a hell of a lot of money. And she doesn't know it. But when she finds out, I suspect she might like to throw it around a little, maybe toward you, when she finds out you helped me find her."

Danny furrowed his brow. "Are you for real? Or is this a load of horse-shit?"

Trick tipped his hat up. "Are you now, or have you ever been, a Texas Ranger, Danny?"

"No."

Trick grinned. "Then I guess you'll never know, will you?"

Danny's face fell. "A hundred bucks, either way?"

"Yes, sir."

"She gave me a hundred to stay quiet."

Trick's heart skipped. "Then I guess you're about to double your money." He pulled out his wallet. "Which mobile home?"

"Number twenty-two. Take the main road and turn right at the end."

Trick handed Danny a hundred bucks and then gave him an extra twenty. "Go get yourself a haircut and a shave on me. A shower wouldn't hurt either."

Danny smirked and took the money.

"Thanks, Danny." Trick headed for the door and glanced at the TV. "Go Yankees." He smiled at Danny and left.

Chapter Seven

Trick approached the small mobile home marked #22. It didn't look much better than Danny's trailer/office. Dirt hid what, at some point, had been white walls, the screens on the windows were torn, the tiny yard was only weeds, and the driveway, where a compact sedan was parked, was mostly dead grass and dry dirt. He took the three steps up the cracked concrete to the faded blue front door, bolstered himself since he didn't know what to expect, and knocked.

He waited to hear footsteps or a lock turn, but nothing happened. He knocked again and listened, but heard nothing. "GQ?" he asked, using his nickname for Lindsey. "You in there?" Still nothing.

He tried the knob, and surprisingly, it turned. He spoke before he opened it. "I hope you're decent." The door creaked as he pushed it back and stuck his head in. He saw a small interior with all the basics, but no Lindsey. "Hello?"

Thinking she'd gone out, he stepped inside and froze when he heard a snore. The bed sheets moved and, looking closer, he saw a bare foot poking out of the end of the bed. He saw a half-filled glass on the nightstand and, scanning the room, spotted various liquor bottles in the dirty kitchen. His mind raced back to the past when he recalled all the times he'd found his mother like this and had to forcefully shove the memories back. Lindsey was not his mother, but his stomach twisted just the same.

Hearing her snore again, he dropped his duffel bag to the floor, closed the door behind him and locked it, and tossed his hat onto the lumpy couch half-covered with her clothes. He stared at the bed and debated waking her, but suspected she needed the sleep. Figuring he better be sure it was her and Danny hadn't lied to him, he walked closer and pulled the blanket back far enough to see short blonde hair against a dingy pillow. He heard her breathing, and she moved enough for him to see her face. His heart pounded at the sight of her, and he gave thanks he'd found her alive.

He dropped the blanket back over her and, looking around, made up his mind and went to work. He grabbed the glass by her bed and brought it to the sink, where he dumped out the contents and set the glass aside. After that, he took every liquor bottle and drained each of them and tossed the empty ones into the trash. Then he cleaned all the dishes, dried them, and put them away. While Lindsey continued to sleep, he grabbed all her clothes and threw them into a pile. After finding the number to the front office, he called Danny from the banged up landline phone in the room and asked about where residents did their laundry. Danny informed him of a nearby trailer that contained a washer and dryer. Trick left the trailer, started up a load, and found Lindsey still sleeping when he returned. He checked the fridge and found only soda, milk and a bottle of pitted green olives. There was a box of cereal and chocolate chip cookies in a plastic container, but that was it for food. After a quick search, he found a piece of paper and a pencil and made a quick list of groceries. He considered whether to go to the store, but didn't want Lindsey to wake up without him there, so he set the list down on the table and spied a black-and-white photo. He'd seen it earlier but now he paid closer attention. He picked it up and studied the picture of an older woman who had Lindsey's smile and eyes, sitting with a younger woman who was obviously a more relaxed Lindsey. Her hair was longer, and her eyes held fewer secrets. The younger version appeared more carefree than Trick had ever seen her.

Wondering where that past Lindsey had gone, Trick set the picture back on the table, along with his list. Thinking of the cookies, he grabbed the container of them, poured himself some milk, and went to sit on the couch, where he flipped on the TV. He found the game Danny had been watching and happily dunked his cookies into the milk and ate them.

After the game ended, he ran out to toss Lindsey's clothes into the dryer and returned. He kept the TV volume low and debated waking her when she stirred and moaned. He muted the TV and waited to see if she'd wake up. When she jerked in the bed, he stood to see if she was okay. He lifted the covers and saw the sheen of sweat on her forehead and her hair plastered against her skin. Her face was a grimace, and she moaned again.

"Lindsey?" His experiences with his mom over the years told him Lindsey was having a nightmare.

She sucked in a breath and jerked again. "No."

He pulled the covers back. "Lindsey. It's Trick. Wake up." Grateful she was clothed, he noted how her thin spaghetti-strapped top was damp with sweat, and she whined under her breath. "Mom?" she whispered.

Trick carefully sat on the side of the bed and jostled her shoulder. "Lindsey. Wake up."

Gripping the sheets, Lindsey cried out and bolted up into a sitting position. Trick almost fell off the bed when her shoulder hit his and he grabbed her automatically to calm her, but it had the opposite effect. She flailed in his arms and shoved him back. "Don't touch me." Her breathing came in gasps, and she fought to get away from him.

"Lindsey. It's me. It's Trick." It was clear she hadn't completely come out of her dream.

"Leave me alone." She got her hand free, and Trick grunted when she punched him in the gut. "Lindsey," he yelled, but she still struggled. "GQ," he yelled louder.

That name stopped her, and she went still. Breathing fast, she stared at her surroundings and Trick and blinked several times. "Wha...what?" she asked.

Seeing she was calmer, Trick let her go. "You back with me?"

Lindsey looked around the room. "How...how much did I drink?" She held her head, which sported her spiky hair, which was either stuck to her damp scalp or pointing up in numerous directions. She shook her head. "Where...How?" She eyed Trick with wide eyes. "Oh, God. Did we...?" She looked at the bed.

Trick grinned. "Believe me, honey. If we had, you'd remember."

She groaned, and Trick winced when he got a whiff of her breath. "What are you doing here?" she asked.

"I've been looking for you. So is Garret."

Looking annoyed, she tossed the covers aside and got out of the opposite side of the bed. "Nobody asked you to."

"Actually, your father did."

Lindsey adjusted the snug shorts she wore. "I'm fine. You can go home now." She grimaced and held her head.

"Must be a hell of a hangover." He noted the dark circles under red-rimmed eyes and wondered again what tormented her.

"That's none of your business." She headed for the kitchen and Trick waited for the outburst.

She stopped, narrowed her eyes, and went through the cabinets. "Where the hell is everything?"

Trick got off the bed. "I cleaned. By the looks of it, it's not your strong suit."

Lindsey searched the kitchen. "You son-of-a-bitch. You threw it all out?"

"I saved your soda and milk." He waved his hand toward the couch. "Would you like some cookies?"

She stomped out of the kitchen and glared at him. "Who gave you the right? I didn't ask you to come here and I don't want your help."

"Lindsey, listen to me..."

She moved around him, opened a drawer in the nightstand, and pulled out a small purse. Ignoring Trick, she headed for the door.

Trick ran ahead. "Where are you going?"

She opened the door, and he blocked it with his booted foot. "I'm going to the liquor store," she yelled. "Now get out of my way."

"Sorry," he said, "but plans have changed."

"I don't want you here. You don't need to rescue me. Now move."

"Lindsey, you're half-dressed, you're not wearing shoes, and you look like you just battled one of those cryptids you love to kill and lost."

"It's Vegas. Nobody cares." She tried to open the door again, but it banged against his foot. "I said to get out of my way."

He took her arm, and she pulled it back. "If I don't need to be here," he said, "then why did you call me, huh? Why did your father ask for my help to locate you? Why is Garret searching for you as we speak?"

Her anger waned and her eyes lost some of their glare. "That's none of your business."

"Maybe so, but I'm here now, and I'm not leaving. And whatever happened five years ago that's tormenting you, it's going to have to wait."

Her glare returned. "You don't know what the hell you're talking about."

He held her gaze and told her the truth. "I know more than you think. Proteus is back, and he's searching for you."

Her face paled, and her jaw dropped. "What did you say?"

"Your dad is scared, and so is Garret. That's why I'm here. Your dad is pulling out all the stops to find you."

She stared in shock. "He's got to be wrong. Proteus is in—"

"Jail? Not anymore. He escaped three weeks ago, and he's looking for you."

Her jaw hung open. "That can't be."

"It's true. Your dad wants you to come in. It's the only way to keep you safe."

Whatever color remained in Lindsey's face disappeared, and she held her stomach.

"You okay, GQ? You're not looking too hot."

She made a noise in the back of her throat, pushed past him, dropped her purse, and ran into the bathroom. The door slammed and Trick imagined she was losing whatever was in her stomach, which wasn't much based on what was in her kitchen. His theory was confirmed when he walked up to the door and heard her retching.

He knocked softly. "Can I do anything?"

She retched again, and he waited for it to slow. After a quick scan of the kitchen, he found a kitchen towel, wet it, and brought it back to the door. He knocked again. "Can I come in?"

He heard a subdued, "Leave me alone," and opened the bathroom door. He peered inside and saw her sitting on the floor across from the toilet with her back against the wall. Her face was as white as the bathroom tile had likely been when it was new. "Do you ever listen?" she asked, her voice strained.

He entered the bathroom and squatted beside her. "I listen plenty. It's the ignoring part I excel at." He handed her the damp towel, and she took it. "Feeling better?"

She looked at him with a sneer. "What do you think?"

Seeing her hair plastered against her scalp, her pale skin, and her shaky fingers, he sighed. "I'll use my masterful powers of perception and guess no."

Lindsey used the cloth to wipe her face. "I feel like shit."

"You look about the same. When's the last time you took a shower or brushed your teeth?"

She lowered the cloth. "I don't remember."

"Judging by the look and smell of you, I'm going to guess not since you arrived."

She held the cloth against her face, leaned her head against the wall, and moaned.

Trick sat beside her on the floor.

"Go home, Texas," she said through the cloth. "I can take care of myself."

"If Proteus came through that door, you'd be a dead woman."

She took a second before she answered. "Maybe that's a good thing."

That surprised Trick. "What's going on, Lindsey? Why is this Proteus after you?"

She lowered the cloth abruptly. "How much do you know? What did my dad tell you?"

"Your dad didn't tell me anything. He protected your privacy."

Lindsey sat up. "Then how do you know about Proteus?" She sucked in a breath. "Garret? That son-of-a...How much did he say?"

Sensing her fear behind her anger, he raised his hand. "Relax. Garret protected you, too. Maybe a little too much, until he didn't have a choice."

"What does that mean?"

He shifted his position on the tile floor. "Proteus located me. He used a housekeeper to get into my hotel room. When Garret learned that, he had to tell me about Proteus."

She wiped her eyes with the wet towel. "How could Proteus have found you? He doesn't know who you are."

"I opened a missing persons' report with the police."

Her eyes widened. "Why the hell did you do that?"

"Because you're a missing person, or at least you were."

"You stupid idiot."

"Your family should have told me what I was dealing with."

"They shouldn't have told you anything at all."

"If you hadn't run off and disappeared, they wouldn't have needed to."

She slumped and fell back against the wall. "What I do with my time is my business."

"You didn't call your dad. Why not?"

She put the towel back over her face and didn't answer.

Trick could almost feel her tense up and sensed something he'd never felt before from her. Shame. "What happened between you and this Proteus?"

His words had an immediate effect. She pulled the towel down and tried to sit up. "You need to go."

Trick stood with her, and when she wobbled, he took her arm to steady her. "Your family is worried about you. So am I."

She pulled back. "You have no idea what you're dealing with."

"I have some idea. Garret and I had lunch. He told me what Proteus can do and what to look for. You can't fight this man alone."

"Who said I'm going to fight anyone?" She tried to step around him, but she wobbled again and held her head. "And Garret should have kept his mouth shut."

He took her arm to support her. "Lindsey, you need help."

She went rigid. "I don't need your help or anyone else's. I want you to leave me alone." Pushing past him, she left the bathroom, but Trick followed.

"Look at you, Lindsey. You can barely stand. You're weak because I suspect you've barely eaten. You've been drinking yourself into a stupor. I noticed that nightmare you had. My guess is that's happening a lot, and you've barely slept. How long to you plan to go on like this?"

Still shaky, she made it to the bed and sat. "For as long as I damn well want."

"Does that mean the next three days?"

She looked up in surprise. "What do you know about the next three days?"

"It doesn't take a mind reader to realize this time of year is the trigger. Your father implied as much. And Garret is almost as messed up as you." He tried to speak calmly, but pushed a little harder to get through to her. "I don't know what happened to you and your family five years ago, but it's obvious whatever it is, that you're carrying most of the baggage and a significant amount of guilt. Now I know that sucks. I've carried around plenty of my own over the years and have used alcohol to try to forget, but it never works because you can't stay drunk forever." He walked closer to her. "Now if this Proteus hadn't escaped, your dad likely would have never called me and you'd have stayed in your alcoholic haze until the anniversary passed, but that's not what happened. Proteus is out there and he's searching for you."

She dropped and held her head.

"And I'll be damned if I'm going to let you give up and sacrifice yourself to him out of some perverse need to atone for something. That's not you, Lindsey."

Still holding her head, she chuckled sadly to herself. "You don't know me, Texas."

Garret telling him the same thing flickered in Trick's mind. "Yes, I do, Lindsey. Better than you think." He sat beside her. "You're just not in the state of mind to realize that right now. I've seen you slay vampires and werewolves without a second thought to your own safety. Don't tell me I don't know who you are."

Her fingers tightened around her temples, and she stayed quiet.

Since she couldn't do it, Trick took the initiative. "What you need right now is a shower, some food and a good night's sleep. Once you have that, then I'll trust your decision making a little more."

She didn't respond.

"Your clothes are in the dryer."

That got a response. "My clothes are what?" She looked up and he could see the shimmer in her eyes.

"I cleaned them." He ignored her when she yelled at him for not leaving her stuff alone. "You need to get in the shower, or better yet, take a long hot bath."

"I am not taking a bath."

"Why the hell not?"

Staring at him, she scoffed.

"Just soak while the alcohol works its way out of your system. I'll go get your clothes, so you'll have something to wear. While you're cleaning up, I'll go to the grocery store and get some food. You'll eat a decent meal, sleep instead of passing out, and then tomorrow, after a decent breakfast, we'll make some decisions."

She made another snort, rubbed her neck and looked away.

"You're safe for now. No one knows we're here. Garret thinks I'm on my way home and he's busy checking hotels, not motorhomes. And Proteus, if he's been tracking me, thinks I've left town too."

"What about your phone?"

"It's on its way to California, in a woman's purse. Where's yours?"

"I left it home."

"So nobody can track us. We've got ourselves a day, maybe two, to figure out what's next."

Lindsey rubbed her eyes. "You plan on staying here with me? Is that your plan, Texas? Because if you think this supposed rescue is going to get me into bed with you, you've come a long way for nothing."

He patted her knee. "Now that's the Lindsey I know. I was certain she was in there somewhere. And for the record, I don't bed damsels in distress. They bed me." He grinned at her. "So the ball's in your court." He gestured at the sofa. "Until then, I'll take the couch."

She studied the floor. "Don't get your hopes up."

"Not to disappoint you, but I'd run the other way if you so much as smiled at me right now. You stink."

That garnered a slight smile from her until she held her stomach again and grimaced.

"Are you going to puke again?" he asked.

Taking slow breaths, she stood, and he helped her up. "I hope not." Finding her balance, she ran a hand through her messy hair. "Okay. I'll take a shower."

"Good. I'll go get your clothes. I'll leave them on the bed."

She nodded. "Get me a toothbrush while you're out. I dropped mine behind the toilet."

He made a face of disgust. "Will do. We'll burn the other one. Where's the car keys to the sedan?"

"Top shelf in the nightstand, along with the key to the house."

"Thanks." Seeing her walk to the bathroom, he spoke with seriousness. "You're going to be here when I get back, right? You better not disappear on me."

She glanced back at him. "I won't disappear."

"You got shampoo? Soap? Maybe some bleach?"

She rolled her eyes. "I do." She made it to the bathroom. "Grab some potato chips while you're out."

"How about tortilla chips and salsa?"

"Fine."

"Okay." He watched as she closed the bathroom door and waited until he heard the water running. Not trusting her, he picked up her purse and shoes, found the car and house keys, and headed for the door. If she was going to run, she'd have to do it in bare feet and no wallet. Taking a last look around, he walked out of the motorhome and closed the door behind him.

Chapter Eight

An hour later, Trick opened the door. He carried the grocery bags inside and closed the door with his foot. He saw the clothes on the bed had been rearranged and the bathroom door was still closed, yet didn't hear the water running. "Lindsey?" he asked. "You still there?" He set the bags on the kitchen counter. "Lindsey?"

Not getting an answer, his heart thumped, and he went over to the door and knocked. "GQ? You better be in there." Eyeing her clothes on the bed, he couldn't imagine where she'd go with no shoes, clothes, wallet or car.

He heard a soft voice. "I'm here."

Trick sighed with relief. "You okay?"

There was a pause. "I'm great."

Her response seemed out of place. "Can I come in?"

He heard a long sigh. "Sure. Why not?"

Frowning, he turned the knob and pushed the door in enough to peer around it. He cursed when he saw Lindsey still sitting on the floor. Her hair was damp and combed, though, and she wore a clean T-shirt and cutoff denim shorts. She also held a half-filled glass in her hand and an open bottle of tequila sat beside her.

He pushed the door in and entered the bathroom. "What are you doing?"

She half-smiled at him. "You missed one."

Trick picked up the bottle. "Where was it?"

"Under the bathroom sink."

Trick recapped it. "I'm not even going to bother to ask why. Why are you sitting in here?"

She giggled. "Because I'm hiding."

Frowning, he held out his hand. "Give me the glass."

She pouted. "Are you going to throw out the booze?"

"I am."

"All of it?"

"Yes."

Groaning, she sipped some more tequila and handed him the glass. "You're not my dad, you know."

"No, but I'm your friend, and right now, you need one, plus a hot meal and some sleep." He dumped the contents of the glass in the bathroom sink.

"Help yourself to the tequila if you want any," she said. "It's good stuff. It shouldn't go to waste."

Wondering what had set her off again, Trick spied the photo from the table on the floor and got his answer. "What's that?" he asked, gesturing toward the photo.

She glanced at it, picked it up and tucked it inside her shirt pocket. "Nothing."

Trick chose not to push. He leaned over and sniffed her head. "At least you took a shower. Can you stand?"

She snorted. "Course I can stand." Grabbing at the edge of the tub, she tried to pull herself up, but fell back to the tile.

"Stay there." Trick returned to the kitchen, set the tequila and glass down, and returned to the bathroom. "Take my hand."

"I can do it." She tried again, but failed.

He took her arm. "Hell. How much did you drink?"

She stood with his help. "A lot. I knew you were coming back." She fell into him, and he held her up.

"You are the most stubborn woman I know." He stooped, put his arm beneath her knees, and lifted her into his arms.

She complained. "What are you doing? I can walk."

"Trust me. This is safer." He carried her into the main room and set her on the edge of the bed. "Now stay put. Better yet, lie down and try to rest. I'll put the groceries away."

Lindsey held onto his arm when he tried to stand. "Hey," she said.

He sat again. "Hey, what?"

She leaned into him. "Why are you really here?"

He stared back at her. "I could ask you the same."

She poked his arm. "You ask too many questions."

"I haven't asked near enough." He paused. "Who's the woman in the photo?"

She looked away.

"Is it your mom?"

Lindsey rubbed her leg. "I don't want to talk about her." She leaned close again. "I want to talk about you."

"Really? What would you like to know?"

Her gaze traveled over him, and she narrowed her eyes at the baseball cap he wore. He'd bought it in the store to look less conspicuous. "What is that?" She reached up and took it off his head. "I Love Las Vegas?" she asked, reading the logo on the front of it.

"Thought I'd blend in more. Proteus will be looking for a cowboy hat."

She tossed the hat aside. "You look much better in the cowboy hat."

"Thank you. I think so too."

Her gaze returned. "You look good out of it, too."

He smiled at her and chuckled. "Are you getting frisky, GQ?"

She took his hand and squeezed his fingers. "I bet you look good out of a lot of things." Her other hand found his thigh.

Her touch made his skin prickle, but he wasn't about to act on her overture. "I bet you do too, but now is not the time to find out, tempting as it is."

She grinned at him. "Have a few shots of that tequila and you'll change your mind."

He moved her hand off of his thigh. "How about we wait until you sober up? Then, if you're still inclined to act on your interest, and you've brushed your teeth, then we'll talk. Until then, you're off limits."

She sighed and shifted to face him. "I know you want me."

Her throaty voice and nearness made his heart race. "You're right. But not like this. And when you're sober, you'll thank me."

Running her hand up his chest and into his hair, she dropped her forehead against his temple. "I want you too, you know?"

His heart raced at her words. "You do?"

"I just don't know how to show it, and..."

Trying to breathe evenly, Trick ran his fingers down her forearm. "And what?"

"I'll only hurt you."

He pulled her hand down and held it. While he hated to see her drunk, he appreciated the effect the liquor was having on her. "You won't hurt me, honey."

She nodded. "Yes. I will."

"Lindsey, why would you hurt me? We're both consenting adults. All relationships carry risk."

She pulled back. "That's why. I can never have a relationship with you."

Not understanding, he sighed. "Why not?"

Lindsey took her hand out of his. "I can't. I don't deserve it. I don't deserve you or anyone else."

The uninhibited Lindsey retreated, and she leaned away from him.

Wondering again what was going on, he thought of the picture in her pocket, and Proteus, and asked the hard question. "What did Proteus do to you, Lindsey?"

Her jaw tightened, and the warm and sexy woman vanished. She turned away and lay on the bed. "My head hurts."

Trick gave up on getting answers because she clearly was not prepared to give them, but his mood darkened at the thought of what must have happened to her. "You rest. I'll make some food."

She nodded and turned her head into the pillow.

Seeing her eyes close, Trick stood and went into the kitchen. Glancing at Lindsey and then the tequila bottle, he uncapped it, poured some liquor into the glass, and shot it back. The heat slid down his throat and bloomed in his gut, and it helped to calm his nerves. Her advances had made his blood rush, and his body react, and he needed to focus, but couldn't help but imagine what would happen if they both came together while sober and without distractions. The images in his mind made him down another shot before he went to the sink and dumped the rest of the booze down the drain. After today, they both needed clear heads and plenty of energy, and right now, Lindsey had neither.

If they were going to survive this, Trick required her to be at full speed, and if that meant pushing her buttons or avoiding them all together, he would do it. Once Proteus was dealt with, then Trick could figure out what to do next. But whatever it was, it would require Lindsey telling him the truth, whether she wanted to or not. Without it, there was no point in pursuing anything with her, no matter how much he wanted her. Recalling her words that she would only hurt him, Trick tossed the empty tequila bottle into the trash and unloaded the groceries.

· · · · •· · • · ·

Hearing footsteps, Trick slid his blanket down enough to see Lindsey enter the bathroom. Sunlight pierced through the bent slats in the blinds that covered the windows, and groaning, he pushed up on the sofa. He'd had worse nights, but he'd definitely had better, too.

After Trick had unloaded the groceries the previous day, he'd made spaghetti with meat sauce and made Lindsey get up and eat. She'd complained at first, but after a few bites, she devoured the food on her plate and came back for more. Trick insisted she drink plenty of water, gave her some aspirin, and after eating, she fell back into bed.

Trick cleaned up, found another game to watch on TV, and after a couple of hours, flipped it off and went to sleep himself. Luckily, he'd found an extra set of sheets in the closet and a blanket. He'd slept fairly well despite the lumpy couch and the couple of times Lindsey had moaned in her sleep and tossed and turned. He'd hoped as she came off the booze, the nightmares would dissipate, but only time would tell.

Hearing the toilet flush and the sink run, he sat up, ruffled his hair, and stretched his back and neck.

Lindsey came out of the bathroom. Still wearing her T-shirt and cutoffs, she sat on the bed, leaned over and held her head.

"How do you feel?" asked Trick.

"Terrible," she said. "I'm completely sober."

"Sorry about that. Did you see your toothbrush?"

"I did. You'll be happy to know I used it."

"So will your dentist, and anyone within a ten-yard radius."

She smirked at him. "Now what, Cowboy? What's your grand plan for today?"

"First up? A shower, and then breakfast." He stood. "Then we'll make a plan."

Her eyes traveled over his frame. He wore boxer shorts and his white undershirt. "How'd you sleep?" she asked.

Glancing at himself to make sure nothing was exposed, he scratched his stomach. "Considering the circumstances, not bad." The two of them had recently shared a cabin in the mountains, so rooming together wasn't new, but her appraisal of him was, or maybe she'd been better at hiding it at the cabin. He gathered the sheets and tossed them on the bed.

"You could have slept up here," she replied. "I would have kept my hands to myself."

He smiled at her, recalling her advances the previous day. "I didn't want to take any chances. That tequila was...relaxing you more than you may remember."

She stared, and her eyes widened. "Did I...? Oh, hell, did I make a fool of myself?" She held her head again and groaned.

"Nothing I couldn't handle." He grabbed some clothes and toiletries. "But you didn't make it easy."

She groaned again, and he chuckled on his way to the bathroom. "Be out in a sec." He walked inside, but stuck his head out. "Don't go anywhere."

Lindsey looked up. Her eyes were still puffy from sleep. "Don't worry. My mortification prevents me from showing myself in public."

He chuckled again and shut the bathroom door.

Fifteen minutes later, he reemerged from the bathroom and smelled coffee. Lindsey was in the kitchen, helping herself to a cup. She'd changed clothes and wore jeans and a fresh T-shirt. She'd brushed her hair, and her eyes looked brighter and less haunted.

"Coffee smells great." He tossed his clothes into his duffel bag and put on his socks and boots. Lindsey brought him a cup of coffee. "There's no cream."

"I know. I didn't see the point of buying any." He took the mug from her. "Thanks." He took a sip and sighed. "That's good." He set his cup on the table. "You hungry?"

She hesitated, but then nodded. "I could eat."

He headed into the kitchen. "I'll make eggs, then we'll talk."

Lindsey followed him into the kitchen. "I'm not going home, if that's your plan."

Trick opened the fridge and pulled out the eggs. "You want some orange juice? I bought some. Plus, we have chips and salsa. Why don't you open them up? We'll snack on them, plus they'll be good with the eggs."

Holding her coffee, she stared at him. "Did you hear me?"

He stared back. "Did you hear *me*? We eat first and then we'll talk." He held her gaze until she huffed and grabbed the bag of chips.

After preparing and eating a hearty helping of omelets, tortilla chips, salsa, and coffee, Trick pushed his plate back and patted his stomach. "That hit the spot."

Lindsey ate a chip. "Can we talk now?"

Happy she'd finished her food and a healthy dose of chips, Trick nodded. "Yes. Now that you've eaten, we can talk."

"Why the focus on food?"

"Because I need you at your best, and you snarling at me because you're hungry and still a little hungover is not your best."

To her credit, she didn't argue. "Okay, well, maybe me being at my best is stretching it, but I'm way better than yesterday, so shoot. What's your plan?"

"We need to get you out of Vegas."

She shook her head. "No. I'm not leaving."

Trick sat up. "Why not? You'd be safer at home."

"Who says? My dad? Garret?"

"Yes."

"And what happens then? Do I stay inside the rest of my life?"

"No. You wait until Proteus is recaptured."

She snorted. "And who is going to do that? You?"

Trick lifted his hand. "Whoever is qualified to do it. You and your family can't be the only ones in the CU capable of stopping this man."

"Which means putting some other family at risk."

"Isn't that what they signed up for? You don't have to make all the sacrifices, Linds."

She froze and gripped her coffee cup. "Don't call me that."

Trick didn't understand. "Don't call you what?"

"Linds. Don't abbreviate my name like that. Call me Lindsey, GQ, honey, a bitch, whatever, but don't call me Linds." She stared down at her coffee.

"Doesn't your family call you Linds?"

"No. They call me Lin."

"Two letters make a difference?"

"A crater-size one." She glared at him.

Trick wondered why, but nodded. "Okay. No Linds."

"Thank you."

"Back to my point, honey bunny—" She rolled her eyes at him. "You've been through enough. Let somebody else deal with Proteus."

"I can't do that. This is my cross to bear. He wants me, then let's use that."

Trick blew out a breath. "What are you saying? You want us to lure him in?"

"Not us. Me."

"The hell that's happening."

She leaned in. "You don't know him, Trick. This man can assume another's identity. He can become anyone. You can't stop him."

"What makes you think you can?"

She shifted in her seat. "Because I *do* know him, and he knows me."

"Which is exactly why you're vulnerable." He straightened and tried to organize his thoughts. "I know you two had some sort of prior relationship. That much is obvious. And my guess is he used you to get to your family."

Her jaw tightened.

"And now that he's out, this is your chance to seek your revenge, but that's dangerous territory, Lindsey. Vengeance is never productive and rarely wise."

"But it sure as hell feels good."

"Assuming it works out the way you hope, but it's rare for that to happen and it usually backfires."

"I know what I'm doing."

"No. You don't. He can fool you just as well as he can fool me."

"He's not perfect. He has his weaknesses, too."

"You mean the whole shimmering thing? Garret told me, but he also said it's subtle and easy to miss."

"I've seen it before, and I know what to look for."

"And that's why you shouldn't do this. You're overconfident and angry. That's no way to catch him."

"You don't know everything, Texas."

"I know enough, honey. And it's written all over you." He paused, and watching her, he sensed something he didn't like. "Is this really about catching him? Or is this about you making amends?" He frowned. "Do you want *him* to catch *you*?"

Her jaw tightened again. "My past with this man and how I choose to deal with him is my business, and not yours. If you want to go home, fine. Please do. This isn't your fight. Now that I'm aware he's here, I can plan for that. Eventually, he'll find me, and when he does, I'll deal with him, and if he wins, then at least he'll leave the rest of my family alone."

Trick scoffed. "Alone? How do you know that? He could just be getting started. And if he does kill you, you think your family can endure that devastating loss? That only makes them more vulnerable, and Proteus knows that. Why do you think he's targeting you first?"

"Because he thinks I don't know he's escaped, and because he thinks I'm wallowing in my—" Her face furrowed, and she looked away and cleared her throat. "He knows what this time of year means, and he wants to use that against me."

"So don't let him. Go home. Regroup with your family and then decide what's next. Do it together. Not alone. That's suicide." He sat back and narrowed his eyes. "Or is that your plan?" He lowered his voice. "Do you want to die?"

Her face paled, and she ran her fingers over her head. "Don't be so dramatic."

"You didn't answer my question."

She met his gaze and held it. "Go home, Texas."

Trick swallowed and debated his response. Arguing with her was obviously failing, so he chose another tactic. "I'll go home if you do one thing for me."

Her eyes widened with surprise. "What's that?"

He stood, went into the kitchen, and grabbed what he needed. After returning, he sat and set two burner phones on the table. "I bought these yesterday. They're activated and ready to use. I figured we'd need them."

She took one. "Probably a good idea."

Trick leaned an elbow on the table. "I want you to call your father. Tell him what you plan to do and why you plan to do it. Explain to him why it makes sense that you have to die." He leaned back. "You do that, and I'll leave."

Lindsey stared in disbelief.

Trick grabbed a chip and bit into it. "I'll wait."

Chapter Nine

Frustrated, Lindsey fell back in her seat and crossed her arms. "I can't do that."

Trick drank some more coffee. "Then I guess I'm hanging around."

"Your reasoning is flawed. Me calling him won't stop me from moving forward."

"I think my reasoning is sound. You don't want to call him because you're scared. You know what he'll say, and you know he won't go for it. And you don't want to tell your father he could lose his daughter."

"He doesn't need to know. It's better if I leave him and Garret and everyone else out of this."

Trick set his mug down. "That's where you're wrong." He sharpened his tone. "I'm not a parent, but I sure as hell can imagine what a situation like this would do to one." He pointed. "Your father has no idea where you are or if you're even alive. He's terrified Proteus will get to you and has no way to stop him. Now he's got his son out here looking for you, who's also at risk. And you don't want to call him? At least tell him you're still breathing and what your plans are?"

Not wanting to think about her dad, Lindsey bit her lip. "We all know what we signed up for when we joined the CU. Anyone one of us could die in the line of duty."

"Your dad never signed up for this. And how exactly is this part of your duty? Last I heard, you all worked as a team. That's your strength. You communicate, strategize, and help each other. That's how we stopped a craver and a dogman, and that's how we'll stop Proteus." He paused. "You're too emotionally involved, and you're not thinking straight. You know it, I know it, and your father will sure as hell know it."

Lindsey looked away. She understood Trick's logic. All of it made sense to him, but he didn't know the entire story. If he did, he'd know why she had to do this alone; why it was her responsibility to deal with Proteus. Something in her gut nudged her to tell him everything she'd bottled up for so long, but the familiar guilt and shame wouldn't let her, and she forced the impulse back. "You don't understand."

"I understand better than you think. You just don't want to hear anyone else's opinion but your own, which is why you won't call Ben. He knows what you're dealing with, and he'll try to breach the walls you've built, and you doubt you can stop him, so it's easier to shut him out, but that's not fair, Lindsey." He took a second and tapped on the table. "If you're going to sacrifice yourself in this personal battle with Proteus, at least have the courage to tell your father you love him and ask him to honor your decision. And if something happens and Proteus gets to you before you get to him, maybe your dad will sleep better at night after you're gone, although I doubt he will." Trick fell back against his seat. "I know I won't."

Lindsey's chest tightened, but before she could allow her emotions to surface, she steeled herself, thought about what she would say, lifted the phone, and dialed. "Fine. You win. I'll call him." She put the phone to her ear and listened to it ring.

• • • • • • • • •

Anxious, Trick watched as Lindsey waited for her dad to answer. He'd hoped he'd gotten through to her, but her determination and resolve were hard to penetrate, and it made it worse that she felt the need to go it alone. He prayed that when she got a hold of Ben, that he would have better luck than Trick on getting his daughter to back down. It was Trick's last line of defense, because if Lindsey chose to leave Trick and face Proteus, there was little he could do to stop her.

After a few seconds, Lindsey straightened and tightened her grip on the phone. "Dad?" she said. "It's me, Lindsey." She listened and nodded. "I'm alive." She eyed Trick. "Trick found me." She paused again. "I'm okay. And I know about Proteus. I know you want me to—"

She stopped and frowned. "Garret? No. I haven't seen him." She looked at Trick and he shook his head to indicate he didn't know where Garret was either. Her eyes widened. "He didn't? When's the last time you spoke to him?" She checked her watch.

Worried, Trick sat forward.

"Where was he staying?" Her face furrowed. "You're what? Where are you?" straightened. "You need to go back." She paused. "Dad, please. Let me and Trick handle it. We're already here. We'll find Garret."

Getting the picture, Trick stood, stacked the dirty plates, and brought them to the sink. He returned to the main room, grabbed his duffel bag, and packed it. Seeing his cowboy hat, he thought fast and made some decisions.

Lindsey stood, too. "Listen to me. We'll go look. You wait until you hear from me before you do anything."

Trick grabbed the Las Vegas baseball cap and put it on. He grabbed his cowboy hat, put it on the table, and grabbed the second phone. He scribbled the phone number and a brief note on a piece of paper from a notepad in the room, tucked it in the band around his hat, and left it on top of the table.

"Promise me, Dad. I'll call you as soon as I know something." She found her shoes and grabbed them. "I will. I love you too and don't worry. We'll find him." She hung up. "Garret's missing. He didn't check in with Dad last night or this morning, and Dad can't reach him." She hastily put on her shoes. "Dad's on his way. He's driving and about an hour out. I told him to hang back, but I don't know if he actually will."

Trick closed his duffel bag. "How long do you have this place rented for?"

"The next three days."

"Good."

Lindsey packed the rest of her stuff into a backpack and found her small purse. "You have a weapon?"

"No. Do you?"

She pulled a small switchblade out of her backpack and stuffed it into the back pocket of her jeans. "It'll do in a pinch, but I'd like something bigger."

"We'll see what we can find while we're out."

Lindsey slipped her backpack over her shoulder. "You realize this isn't part of the deal? I called Dad like you asked. You should go home."

"You called him, but you didn't tell him everything. And now, with Garret missing, you need me, whether you want to admit it or not."

Lindsey grabbed her car keys. "You sure you want to do this, Texas? You get involved in this, and Proteus will target you too."

"He's already targeted me. He knows I'm here, and he called me. So I'd say I'm involved."

Lindsey's eyes rounded. "When did he call you?"

"Yesterday, at lunch with your brother." Trick chastised himself. Proteus had obviously been watching them, but Trick had thought little of Garret's safety. "That's why I dumped my phone."

"Damnit. Garret should have known better. He's always been over-confident."

"Sounds like his sister."

Lindsey ignored his comment. "You have to be careful. If Proteus gets close, he'll use you to get to me, or vice versa. He's good at using people's weaknesses against them."

Trick picked up his duffel bag. "Then let's not give him what he wants."

"But if he gets that far, can you do that? Can you sacrifice me to get to him?"

"Can you do the same?"

She hesitated. "I'll do whatever it takes to get this man. He's that dangerous, and it's crucial that he doesn't leave this city alive. For both our sakes. And if he has Garret, he'll use him, too."

Trick sighed, hating to say his next words. "Then consider yourself expendable."

She nodded. "Good. You too."

Trick wondered if they both meant it, but didn't have time to reconsider his decision. They stood for a moment, holding a shared gaze, before Lindsey broke the look and opened the door. "Let's go."

Chapter Ten

Trick entered the lobby of the Hotel Olympic where Garret was staying. Ben had given Lindsey the name of the hotel and Garret's room number. After entering the lobby, Trick noted the peeling paint and worn carpets. Most of the patrons had either a cigarette or a drink in their hand and had the pasty look of people who wasted too much time indoors in front of a slot machine. "You and your brother don't spend much on accommodations, do you?"

"We're in Vegas. The cheaper and less obvious, the better." Lindsey scanned the lobby. "Keep your eyes open."

"What am I looking for?"

"Anything out of place."

Trick stepped back as an older gentleman with wild gray hair, wearing socks with sandals, and an old bathrobe over his torn shorts and a stained T-shirt, headed toward a slot machine. He pulled a handful of change out of his pocket and started feeding it into the machine. Trick pointed at him. "Does that count?"

Lindsey glanced at the gentleman. "Around here? No."

"If Morphman can become anyone, that could be him."

She headed toward the reception desk. "He wouldn't be caught dead in socks with sandals."

Trick followed. "Glad to know he's got fashion sense. Where are you going?"

"We're going to need a key to Garret's room."

"How are you going—"

Lindsey smiled and approached a short man in a dingy gray uniform and a bad comb-over standing behind the counter. "Excuse me, sir?" she asked.

He looked up with dull eyes. "Yes?"

"Can I get the key to room 809, please? It's under Garret Cobain."

"And you are?" He punched some keys into a keyboard.

"I'm his wife. Lindsey Cobain." She leaned over the counter. "He doesn't know I'm here. I came to surprise him."

Still looking bored, the man stared at the monitor. "Can I see some ID, please?"

"Sure." She dug through her purse and pulled out her wallet. "Here." She handed him her ID.

The man perused it. "That says Lindsey Eilish."

"I kept my maiden name." She put her ID away.

The man stared at her and then at Trick, who hung back behind Lindsey. "I'll need to call Mr. Cobain."

Lindsey smiled bigger. "But he's not in his room, and if you call, it will ruin the surprise."

He huffed. "I'm not supposed to give out keys if you're not listed as a guest."

"I understand." She leaned forward. "What's your name?"

"Roger."

"Roger." She lowered her voice. "Listen, Roger. I can certainly appreciate your professionalism, and I admire it. But do you think you could make an exception for me?"

Roger hesitated and offered her a flat look. "Are you really his wife?"

Lindsey paused, pursed her lips, moved closer, and whispered something to Roger. Her movement brought her breasts against the counter, and her snug T-shirt provided an ample view that Roger appreciated. Trick fought the urge to tug Lindsey back and shove Roger back behind his monitor.

As she spoke, Roger's eyes rounded, and he shot a look at Trick and leaned back. "Really?"

Lindsey nodded. "Really. So, can I have the key?" She crossed her fingers and held them up. "Please, Roger?"

Roger looked around, typed something, waited, and then handed Lindsey a keycard. "Don't tell anyone."

"Not a soul," Lindsey whispered. "You're the best, Roger."

Roger smiled and looked at Trick and glanced around again. "Any chance I could book you, too?"

Lindsey stepped back from the counter. "Oh, Roger. You couldn't possibly afford me." She tipped her head at Trick. "And he's even more expensive."

Roger's gaze traveled over Trick. "I bet."

Lindsey tucked the card into her back pocket and winked. "Thanks, Roger."

Roger nodded and watched as Lindsey and Trick headed to the elevators.

"I'm afraid to ask what you told him," said Trick.

An elevator arrived and opened, and Lindsey stepped inside. She hit the button for the eighth floor. "I told him we were here for a threesome with Garret."

Trick stared at her in surprise, but then chuckled and shook his head. "You're damn right I'd be more expensive than you."

The elevator slowed to a stop, and Lindsey snorted. "You wish." The doors opened, and she stepped off.

Trick joined her. "This way." He pointed down the hall and stopped in front of 809. "You ready?"

Lindsey pulled out her small knife and flicked it open. "Remember what we said."

Trick recalled their agreement vividly. "You're expendable."

"So are you."

"What about Garret?"

"Only as a last resort."

"Isn't that a given for any of us?"

She didn't answer and stepped to the side of the door. Trick stepped to the other side and knocked. "Garret? It's Trick. You in there?"

Hearing nothing, Trick knocked again. "Garret?"

Still not getting a response, Lindsey pulled out the keycard and swiped it. The reader turned green, and she opened the door. "Garret?" She peeked and stepped inside. "Hello?"

Trick followed her in and saw a messy room and an unmade bed, but no Garret. He closed the door behind him.

Lindsey checked the bathroom, and Trick opened the closet. "Nothing," said Lindsey.

"No sign of a struggle," added Trick.

Lindsey put her knife away and pulled out her phone. "I'm going to call him."

Trick put his hand on her wrist. "Use the hotel phone."

Lindsey nodded. "Good idea." She went to the landline and called Garret. "Nothing," she said, listening. "It goes to voicemail." She hung up. "Something is very wrong."

"His bag is here." Trick gestured to a small knapsack. "He hasn't checked out. Where would he go? He's looking for you. Maybe he thought he found you and he's staking the place out?"

"Then why wouldn't he call Dad and check in?"

"I don't know." Trick pulled out his burner cell. "Let me make a call."

Lindsey walked around the room, opening drawers. "Who are you calling?"

"The LVPD." He found the number and dialed.

"What for?"

When someone answered, Trick asked for Officer Novak.

Lindsey frowned. "Who's that?"

"My contact. I opened the missing persons' report on you with her. She knows me."

Lindsey's frown deepened. "How well does she know you?"

Trick almost smiled. "You worried?"

"No." Lindsey looked away. "What you do with your time is your business." She pulled back Garret's bed sheets and kept searching.

"Shocking as it may seem, I don't think she's interested."

Lindsey dropped the sheet. "Smart woman."

Trick smiled and heard a female respond over the phone. "This is Novak."

He spoke and was surprised when she told him she'd been trying to reach him. He explained that he'd had to change phones and wondered what her update was since he'd already located Lindsey. "What's the update?"

"A patrol spotted a woman matching the description of your missing person."

Trick raised his brow. He put the phone on speaker and waved Lindsey over. "You spotted Lindsey? Where and when?"

Lindsey came over and listened with interest.

Novak was gone for a second and then answered. "Yesterday evening. A patrol was responding to a noise complaint at the..." she paused and came back on the line. "...The Olympic Hotel."

Lindsey dropped her jaw.

"One of the responding officers believes he saw a woman that matched the description of Lindsey. He stopped her, but she insisted he had the wrong person. She was with a man, and the officer let her go, but he still made the report."

"Who was she with?" asked Trick, suddenly uncomfortable.

She paused. "The officer talked to him, and the man said his name was Garret, but gave no last name. The two of them walked off, got into a car and drove away."

"Did the officer get the plates?" asked Trick.

"He did."

"Did you run them?"

"I did. Car belongs to a rental company."

"Any chance you contacted the rental company?"

"I might have."

"Good for you, Novak. What did you learn?"

"The car's rented to Ben Sinatra with a San Diego address."

Recognizing the alias of Lindsey's dad, an icy chill ran up Trick's spine. Lindsey looked up at him with surprise.

"You still there, Mr. Monroe?" asked Novak. "Do you know that name?"

"I do," said Trick, "But I suspect it's a fake."

"Why do you say that?"

"Because Ben is not currently in Las Vegas."

"Then who rented the car?" asked Novak.

Lindsey paced.

"I don't know," said Trick. "But I need to open another missing persons' report, Novak."

"On who?" asked Novak.

"Garret Cobain. The man seen with the woman who met Lindsey's description."

"Are you telling me they're both missing?"

Trick eyed Lindsey. He suspected what was happening, but couldn't tell Novak. "That's what I'm saying."

"I'll need you to come in to file it."

"I can do that."

"The sooner the better, and maybe you can fill me in on what's going on here, Mr. Monroe."

Trick eyed his reflection in the mirror on the wall and wondered how he'd found himself in yet another giant mess. "I'll do my best, but you may not believe me."

"When can you be here?"

"I'm on my way."

"I'm off in an hour."

"I'll be there." He hung up and gaped at Lindsey. "What the hell does that mean? Garret walked away with you? Was it Proteus?"

"Well, it sure as hell wasn't me." Lindsey held her head. "That stupid idiot. Garret should know better. What was he thinking?"

"I think he thought he was with you. The question is, did he really think it was you, or was he pretending to think it was you?"

Lindsey continued to pace. "I have to think."

"How can Proteus become you when you weren't with him?"

Lindsey cursed. "Because...because he's done it before." Her voice tightened. "He became me once." She took a deep breath and groaned. "And once he does it, he retains the memory of it, and can do it again, whether I'm there or not. But Garret knows that, and he should have been prepared for it."

"Maybe he's not as prepared as you think, or maybe he went thinking he'd play along until he could get Proteus alone."

"If he did that, he could be dead."

"Or he's still hanging out with Proteus, thinking it's you."

She shook her head. "It's been too long. Proteus can't maintain a transition for that amount of time."

"Maybe his skills have improved."

Lindsey shot a look at him. "Don't even say that."

"I have to. He's been imprisoned for five years. Do you know anything about what's happened to him during that time?"

"No."

"Then you need to prepare for anything. If he's had five years to plan for this, there's no telling what he can do."

Lindsey cursed again. "I need to call Dad, but what do I tell him?"

"The truth."

"Then he'll rush right into this. I won't be able to stop him. Or protect him."

"That's his choice. You want him to honor your decisions, then you have to honor his."

Lindsey sat on the bed and rested her head in her hands. "You don't understand, Texas."

"Everyone keeps saying that." He sat beside her. "What don't I understand?"

Lindsey stared at the floor. "I...I can't..."

"You can't what?" Trick wished she would tell him everything. "You can talk to me."

A quiet moment passed, and Lindsey sniffed, but appeared to gather herself. "We can't just sit here. We have to find Garret." She straightened and wiped her eyes. "Let's go talk to Officer Novak."

Chapter Eleven

T rick sat in Lindsey's rented car outside the police station while Lindsey spoke with her father on the phone.

"I will, Dad. I promise. You too." She nodded. "Love you." She hung up and slid her cell into her pocket. "I got him to agree to wait on meeting up with us. He's here, but he'll stay on the outskirts of town and reach out to his connections in the city, and he'll look for a place for us to stay tonight."

"What, you don't want to go back to your fancy mobile home?" asked Trick.

She smirked at him and opened the door. "Let's go speak with your Officer Novak."

He got out with her. "Don't you think you should stay in the car? There's a missing person report out on you."

"Let me handle that. I want to be there."

"What about Proteus? If he's looking for you to come out into the open, this is a good place to start."

Lindsey looked around. "Let him look." She shut the car door.

Trick chose not to argue with her and headed into the building. He asked for Officer Novak at the front desk, and they were told to wait. They sat on a bench until Novak came around a corner.

Trick stood. "Novak."

"Mr. Monroe." Her hair was pulled back in its usual style and her striking green eyes perused Lindsey, who stared right back. After a few seconds, Lindsey glanced at Trick with an unreadable expression.

Novak's brow furrowed, and Trick sensed her questions, but Novak gestured toward the hall. "Come on back."

"Thanks." Trick followed her down the corridor and into a small office.

Novak sat behind a desk and Trick and Lindsey sat in the two chairs across from her. Novak looked between the two of them. "Before we get started, I'd like to ask the obvious question."

"Shoot," said Trick.

She pointed at Lindsey. "Isn't this the woman you're looking for?"

Trick glanced at Lindsey, who answered. "Yes, and no."

Novak set her elbows on her desk and interlaced her fingers. "You care to explain that?"

Lindsey settled back in her seat. "The woman who is missing is my twin sister."

Trick rubbed his chin and fought not to react.

"Your twin?" asked Novak.

"Yes. I'm Lindsey and the woman who is missing is Linda."

"But I thought Lindsey was the one who's missing," said Novak with a frown.

Lindsey rolled her eyes and shot an annoyed look at Trick. "He never could tell us apart."

Trick narrowed his eyes at her, but didn't say a word. If Lindsey wanted to explain all of this, he was going to let her.

"So, Linda is the actual missing person?" asked Novak.

Lindsey nodded. "Yes. And my brother Garret is also missing. He's the man Linda was with yesterday outside the Hotel Olympic."

Novak scratched her cheek. "If that was them outside the hotel, then they're not technically missing. And I can't keep a missing persons' report out on either of them."

Trick wondered how Lindsey would handle that one.

"I understand," said Lindsey, "but I believe they're currently in trouble. They don't respond to phone calls, nor have they returned to the hotel."

Novak sat back. "Just because they don't want you two to find them doesn't mean they're missing. And I need more to go on than they're in trouble. According to the officer who spoke to them yesterday, they were fine."

Lindsey tapped her fingertip on the armrest. "The problem is Linda is unstable. She recently...was released from a mental health facility. My father believes she's gone off her medication and is dangerous."

"Why would she want to hurt her brother?" asked Novak.

Trick waited to hear the answer.

Lindsey responded. "My brother is, or I should say, was responsible for sending her to the mental facility. She blames him for her, as she calls it, incarceration."

"Then why did he walk off with her?" asked Novak.

"My sister can be very convincing. She likely told him a lie, and he believed her, or he thought he could help, which he tends to do, without telling anyone his plans."

Novak nodded, but still seemed unconvinced. "How dangerous is Linda?"

Lindsey hesitated and sighed. "Off her meds? There's no telling. The whole reason she was sent to the facility in the first place is because..."

Trick waited.

Lindsey cleared her throat and shifted in her chair. "She hurt someone." She expelled a long breath. "If Garret doesn't handle her properly, and he can have a temper, I worry she'll hurt him too, and possibly kill him." She leaned in. "Any officer that sees them should approach with caution."

Novak studied Lindsey and sat back. "What facility was she in?"

Lindsey didn't miss a beat. "My father can get you all the details. Right now, I'd just like the LVPD to be on the lookout for both of them. I'd hate for something terrible to happen and have the LVPD blamed for not taking me seriously."

Novak pursed her lips and narrowed her gaze at Lindsey. "I can see your point." She glanced at Trick. "And what's your role in all of this?"

Trick pushed up in his seat. "I'm—"

"He's my father's illegitimate love child," Lindsey blurted. "We learned about his existence last year. My father's convinced Trick's interests are only to get to know the family, but personally, I think he's got his eyes on the inheritance."

Trick widened his eyes, but shut his mouth.

"He says he's trying to get to know us, but can't even tell the difference between me and Linda." Lindsey sat back with a huff. "That should tell you something." She crossed her arms. "Personally, I think he should mind his business and go home."

Trick rested an ankle on his knee. "Dad asked me to help, and maybe if you could accept that and try not to handle all the problems by yourself, we might find Linda and Garret a lot faster." Lindsey glared at him and looked away. Trick eyed Novak. "Sisters. They're such a pain in the ass."

Novak picked up a pen from the desk and waved it between the two of them. "So you two aren't a couple?"

Lindsey scoffed. "Hardly."

Trick waved his hand. "No. We are not. I can barely put up with her as a sibling." Unable to help himself, he grinned at Lindsey. "But if we weren't related...I think it could be interesting." He sat forward. "Don't you, Lindsey?"

Lindsey frowned back at him, but didn't respond.

"How come you didn't mention she was your sister when you filed the initial report?" Novak asked Trick.

"I didn't?" Trick shrugged. "I guess it never came up."

Lindsey scoffed and rolled her eyes.

Novak looked between them with suspicion, and after a quiet perusal, put her pen down. "Okay then." She pulled her keyboard over and started typing. "Let's amend your current report and get a new one started."

· · · · · ● · · ● · · ·

After their meeting with Novak, Trick and Lindsey left the station. As soon as they were out, Trick faced Lindsey with a scowl. "An illegitimate love child?"

Lindsey shrugged and pulled out her phone. "It sounded reasonable enough."

"What's wrong with just being a family friend?"

"Because the crazier the story, the easier it is for people to believe."

Trick had to admit that was true.

"I have to call Dad and tell him to prepare in case Novak calls." She dialed and headed toward their car.

"After that whole act, she'll definitely call. She'll want to be sure she's not getting sucked into some family drama."

Lindsey put her phone to her ear. "She is getting sucked into some family drama."

They headed into the parking lot while Lindsey talked to Ben and explained their conversation with Novak. Trick listened and after reaching the car, he waited as she finished her conversation and hung up. "Let me ask you something," said Trick. "You think it's smart to involve the police in this?"

"It's not great, but we need all the help we can get. Dad's got Marcy and Trey monitoring the activity from home, and other local connections keeping their ears open. If the police spot something, we'll know it."

Trick recalled meeting Lindsey's other two siblings, Marcy and Trey, at their secret base closer to home, and knew they had the tech to do what Lindsey suggested. "That doesn't mean we can get to Proteus and Garret first if a cop sees them."

"Proteus isn't going to let a cop subdue him. And if Garret is found, he'll know how to handle it. All we can hope for is that if they're spotted, we can get there in time to stop Proteus and help Garret."

"And if someone else gets hurt? Or Proteus morphs in front of your local LVPD officer, or worse, morphs *into* an officer?"

Lindsey put her hand on the roof of the car. "I don't know. All I can say is that we'll figure it out when the time comes. We don't have any other choice. We have to use the resources we have if we expect to find Proteus."

"I hope you're not inferring that others are expendable, along with each of us."

"That's not what I'm inferring." Lindsey opened the car door but paused. "Are you worried about Officer Novak?"

Trick put his hand on the edge of the door. "I'm worried about any officer who may confront Proteus."

"Novak seemed pleased you and I weren't involved. She may be more interested than she's letting on."

"Are you jealous?"

"Just making an observation. She's an attractive woman and just your type."

Trick ignored her attempts to goad him. "Never mind about Novak. If Proteus gets cornered, what will he do? Does he have a weapon?"

Turning somber, Lindsey leaned against the car. "No. He doesn't carry a gun, although he's skilled enough to use one. He's also trained in close combat, and he's lightning quick. If you come up against him, he won't be easy to bring down."

"Then how did you catch him the first time?" Trick closed the door and leaned a hip against it.

She crossed her arms and eyed the ground. "He was weak. He'd morphed, and the energy required to maintain it drained him. Garret, Dad, and Trey subdued him long enough to let Marcy inject him with a sedative."

"Where were you?"

She looked away and ran a clenched hand through her hair. "That's not important."

He sensed it was. "Where did this happen?"

Looking down, she scuffed her foot over the ground. "At our base."

"Where you work now?"

"No. After the incident with Proteus, we were compromised, and we...we couldn't stay after what happened. We were moved to our current base that you're familiar with."

Trick remembered the fancy home with the secret basement, where Ben's branch of the CU operated. "So, Proteus doesn't know about the new location?"

"No. He doesn't."

"Good." He considered another question. "You've told me all about how Proteus can morph into others, but what you haven't mentioned is who he is when he isn't morphed. What does he look like? Does he have an actual name?"

Her jaw tightened. "His actual name is unknown, although..." Tense, she looked everywhere but at Trick.

"Although what?"

"He called himself Michael, but I doubt he'd use that name now."

Trick wondered what role Michael had played in Lindsey's life. "What's he look like?"

Lindsey clenched her eyes shut for a second and opened them. "He's tall. Dark hair and eyes. Strong jaw and prominent cheekbones. Heavy brows. Lean and muscular."

"Sounds like he could model clothes in a magazine."

"Yeah." Her voice had softened, and all the confidence she'd displayed in Novak's office faded away.

Trick turned to face her. "What's going to happen when you see him again?"

Her face paled, but she straightened. "I'm going to kill him."

"You sure about that?"

Subdued, she looked away.

Seeing her insecurities bubble up at the mention of Michael concerned Trick. Lindsey rarely seemed unsure of anything, especially men. "All of that stuff about your sister Linda being in a facility? Were you referring to yourself or Proteus? How close to the truth was that?"

Lindsey abruptly pushed off of the car. "We need to go."

Guessing he'd hit a sore spot, Trick stepped out of her way and didn't pursue it. "Okay. Where would you like to go?"

She opened the door. "We'll go back to the hotel, watch and wait. Maybe Garret will come back or the police or one of Dad's contacts will see or hear something."

"That's a long shot."

"Then what do you suggest?" she asked, holding the door open.

Trick wanted to ask her to return to the mobile home and tell him everything about Michael, but his history with his mother, experiences with the Rangers, and all he'd seen and done since convinced him that Lindsey was suffering from an acute case of PTSD. Until she was ready to deal with it, all he could do was stick around until she felt safe to reveal her secrets. He decided to probe the waters. "You know you can talk to me, don't you?"

She stiffened. "About what?"

"About whatever happened between you and Michael."

The crease between her eyebrows deepened. "There's nothing to talk about."

Determined, he softened his voice. "Talking to family can be hard. There's all the emotion, drama and baggage. So, it may be easier to start with a friend. I'm a good listener, at least that's what Red tells me, and believe me, he's told me a few things."

She gripped the edge of the door. "I'm fine. There's nothing to discuss."

"You know that's bullshit. You're carrying a load heavy enough to cripple Superman, and eventually, it will break you. And if Michael knows that, he'll use it as a weapon against you."

"Stop calling him Michael. He's Proteus."

"Call him what you want, but you need to deal with whatever went down between you two." He stepped closer. "I'm your friend, Lindsey. Let me help you."

She stepped back. "You can't help me because I don't need help. And you're not exactly the poster child for mental health, so stop acting like you're some sort of expert."

Her pushback didn't surprise him. "Sometimes, broken people are your best source of support. We know what the other needs because we've been there."

She raised her voice. "Just leave me alone, Texas."

He gently touched her forearm. "That's what everyone's been doing, haven't they? Leaving you alone. Giving you time. Letting you work it out. Allowing you to push them away when they get too close. Well, I don't push so easy. Ask Red. He tried his damnedest to get me to leave him alone when I confronted him about his addiction, and our friendship suffered, but I didn't give up, and eventually he caved."

"You're comparing me to an addict?"

"I'm comparing you to the most stubborn man alive, and if I could get through to him, I can get through to you."

She huffed. "You have no idea what you're up against."

"I've got an idea."

She turned away from him. A gust of wind blew her hair, and she brushed it back roughly. "Like I said, you don't understand."

"Then enlighten me."

"I'm not strong enough." She studied the ground. "I'm not ready."

"Red said the same thing, but he got through it, and he's stronger now than he's ever been."

A few quiet seconds passed, and he hoped she was considering it. After a few seconds, she turned to face him with shimmering eyes. "As much as I hate to admit this, I care about what you think of me, and once you know, you'll never look at me the same way again, and...and I'm not sure I can bear that." She gritted her teeth.

He wrapped his fingers around her wrist and slid them into her hand. "Nothing you say will change the way I feel about you. You already drive me nuts. How much worse can it get?"

She squeezed his fingers. "Pretty bad."

Happy she was ready to at least start the conversation, he gestured toward the car. "Let's get in, and you can tell me whatever you're ready to. We'll take it slow."

She wiped away an unshed tear and shook her head. "I...I don't know."

"Hang in there with me, GQ. Don't get spooked. You can do this."

"God..." She took a shaky breath and sniffed. "I hate being scared."

"Join the club." He pulled on her hand, and she stepped closer. Another gust of wind blew, and he brushed a strand of her hair off her cheek. "Red and I met with his addiction counselor, Tarina, once. She told us scared just means you're almost past the worst of it. The closer you get to facing it, the scarier it gets. But it's just an illusion designed to keep you right where you are. That's why it's important to face your fear, and when you do, you realize there was nothing to be afraid of."

Her face tightened, and she groaned. "Why can't you just leave me alone?"

Trick thought of his mom. "Because I've seen what can happen if you leave someone alone, or if you don't and they refuse your help. You end up in a rundown mobile home park drinking yourself to death with tequila. It's a hard road, honey, and you deserve better."

"I'm not too sure about that."

"Let me be the judge. If I think you should spend eternity in the fires of hell, I'll let you know, but don't count on it. I tend to be lenient when it comes to eternal damnation."

She surprised him when she got closer and dropped her head on his shoulder. "I may be the exception."

Hearing the pain in her voice, his chest tightened. He put his free hand on the back of her head and stroked her hair. "You've done a lot of good in this world, GQ. That counts for something."

She let go of his hand and wrapped her arms around him. Hugging her back and feeling her body against his made his heart thump. And although people walked to and from the parking lot on their way in and out of the police station, Trick barely noticed them. "You ready to try?" he asked.

She nodded and pulled back. "No promises, though. I may clam up on you. And if I don't, the ugly cry is a guarantee."

"No promises required. Just do your best. And the uglier, the better."

Wiping her eyes again, she stepped back and looked up at him. "Every time I think I have you pegged, Texas, you surprise me."

"It's part of my charm. It drives my mom nuts." He stepped around her and pulled the door open for her.

She hesitated, but then took a shuddered breath. "Okay, let's—" She took a step and froze. Looking behind Trick, she stared with wide eyes. "No," she said, her face draining of color.

"What's wrong?" Trick swiveled to look behind him, but only saw parked cars, the road, and pedestrians.

"It's him."

Before Trick could ask who she was seeing, Lindsey cursed, darted around Trick and took off in a dead run.

Chapter Twelve

Lindsey shot through the lot, passing parked cars, and headed toward a small strip mall that bordered the parking lot near the police station. She couldn't believe it when she'd spotted Proteus standing against the side wall of the mall, watching her and Trick. At first, he'd appeared as just another person near the busy road that led to the police station. But something about his stance, his familiar features, and the way he studied them made her hair stand on end, and she'd known immediately it was him.

As soon as he'd caught her eye, he'd darted around the wall toward the front of the row of shops and disappeared. Running fast, she raced to catch up to him. Her logical mind told her to be careful, that this could be a trap, and not to go alone, but her emotional side raged with the need to stop him and find Garret. Proteus had already taken so much from her, and she couldn't allow him to take more. With no thought of whether Trick was even behind her, she made it to the corner of the mall and turned around it. She heard and saw the cars driving down the busy street. A few patrons walking along the sidewalk moved back as she ran by. A homeless woman pulling a cart stepped up onto the curb in front of her, and she spotted Proteus at the opposite end of the shops racing across a side street. She ran down the front of the shops. A couple yelled at her, but she ignored them and kept going. Dodging people, she ran across the street and into the parking lot of an apartment building. Not seeing Proteus, her heart raced with adrenaline and fury. Moving farther into the complex, she stopped when she saw a figure dart over a concrete wall with iron bars extending above it and disappear into a lot where several unattached box trailers were parked. Not hesitating, she pursued.

· · · · ● · · ● · · ·

Trick took off after Lindsey. Not seeing what had set her off, all he could do was stay behind her, but she was quick. She ran toward a small strip mall that faced the street they'd driven in on. She raced around the corner and out of his sight, but he picked up his pace to close the distance. Rounding the corner, he ran straight into a homeless woman pulling a small cart. Trick, trying to avoid colliding with her, ran straight into the cart, stumbled and fell to the concrete. His elbow and knee flared from the impact and the cart broke; the various items within it spilling out onto the concrete.

The woman started screaming at him and hitting him with her large purse. Trick did his best to apologize and dodge the blows before jumping up and running off to chase Lindsey. He barely caught sight of her as she crossed a nearby street and ran into an apartment complex. Picking up his speed despite his sore knee, he raced to catch up with her.

· · · · ● · · ● · · ·

Lindsey stepped up onto the waist-high concrete barrier between the apartments and the trailer lot and carefully jumped over the iron bars. She landed in the parking lot where several long trailers sat empty. It was quiet, and no one was around, but she knew this was where Proteus had gone. She carefully weaved her way around the many trailers, trying to catch her breath. Looking for any sign of Proteus, she pulled her knife from her belt and flicked it open.

· · · · ● · · ● · · ·

Trick entered the apartment complex and scanned the area, but didn't see Lindsey. Slowing his pace, he walked through the main buildings. There were only three, so it didn't take long, but there was no sign of her. He ran to the back of the buildings where he saw parked cars, dumpsters, and a low concrete wall with iron bars above it that separated the complex from a lot full of empty box trailers. Wondering if she could have gone there, he stepped up onto the concrete barrier and held onto the iron bars. Looking around, he didn't see her and was about to pull himself over the bars when he heard her call his name.

Swiveling back toward the complex, he hopped off the concrete wall and back into the apartment parking lot. "Lindsey?" he yelled. "Where are you?"

She poked her head out from behind her dumpster. "Here. I'm over here."

Relieved she was okay, he ran toward her. "What the hell did you see?" He stepped behind the dumpster and grimaced at the smell. "Why are you back here?"

She stared over the wall and into the lot of trailers. "Shh," she said. "He's over there."

He came up beside her. "Who is?"

A second passed, and she straightened. She stared at Trick and smiled.

"Lindsey?" he asked. "You okay?"

She took a step toward him. "I can see why she likes you."

Trick frowned, wondering what she meant, when a barely perceptible ripple traveled over her skin. Before he could react, she grabbed his wrist, and the effect was immediate. His legs buckled, and it felt like warm cement ran through his veins. Trick tried to speak, but it was hard to form words. Unable to hold himself up, he dropped to his knees.

Lindsey leaned over him, but he knew it wasn't her. "Sorry," she said. "But she and I need to talk."

Trick wobbled, trying to stay upright. "Leave...leave her...alone." He fell forward, his hands on the hard cement, and then tipped over to his side. He blinked several times and tried to stay conscious, but his strength vanished, and just before he lost consciousness, he watched in shock as Lindsey's face morphed into his own.

· · • • • • • • · ·

Frustrated, Lindsey walked through the narrow passages created by the parked trailers. She looked under and around them but saw nothing. Angry that Proteus had gotten away from her, she left the back of the lot and headed toward another lot that backed up to the trailers. Studying it, she saw a junkyard cluttered with old cars, machinery, wood, bricks, and discarded, used equipment she guessed was all for sale. It would be a perfect place to hide. Heading into the area, she stopped when she heard her name called. Trick came around a trailer just down from her and ran over. "What are you doing?" he asked, breathless.

Worried Proteus was watching, she pulled him behind a trailer. "Get back. He's out here."

"Who?" he asked.

"Proteus. He was watching us outside the police station."

Trick looked both ways. "And you think he's here?"

"I followed him."

Trick raised a brow. "Are you sure? Why would he come here?"

She pushed him against the trailer. "Just be quiet. Stay here and let me look."

Lindsey started to walk toward the junkyard, but Trick stayed right behind her. She stopped and looked back. "What are you doing?"

"Sticking close. I want to protect you."

"I can protect myself."

He snickered. "You always were bossy."

Something in his voice caught her attention. "What's the matter with you?"

He stepped away and casually leaned against the trailer. "Me? I'm fine. How are you?"

Concerned, she studied him. "Now is not the time to get cocky. I have to find Proteus."

Trick pushed off the trailer and approached her again. He lowered his voice and grinned at her. "It's quiet back here." He ran a fingertip down her arm. "Ever get frisky in an empty trailer lot?"

Seeing his smile, her skin prickled. She leaned back, but he leaned with her and stayed close.

He chuckled. "What's the matter, Linds? Not in the mood?" His smile fell. "Since when?"

The nickname confirmed her worse fears. It wasn't Trick she was talking to.

Chapter Thirteen

Lindsey brought her knife up, but Proteus was faster. He grabbed her wrist, put his other hand around her throat, and shoved her up against the trailer. Her head hit hard, and she lost her breath. She expected the warm heaviness to hit her as it had done the last time he'd assaulted her, but it didn't happen. She remained conscious, but her limbs tingled with a strange electricity. Attempting to push back, she struggled against him, but he laughed at her.

"There's no point," he said, tightening his hold on her throat.

Her throat constricted but still able to breathe, she grabbed his wrist with her free hand. "Let me go," she said, her voice strained.

"So you can stab me? No. I don't think so." He tightened his hold on her wrist and banged it against the trailer until she dropped the knife. Still holding onto her, he brought his face close to hers. "I've missed you."

Lindsey fought to recoil, but had nowhere to go.

He was so close, his lips grazed her cheek. "Did you miss me?" he asked.

She averted her gaze. "No."

He pushed his body against hers. "I thought about you all the time. I had a lot of it. Prison, at least the one I was in, doesn't allow for much else."

Lindsey squirmed to get away from him, but only succeeded in moving against him.

"What's the matter?" he asked. His face, which was morphed into Trick's, twisted in a sneer. "You used to love it when I touched you. You and I couldn't get enough of each other, remember?"

Lindsey's stomach lurched at the memory.

"Those were the days, weren't they? I remember them fondly."

"Where's Garret?" She was desperate to get him away from him and not join him in his reflections of the past.

"Alive. For now." He leaned in and smelled her skin. "Your family needs to be more careful."

"Don't hurt him."

"That's up to you, provided you do as I say."

Her heart thumped harder when she thought of Trick. "Where's Trick?"

His smile grew. "Behind some dumpsters."

Still trying to pull his hand from her throat, she dug her nails into his wrist when she feared the worst. "No."

"Don't worry, kitten. He's alive."

Relief raced through her. "Leave him alone. He's not a part of this."

"But he is. I saw you two together." He clenched his fingers tighter around her neck, and she clutched at his hand when her air cut off. "What do you see in him?" he asked. He looked at himself. "Is this what you like? His body? His face?" He loosened his hold. "Does he make you cry out in pleasure like I did?"

She didn't answer but sucked in a breath to get much needed air.

"You disappoint me," he said. "After all this time, he's the one you choose? I expected more from you." He moved closer, and his breathing deepened. "I bet we could rekindle those memories, right here and now, and you could see what you're missing."

Her stomach flipped, and she wanted to scream but didn't have the lung capacity to do it. "Don't touch me," was all she could muster.

He pulled back, but remained close. "Too bad. But I can see why you're distracted." He paused. "Tomorrow is the big day, isn't it?"

She whimpered under her breath.

"Five years." He closed his eyes. "Since I took what I wanted." He drew a deep breath and blew it out. "I relived that moment every day in my cell."

He opened his eyes. "It's what motivated me, encouraged me, and gave me hope that one day," he dragged his lips over hers, "I could do it again."

Lindsey fought to turn her face away from him.

He pulled back. "Why the resistance? I am him, after all. Don't I turn you on?"

"You're not him," she whispered. "I don't care what you look like."

His face fell. "Aww. That's sweet. You truly care for him, is that it?" He lowered his voice. "Do you have feelings for him? Is it love?"

Lindsey struggled again to get loose.

"Seems I hit a nerve. Maybe when I'm done with you, I'll return to your boyfriend and finish the job." His face twisted again. "It's the least I could do, especially on such a special anniversary."

"Don't. Leave him alone."

He stared down at her, and his eyes narrowed. "Do you think you have a future with him? After what you did? After your failure?" He shook his head. "Does he know? Have you told him?"

Tears sprang into Lindsey's eyes.

He smiled softly. "No?" He chuckled. "That's good, because once he knows, he can't possibly love you in return. Maybe your family can look the other way. They have no choice. But he does." Proteus whispered in her ear. "What you did is unforgivable."

Lindsey groaned. "I didn't do it. You did."

He whispered again. "You know that, but *she* never did. Such a shame."

The memories swirled again in Lindsey's mind, and the overwhelming grief and guilt surged through her. "Leave me alone." A tear escaped and trickled down her cheek.

He grazed his lips from her ear to her mouth. "I will never leave you, or your family, alone, until you are all destroyed."

Lindsey tightened her lips, and he moved his face away from hers. "But you will be the last, Linds. I'll take everyone else first. And when I take you, only then will you feel the release from your pain—when you take your final breath."

Her eyes filled with tears, and she pulled on whatever strength she had left. "Not if I kill you first."

He ran his thumb over her neck. "Better be sure it's me, then. I'd hate for you to kill someone you loved...again."

Lindsey cursed at him and called him an ugly name.

"That's the lady I remember." He sighed. "I always loved that about you. Your fight. And your confidence. You were a challenge I loved conquering. I liked our dance and using you to get what I wanted. And it was so easy. You fell like a stone in water, and I relished my victory."

Lindsey gathered what remaining saliva she had in her mouth and spat in his face. It hit him in the cheek and ran down his skin.

His expression darkened, and his grip tightened. "Be glad I'm not ready to kill you yet."

Trying to get oxygen, Lindsey clawed at his fingers. Seeing stars, she fought to stay conscious. When he eased off, she sucked in a gulp of air and fought to speak. "Kill me now."

He tipped his head. "Nice try, but not yet. There's more to do. Aren't you worried about Garret? And Ben? And Marcy and Trey?" He let go of her wrist, wiped the spit from his face, and brought his hand to her jaw and stroked it. "They're all next, you know? After Garret."

Her wrist free, her arm dropped, and she fought to raise it, but that strange tingling had taken all her strength.

"I might change my mind though, provided you do as I ask. Not everyone has to die."

She forced her free hand up and weakly pushed against his arm. "What do you want?"

"It's about time you asked." He loosened his hold on her throat. "I thought about this day frequently while lying in my cell." He glanced at the sky. "I never saw daylight other than from a small window. Do you know that? I understand why. No one could come near me for obvious reasons. Until I befriended a very nice guard. We spoke for months before I finally convinced him he could trust me. Then one day, he came into my cell to help me when I collapsed and fell ill. That's when I became him, killed him, and walked out of that prison minutes later." He ran his hand over her hair. "And now I'm here. Talking to you. And everything is falling into place, just like I imagined it."

Able to breathe easier, Lindsey tried to stop her voice from shaking. "What did you imagine?"

"My revenge."

"You took your revenge when you betrayed me."

"But I'm not done. After your family put me in that place, I had plenty of time to plan, strategize, imagine, and now that I'm out, I want to savor my freedom and the unfolding of my vision. There's no rush to take everyone at once. I want to enjoy my time with you, and this is one way to do it."

"Where is Garret?" she asked again.

He glared down at her. "He keeps goading me, you know? Tells me to leave you alone, to take him instead. He's a noble brother. So, I figure, why not let you both decide what happens next?"

Lindsey's stomach rebelled and she almost retched. "What do you want?"

He lowered his hand, reached into the pocket of his Trick lookalike jeans, and pulled out what looked like Garret's wallet. He held it up to her and tossed it to the ground. "There are instructions inside. Follow them, and you'll see your brother again. If not, I'll kill him, and tomorrow will have a whole new reason for you to mark the day."

She squirmed again, and he tightened his hold on her.

"And leave everyone else out of it. If your father, or Trick, shows, I'll kill them both." His sneer returned. "And don't even think of taking yourself out of this fight. You disappear or off yourself, know that what you have experienced will pale compared to what I'll do to the ones you love."

Disgusted, Lindsey pushed against him, but he didn't budge. "Let me go," she pleaded.

He brought his lips close to hers again. "It's been nice to reconnect. You look as good as always. Too bad we can't relive old memories." He slid his free hand down her shoulder, to her hip and thigh.

She froze, hating his touch.

His gaze held hers. "I bet you're not the ice queen for him." He squeezed her butt. "I could go back to the dumpster. Give him a few pointers."

A flare of strength allowed her to shove his hand away from her. "As I recall, you weren't that memorable. I faked most of my interest."

His smile dropped. "I think we both know that's not true."

She sucked in some air. "But you'll never know for sure."

His gaze held, but then he eased off. "You're good. But not that good."

"I could say the same."

"We'll see about that. You don't know everything. Just remember I took from you before, and I will take from you again. Your family can hide in their little lair, but it won't stop me from finding them. I did it once, and I can do it again. Just look at Garret. He came out in the open to rescue you, and now you have to rescue him."

Her limbs heavy and her head foggy, she refused to back down. "I'll find a way to stop you."

"Good. That means you and I will continue our little dance. Just be sure no one else gets in the way, especially Mr. Monroe. I have no issue taking him next. In fact, it would be a delight." His eyes twinkled. "Especially if he thought his attacker was someone he trusted."

Thinking of the past and Trick's safety, Lindsey considered the only thing that could protect him. "I'll get rid of Trick."

"That's up to you. I'm not the jealous type." He trailed a finger down her cheek again. "It was nice to see you again. I've enjoyed reconnecting, even if it was as him." He made a face of displeasure. "But maybe you'd like to remember me as I was? Will that warm you up?" He stilled and closed his eyes.

Seeing his skin ripple, Lindsey watched as his features softened and shifted, and his face and body became the person she recognized as Michael.

"Is that better?" he asked with a shiver. "It is for me."

"You looked better before," she said.

He laughed. "Same old Lindsey. It's a shame we had to break up." His lips hovered over hers again. "Admit it. You missed me just a little."

She turned her face away from his. "Get away from me."

His features hardened, and he forcibly kissed her. She mashed her lips together and endured his assault until he abruptly pulled away, released her throat, and stepped back.

Free from his grasp, she collapsed to her knees and went to all fours, sucking in deep breaths.

He touched her head. "Until we meet again, kitten."

Recoiling and holding her throat, she waited until the stars faded from her vision, her head cleared, and when she looked up, he was gone.

• • • • • • • • • •

His awareness returning, Trick moved his head and felt the abrasive concrete beneath his cheek. Moaning, he wondered where he was and cracked his eyes open. His head throbbed, his limbs felt heavy, and it hurt to move. Getting his hands beneath him, he tried to push up but barely had the strength. He fell back to the ground, took a second to gather himself, and pushed up again. Groaning, he got himself up to a sitting position. Rubbing his eyes, he took several deep breaths and tried to remember what had happened. His mind slowly cleared, and he recalled looking for Lindsey. They'd left the police station, made it to the car, and then she'd run off. He'd followed and... Trick straightened when he had a clear recollection of Lindsey calling him from behind the dumpster. He'd run over, but it had been Proteus. Horrified, Trick remembered Proteus grabbing him and morphing into Trick. Fearing for Lindsey, Trick gritted his teeth and forced himself to his feet. He had to find her.

Putting his hand on the dumpster for balance, he checked his watch and was shocked to see he'd been out for almost an hour. He cursed to himself, shook his head to clear the cobwebs, and stepped out from behind the dumpster.

No one was around, and he saw the trailer lot behind the apartment complex. He'd been about to go over the wall when Proteus had derailed him. Trying to walk fast but struggling, he made it to the wall but didn't have the strength to pull himself over it. Frustrated, he followed the wall back around to the front of the complex, where he walked through the entrance and into the lot filled with empty trailers. He didn't see anyone and chose one side of the lot and made his way through the narrow spaces. Not seeing her, he cursed when he thought of his phone. He pulled it out and was surprised to see it was dead. Sliding the phone back into his pocket, he kept looking and prayed Proteus would not return. Another attack from him would doom Trick and likely Lindsey too. Staying alert and his strength improving, he headed down another aisle. He stooped low to look beneath the trailers and saw someone sitting on the ground several trailers over. Not sure if it was Lindsey, he ran down to the end of the corridor and past several trailers until he found the right aisle.

Seeing Lindsey sitting on the ground, he raced over to her. "Lindsey?" Sitting cross-legged, she jumped when he approached, and he squatted next to her. "Are you okay?"

Her face clenched, and she leaned away from him. That's when he saw the bruises on her throat. "What happened?" He reached for her, but she pushed him away and got to her feet.

Seeing her wide eyes and pale face, he softened his approach and made a guess about why she didn't want him near her. He raised his hands. "It's me, GQ. It's Texas. I'm not Proteus."

Clearly uncertain, she backed up until her back hit the trailer. "Don't. Just stay back."

"You're safe. I won't hurt you." He noticed she held a wallet in her hand. "What did he do? Are you hurt?"

She touched her throat and seemed confused. "I'm fine."

"No, you're not. Let me help you."

She moved away at his approach.

He spoke softly. "It's me, honey. I promise."

Her gaze traveled over him. "How did we meet?"

Trick thought back. "I was with Kyle. We were on a case and looking for Jackson Trammel. It was in a bar called Bullard's. I noticed you the moment you sat at the bar and made my move, but you shot me down like a spy plane. I didn't know at the time that you were following us."

She stared at him, and a moment passed, and she nodded. "Are you okay?"

He rubbed his tingling arms. "I'm getting better. I'm going to take a few steps toward you, okay? Don't freak out."

She didn't move, and he walked up to her. Seeing her neck, he felt the bile rise in his throat. "What happened?" He tried to touch her bruises, but she stiffened.

"Nothing. I'm fine."

"Your neck is half-purple."

Lindsey stared off. "It's okay."

Trick didn't like her faraway look. "What's wrong, Lindsey? Talk to me." He tried to take her hand, but she pulled away.

"I don't want to talk about it."

"Proteus approached you as me, didn't he?" Trick wanted to punch the side of the trailer.

Her face fell, and she looked away. "He...he..."

He tried again to touch her, but she wouldn't let him. "Take it easy," he said.

Lindsey closed her eyes and opened them. "He has Garret."

"What did he tell you about Garret?"

She took a heavy breath. "He gave me Garret's wallet to prove he had him. He told me...he..." She bit her lip and held her head.

Trick eased up beside her, but didn't touch her. "Is Garret alive?"

She nodded. "Yes. Proteus said...he told me to wait, and he would be in touch."

"About Garret?"

"Yes."

"When?"

She swallowed and grimaced. "Tomorrow. Sometime tomorrow. I don't know when."

"Did he mention what his plan was?"

She shook her head. "No."

Trick suspected there was more to Proteus' visit than just Garret. "What else did Proteus say?"

She studied the wallet. "Nothing."

Trick sensed the lie. "What are you hiding, Lindsey? What did Proteus really want?" He paused and asked the question he dreaded the answer to. "Did he touch you?"

She shook her head. "No. He threatened it, but that's all." She gingerly touched her neck.

"Why did he hurt you?"

"Because that's what he does," she said sharply. Holding her throat, she stepped away from the trailer. "I need to call Dad."

"Wait a minute. Don't shut me out, Lindsey. I know there's more."

She turned on him. "You can't help me."

Trick stiffened. It was obvious Proteus had messed with Lindsey's head. "What did he say?"

"Nothing. Just let it be." She started to walk away.

"Don't do that. He's playing games with you. Don't let him win."

She whirled to face him. "You don't know what you're talking about. This has nothing to do with you." She clenched her eyes shut. "It's better if you leave."

Trick forced himself to relax. Proteus had pulled Lindsey back into the dark mindset that had brought her to Vegas and the last thing she needed was Trick telling her what to do. He recalled their conversation in the parking lot and how close he'd come to getting her to open up to him. "I can't do that."

She opened her eyes and glared. "Yes, you can. If you care about me, that's exactly what you'll do."

"It's because I care about you that I won't."

"Damn it. Why won't you listen to me? I don't want you here."

"Your father does."

"He wanted you to find me, well now I'm found. Your job is over."

Trick took a breath. "I want to help you, Lindsey."

"I didn't ask for your help," she yelled. "This is my battle to fight." She lowered her voice. "So please go home."

The sound of defeat in her voice made Trick want to take her in his arms and hold her. "I'll make you a deal. If Ben tells me to leave, then I will."

She shot a look at him. "That's not fair. You know he'll side with you."

"Then I guess you're stuck with me."

Scowling, she turned and walked away.

Trick followed, wondering what he could do or say to get the confident Lindsey back. "You're not going to find a bottle of tequila, are you?"

She didn't answer, but kept walking.

"You can try to shut me out, but I like I told you before, I'm not going anywhere. I'm your friend, Lindsey."

She walked through the lot. "If you were my friend, you'd do as I ask, and leave."

Trick followed, glad his strength had returned and the tingling in his limbs was gone. Hearing the tone in Lindsey's voice, he had another theory. "Is this about you, Proteus, or me?"

She turned to face him. "It's about all three of us. I can't do what I have to do if I have to...to..."

"To what? Protect me?"

She turned around and kept walking.

He stayed behind her. "You don't have to protect me. As you so often like to say, I can take care of myself."

She whirled again and waved her hands. "He became you. He walked right up to me, and I didn't know. Now he can do it whenever he wants. He can become me, and you wouldn't know the difference."

Trick recalled her shouting his name from behind the dumpster. "We can still stop him."

"No, you can't. I'm not even sure I can. And I'm not going to watch anyone else die." Her eyes sharpened. "This is my battle to face. I screwed it up the first time around, but I don't have to screw it up again. You're a distraction, Trick. If I worry about you, it could get me killed, and if you worry about me, it could get you killed. So, please stop staring at me like I'm some pathetic woman on the edge and pretending like you have all the answers because you don't. He got to you once and he can do it again, and I can't afford any more loose ends."

He stared back at her, uncertain of what to say.

"You're a liability, Trick. And I don't need that right now. Stop trying to be my hero."

His heart hammering, Trick found himself at a loss for words. Was she right? Was he only adding to the danger and putting her and himself at risk? "The last thing I want to do is hurt you."

"If that's true, then you know what you have to do." Her voice tight, she turned back toward the exit of the lot. "I'm going back to the car. If you're ready, I'll drop you at the airport. The sooner you leave, the better."

Stunned, Trick watched her walk away.

Chapter Fourteen

Finally free for the day, Samantha Novak walked out of the police station, although she'd left later than planned. After updating the missing person's report for Trick Monroe and his supposed sister, Lindsey, Novak had been about to leave when her superior, Captain Filmore, had called her into his office and asked to assist a new rookie, Officer Collins, with the new database and reporting system. Novak had informed him she'd just gone off duty, but he'd asked her to do him a solid and help him out. The officer assigned to train Collins had called in sick and his replacement wouldn't be in for another hour. Filmore had a meeting to get to and didn't have the time to deal with Collins.

Guessing Filmore's meeting was at the golf course with his police cronies, Novak agreed to help because she wanted to make an impression and get on Filmore's good side. Being a rookie officer herself, plus a young, attractive female, she knew she'd have to work harder to get the respect of the more seasoned male officers on the force, so she agreed to stay until the replacement officer arrived. Filmore had smacked her on the shoulder, told her he'd remember her good deed, and left.

Novak spent the next hour trying to teach Collins how to search the database, make reports, and run plates until the replacement officer arrived. Once he did, she headed to the locker rooms. She changed out of her uniform into street clothes and took her hair out of the tight bun and brushed it out. After hooking her badge and holstered gun to her belt, she threw on her jacket, grabbed her purse, and left.

Glad to be out of the station, she took a deep breath and appreciated the sunshine. It was warm outside, but not too hot, and she debated what to do with the rest of her day.

"Hey, Novak. Lookin' good."

She looked over to see Charlie Hanson, an experienced officer who'd trained her for a short time before another officer took his place. Novak wondered if the change had something to do with Hanson's frequent sexual innuendos and flirty conversation.

"Hanson," she said, and kept walking, although she didn't miss his perusal. It happened frequently with certain colleagues, but she did her best to ignore it.

"Going somewhere fun?" he asked. "Want some company?" He passed her and turned to walk backwards.

"I'm good. Thanks." She headed toward the parking lot and didn't look back.

"You change your mind, you let me know," she heard him shout back.

Ignoring him and rolling her eyes, she adjusted her purse over her shoulder and wondered if she could put up with this crap long enough to become a detective. Her father had been a revered one, and it was all she'd wanted to do since she was a little girl, but the price to pay to get there was high. She'd always been determined and stubborn, though, and she'd get there, even if it meant moving to another city where it might provide more opportunity. For now, though, she'd stick to where she was, get more experience, and see where the road took her.

Thinking about the future and maybe stopping at the grocery store on the way home, she glanced to her right when she heard arguing. As she stepped into the parking lot, she saw a man and woman in a heated conversation near where she'd parked her car. She almost ignored it, but stopped when she recognized the couple. It was Trick and Lindsey, the two who'd reported their sister and brother missing.

Frowning, she wondered what they were still doing at the station, since they'd made their report over an hour ago. Hearing bits and pieces of their conversation and recalling the story they'd told about the missing twin and a brother named Garret, Novak's suspicion grew. Trick's initial report about the missing Lindsey, and then the updated report about the missing twin Linda, had made Novak question the truth of their account. After the two had left the station, she'd even brought the information to Fillmore to ask if she should investigate their story.

Fillmore had chuckled, told her to stop overthinking and file the report. He'd said it was Vegas and suspected the two missing siblings were likely drinking and gambling and would turn up in either a ditch somewhere or passed out on the sidewalk. Or they wouldn't turn up at all. Novak hadn't argued with him and completed the report.

Seeing the couple again, though, her curiosity got the better of her. They were so caught up in their argument, they were paying no attention to anyone around them, so Novak stooped low, walked past a few rows of cars, and came up the row near where Trick and Lindsey were parked. Crouching down on her hands and knees, Novak eavesdropped on their conversation.

· · · · ● · ● · · ·

Trick tried hard to rein in his anger. On the walk back to the car, he'd stayed quiet and so did Lindsey, but the more he thought about their conversation, the angrier he became. Especially when he realized Lindsey had played the same mind games with him that Proteus had played on her, and he'd fallen for it.

She'd made him doubt himself, question his decisions and think this dire situation between Proteus and her family would suffer if he stayed. Returning to the car, though, he chucked all that crap to the curb, and as

Lindsey approached the driver's side of the car, he walked up next to her. "I'm not leaving."

Lindsey cursed and faced him. "Are you deaf? I don't want you here."

"I hear fine, thank you, and what do you care if I stay? We're expendable, remember? Didn't we agree to that?"

"Why be expendable if you don't have to be?"

"Why do you really want me to leave?"

"Because, damn it, you're a pain in my ass. Just like Garret. And look where Garret is. If you stay, that's one more person at risk."

"If I stay, that's one more person to help. You can't do this on your own, which I suspect is your plan."

"My plan is none of your business," she yelled.

"Yes, it is. I've come too far to stop now. Proteus attacked me and now he can become me. You think I'm just going to hang up my hat after that?"

"If you're smart, yes."

"Then I guess I'm stupid."

"You're right about that much."

Trick opened his mouth to respond when Lindsey's phone rang.

She took it from her purse. "It's Dad."

Trick took his baseball cap off of his head and ruffled his hair. "Answer it and tell him what you want me to do. If he agrees with you, I'll take the next flight out." He put his hat back on and waited.

She glared at him and answered her phone. Stepping away, he heard her talking and picked up on some of the conversation. She was telling Ben about making the report with Novak and about what happened afterward. When she got to the part about Proteus, she mentioned Garret, but said nothing more about her interaction with Proteus. Then she started talking about Trick.

Lindsey's voice hardened and her voice rose, and after listening to her dad, she simply responded, "Fine." Before hanging up and returning to the car. "Shocking. He doesn't want you to leave. You win."

"This is not about winning, Lindsey." Trick fought to keep his anger at bay. "This is about you and your family, and Proteus, and making sure he's stopped."

She put her hand on the hood of the car. "And you think your presence changes anything? It doesn't."

"Your father can see the big picture. Why can't you? The whole reason Garret is missing is because he was alone, which made him vulnerable. There's safety in numbers, Lindsey, and the only way to stop Proteus is to do it together."

"How are we going to do that if we can't even be sure who's safe and who isn't? How do we know who we're even talking to?"

"There are ways around that. Proteus doesn't know everything. He doesn't know our past, or personal information. We can use that. And if you'd take two seconds to consider that, you'd agree with me."

"Is that what this is about? Agreeing with you? Is your ego that sensitive?"

Trick bit back an unhelpful retort. "You know it isn't. Why are you so determined to fight with me and your father? Why are you so convinced you're right and we're wrong?"

She pointed at herself. "Because I'm the one whose neck Proteus wrapped his fingers around. I'm the one he threatened with all the things he's going to do to the people I love. He wants to hurt me. He's pissed about his incarceration, and he blames my family. Now you can stand there and claim to know what to do, and Dad can agree with you all he wants, but neither of you were...were..." Her face red, she turned and kicked the side of the car. "Neither of you know him like I do."

Seeing her frustration and anguish, Trick softened his voice. "That's because you won't tell us anything."

She turned away and crossed her arms. "Not this again."

"Yes. This again." He walked up behind her. "If you want us to successfully deal with Proteus, or better said, if *you* want to successfully deal with Proteus, you have to discuss what happened to you."

"My family knows enough, and I don't need to tell you a thing." She turned around. "I've revealed all I'm going to. If I thought for one second it would help, I'd shout it from the rooftops, but it won't, so leave me alone."

Trick put his hands on his hips. "You keep carrying this, you're going to end up in the same situation as Garret, and none of us may be able to save you."

She stared up at him, and her expression hardened. "Maybe that's for the best."

"Damn it, Lindsey..."

Not saying anything, she walked to the car and opened the door. "Dad found us a place to stay. He texted the address." She looked back at him. "So, if you're coming, get in." She slid into the seat and shut the door.

Hoping she wouldn't drive off without him, Trick jogged around to the other side and got into the passenger side. Buckling his seatbelt, he tried again. "Lindsey," he said.

She pointed. "Not another word, unless you decide to leave."

Tabling his argument for another time, he shut his mouth as she started the car, backed out, and drove off.

· · · · ● · ● · · ·

Novak stood as Lindsey and Trick drove away, wondering what exactly was going on. Based on what she'd heard, the two were involved in way more than locating missing siblings, and a man named Proteus, who they hadn't mentioned when making their report. And she had serious doubts that Trick and Lindsey were actually siblings. Making up her mind, she ran to her vehicle, opened the door, and tossed her purse in. She got in, quickly started the ignition, and zipped out of the lot. Seeing the car with Lindsey behind the wheel stopped at the corner as they waited to exit, Novak slowly pulled up behind them, and as they turned the corner, Novak followed.

Chapter Fifteen

Trick studied the street as Lindsey drove through the upscale neighborhood. Tall palm trees, gated driveways, and manicured lawns sporting bubbling fountains were in abundance as Lindsey wound her way past the homes. "Nice area," he said.

"Dad's not one for mobile homes."

"I can see that. But I thought he preferred smaller quarters and sleeping on cots."

"That's his military background. But places like these have better security."

Trick nodded. "Makes sense." He pointed. "Take a left at the stop sign."

Their drive had been a quiet one. After getting in the car, Trick had plugged the address into his phone and provided directions. Since he had no plans to leave Vegas, he honored Lindsey's request not to speak. And based on her body language, she was in no mood to talk.

Thinking they needed a break anyway, Trick settled back and tried to think about what to do with Proteus and what his plans with Garret might be. The obvious choice would be to lure them all out into the open, where he could use Garret as a pawn. But a pawn for what? Did he want to exchange Garret for either Lindsey or Ben? Did Proteus plan to kill Garret in front of his family? Or did Proteus plan to kill all of them? Not knowing Proteus, Trick could only guess what could happen the next day. Lindsey had only said that Proteus would be in touch, but what did that mean?

Would he call? But if he did, that would mean he had one of their numbers. And if he had that, he could track them with the right resources.

Concerned since they were heading to their safe house, he glanced at Lindsey. "How is Proteus supposed to contact us tomorrow?"

Lindsey gripped the wheel. "I told you. I don't know."

"Well, the only way to do it is for him to join us at the house, which I'm guessing is not the plan, or he'll call. But how is he going to call unless he has a number to reach us?"

Lindsey set her jaw.

"And if he has that, then he can find us." He paused. "Which means he'll know where we're staying."

"He won't know."

"How can you be sure?"

Lindsey fixed her stare on the road. "Are we close?"

Trick narrowed his eyes at her. "What aren't you telling me?"

"Nothing," she said, but her quick response betrayed her.

"You already know where the meet is, don't you?"

"Don't be ridiculous. You're as bad as Dad."

Trick didn't buy it. "That's why you're not worried about Proteus knowing where we are, because the meet is already set."

Lindsey looked out her window. "Are you going to tell me where we're going, or am I driving in circles?"

Trick checked his phone. "Take the next left. Then it's the third house on the right."

Lindsey slowed as the turn approached. "And for your information, we can never assume we're safe. If Proteus wants to find us, he will. That's why we need a place with security that allows for plenty of surveillance. And getting our phone numbers is not impossible. If he can access the LVPD records, he can get our information, so we have to assume he'll find us eventually."

"Then why aren't you worried?"

"Who said I wasn't worried?" She turned, drove down the tree-lined street, and slowed in front of the third house, which had a long, gated driveway, manicured lawn, and tall palm trees. It was a large corner lot with plenty of landscaping and a high fence. "But coming here involves risk. We're familiar with the area, and he isn't. Plus, we'll be prepared." She stopped at the gate and rolled her window down. "Proteus plays the odds and since it's only him, the odds aren't good if he comes here." Before she could hit the intercom, the gates started to open. "See?" she said. "Dad's watching and knows we're here. He's probably got this place hooked up to base at home, and Marcy and Trey have eyes on us."

The iron gates slowly opened. "So what you're saying is there's safety in numbers?" asked Trick, rubbing his chin. "Huh. Where have I heard that before?"

She smirked at him. "But we can't hole up here and expect to catch him. We can't hide forever. If we want to stop him, we have to get creative." She drove up the driveway and stopped in front of a large two-story Spanish-style home with an orange-tiled roof and brown stucco walls. A burbling fountain, tiled in elaborate colors, sprayed water down the sides and into a small pond.

"Exactly my point," added Trick. "We get creative, and we work together to do it."

Lindsey parked and didn't answer. She opened her door and got out just as the ornate yellow front door opened and Ben stepped outside. An older version of Garret and just as tall, he wore blue jeans and a long-sleeved shirt with a vest and stepped down the front walk.

Trick exited the car as Lindsey greeted her dad, who wrapped her in a bear hug. "Thank God you're okay," said Ben.

Trick grabbed their things from the back seat and carried them to the front of the house.

Ben let go of Lindsey and frowned. "What the hell happened to your neck?"

Lindsey touched her throat. "It's fine. No big deal."

Ben's frown deepened. "No big deal?"

"Leave it alone, Dad." She took her backpack from Trick. "And you didn't need to send Trick." She walked into the house.

Staring after his daughter, Ben sighed and faced Trick. "Good to see you, Trick." He shook Trick's hand. "Thank you for bringing my daughter back to me."

"You're welcome, sir, but I don't think she's appreciative."

Ben stopped on the front walk and eyed the door. "She's mad at me, isn't she?"

"She's mad at everyone, it seems."

Ben sighed again and shook his head. "Come on in."

"Thank you, sir."

"I told you. It's Ben."

Trick threw his knapsack over his shoulder and entered the house. "Okay, Ben." He walked into a large front entry that led to an open living area, kitchen, and dining space with a bar. "Nice digs."

Ben closed the door behind them. "All the comforts of home." He gestured toward the back of the house. "I've set up our command center in the office. There's two bedrooms upstairs and two down. I'm taking the couch." He nodded toward a long leather couch facing a wide-screened TV.

"You got something against beds?" asked Trick. He walked to the back window to look outside.

Ben chuckled. "I don't like to get too comfortable in a situation like this. Plus, the couch is more my speed, and it's close to the command center. I figured you and Lindsey can take the bedrooms upstairs." He looked between Lindsey and Trick. "In case you two want some privacy."

Lindsey scoffed and dropped her backpack on the couch. "We don't need privacy, Dad. Stop playing matchmaker."

Ben raised his brow. "I call 'em as I see 'em."

"There's nothing to see," said Lindsey, sliding her jacket off and dropping it next to her backpack.

Trick slid his knapsack off his shoulder. "The rooms upstairs are fine, Ben. Thanks." He shot a thumb toward the window. "That's quite the backyard. Is that a guest house out there?"

"Behind that fancy garden?" asked Ben. "Yes. But it's locked up tight. There's also a large garage with a boat trailer inside. Plus, there's a cold plunge pool and a sauna if you want to relax."

Trick looked out the window and whistled. "That is a nice garden. Somebody must pay a fortune for water."

"And pay off the water police." Ben joined him at the window. "There's even a stone path that winds through trees and shrubs to get to the guest house. It's a pretty space if you enjoy being outside."

"I can see that." Trick turned from the window and eyed Lindsey. "Care to go for a plunge, swim and sauna later? It might help you relax."

Lindsey rolled her eyes at Trick and turned. "I'm going into the command center."

"One second, Lin," said Ben, walking away from the window. "We need to talk."

Lindsey glanced back. "There's nothing to talk about."

"The hell there isn't." Ben's friendly tone hardened. "You disappear for days without telling anyone where you are, and you don't get in touch?" He took a few steps toward her. "That's not the way we work, and you know it."

Lindsey hesitated. "I'm a big girl. I can take care of myself."

"Don't give me that BS. In our line of work, there's no room for 'me' time. What you did was reckless. If Trick hadn't found you—"

Lindsey glared. "I'd still be in that mobile home minding my own business."

"While we all searched frantically for you. And if Proteus had found you first—"

"But he didn't, did he?" She waved her hand. "Not until Garret showed and made himself a target. If anyone did anything stupid, it was him."

Ben raised his voice. "I sent Garret here to look for you."

"No one told you to do that," she yelled.

Figuring Ben needed to get some things off his chest, Trick stayed out of the conversation.

"What did you expect me to do?" asked Ben. "Let you stay out here, knowing what you were doing? And knowing why Proteus wanted to find you?"

"Yes," said Lindsey. "I can handle my own problems."

Ben's face turned red. "These aren't just your problems to handle. When are you going to let yourself off the hook?"

Lindsey's cheeks turned as red as Ben's. "They are my problems to handle, and you know why."

Ben clenched his jaw. "What happened between you and Michael—"

Lindsey pointed. "Don't you say his name." She shook her head. "I told you to never say his name."

"Fine," said Ben. "Proteus. What happened between you two isn't your fault."

"How can you say that?" she said. "It is my fault. It will always be my fault." She smacked her hand on her chest. "And I came here to deal with it and not involve you or anyone else who suffered because of me. So stop acting like you don't understand why I left."

Ben softened his tone. "Lindsey, honey. Please. How many times have I told you we don't blame you?"

"It doesn't matter," yelled Lindsey. "I blame me. I always will. And that means sometimes I'm going to disappear for a while. And I'm sorry if you don't like that."

"It's not about you going away, Lin. It was about you coming back." Ben took a heavy breath and took a second to respond. "I was terrified you wouldn't." He held Lindsey's gaze. "And that had nothing to do with Proteus."

Lindsey stared back and swallowed. "You worry too much."

"Do I?" asked Ben. "Because I'm not too sure. If Proteus hadn't escaped..."

Lindsey straightened. "But he did, and Trick found me. Let's move on." She cleared her throat. "Any word from Marcy or Trey?"

"No," said Ben. "And if you think you've successfully changed the subject, you're wrong. We're just getting started."

Lindsey put her hand on her head and groaned. "Dad, please."

"What really happened between you and Proteus this afternoon?" asked Ben. "Because you bypassed that subject almost as fast as any time your mother is mentioned."

Lindsey looked away.

"What did that miserable bastard tell you?" asked Ben. He waved his hand. "I assume he gave you those bruises."

Lindsey shut her eyes.

Trick answered. "Proteus did a number on her. He took me out, morphed into me, and approached her as me. He half strangled her. Then he threatened you and your family. He's angry about his incarceration and blames you and your loved ones, Ben, and he's going to take it out on Lindsey."

Ben's face turned stony. "That son-of-a-bitch."

Trick didn't back off when Lindsey's glare found him. "That's why she wants me to leave. To protect me and to face Proteus alone."

Lindsey's expression didn't change. "I can handle Proteus."

"The hell you can," yelled Ben. "Don't you see he's baiting you?"

Trick braced and told Ben the rest. "And I suspect Lindsey hasn't told us everything about tomorrow. I think Proteus set up a meet between him, Lindsey, and Garret, and Lindsey isn't sharing." Lindsey narrowed her gaze at Trick and if looks could kill, Trick felt sure he'd be dead.

Lindsey grabbed her knapsack and jacket. "What happens tomorrow is between me, Proteus, and God."

Ben put his hands on his hips. "If you think you're going alone, you don't know me very well."

Lindsey slung her backpack over shoulder. "Where I'm going is upstairs."

"Lindsey," yelled Ben. "We need to talk about this."

Lindsey stomped over to the staircase on the far side of the living room and headed up.

"Lindsey," repeated Ben.

She ignored Ben and kept walking.

"Let her go, Ben," said Trick, watching Lindsey disappear into the upstairs hall. "Give her some time. I think she's pretty rattled after this afternoon, although she'll die before she shows it."

Ben cursed and turned. "That girl's gonna be the death of me."

Trick heard an upstairs door close and wished he knew what to do or say. "If she gets her way, her plan could be the death of all of us."

• • • • • • • • • •

Lindsey shut the door behind her and tossed her backpack on the floor. Her eyes burning and her head pounding, she sat on the edge of the bed and dropped her forehead into her palms. Her dad's words echoed in her ears, and she hated the worry in his voice. If the situation were different, she'd attempt to talk to him, but she had more pressing matters to deal with.

Her throat tight and fighting back tears, she clenched her eyes shut and willed the tears away. Her headache flared, but she ignored the pain. She couldn't afford to fall apart now. The next twenty-four hours would decide the fate of her and her family, and she couldn't risk anyone else getting hurt. She wasn't even sure she could get Garret out alive, but she would try. If stopping Proteus meant sacrificing herself, then it was well worth the cost, no matter what her father or Trick said.

Getting control of her emotions, she ran her hands through her hair, rubbed her shoulders, and tried to think. Now that Trick had guessed correctly that Proteus had given her instructions for tomorrow, she had to find a way to keep him and Dad from joining her.

Collecting herself after a deep breath, she reached into her jeans pocket and pulled out the picture of her and her mother. She stared at it, refused to cry, and put it away. Then she pulled out the note Proteus had left for her in Garret's wallet. She opened it again and read it.

Meet me at warehouse nineteen at ten am. Come alone and unarmed. Break the rules and your brother will end up like your mother.

Beneath Proteus' scribbling was an address, which Lindsey guessed was in an industrial district. Proteus would want a place where he could be undisturbed, hold on to Garret, and torment Lindsey.

Her vision blurring with fatigue, she closed the note and put it back in her pocket. Thinking, she dropped her head back into her hands. Her background with Proteus gave her an edge because she could anticipate his actions. If she could keep Dad and Trick away, she wouldn't have to worry about Proteus morphing into either of them, and that would give her another advantage. And if he morphed into Garret, Lindsey felt confident she would know it.

Despite her attempts to ignore her father's concerns and disregard her warring emotions, an image of her mother flared in her mind, and she heard her mom's voice in her head.

It's not your fault, honey.

Her mom tried to say more, but Lindsey pushed her out as she often did. Without the tequila, though, it was harder to do, but with sheer will and determination, she succeeded. No matter what her mom had to say, Lindsey couldn't accept her, or anyone else's, forgiveness.

Her mind finally quiet, Lindsey laid back on the pillow, refocused, and came up with a plan.

Chapter Sixteen

Trick studied the monitors in the office. Ben had done an impressive job creating a command center where he could monitor the house and stay up to speed with any information Marcy and Trey learned. So far, though, there was little to report. There'd been no police activity regarding Garret, or the fake twin named Linda, so Trick suspected Proteus was biding his time until the anniversary of whatever horrible thing that had occurred between him and Lindsey.

Eyeing the footage from the cameras located around the property, which was displayed on the monitors, Trick sat back in the office chair and debated again whether to try to get Lindsey to talk. He'd come so close that afternoon, until Proteus had intervened, and Lindsey had retreated into her shell.

She'd come downstairs only briefly since disappearing into her bedroom. She'd made a sandwich and drank some water, but as soon as Trick and Ben pressed her about the meeting with Proteus, she'd left the house and walked the grounds, and when she'd returned, she gone back to her room after Ben told her she wasn't going anywhere again until she talked to him.

That had been an hour ago, and as night fell and the moon rose, Trick considered going upstairs and pounding on her door. Time was running short, and if they planned to confront Proteus the next day, they needed to discuss it. He wasn't worried about her sneaking out because the cameras would catch it, and if Trick or Ben didn't notice, Marcy and Trey would.

Checking his watch, Trick told himself he'd give her thirty more minutes before he went upstairs and insisted she talk. Frustrated with waiting, he leaned his head back and closed his eyes, but opened them when Ben came into the room.

"If you need to catch some z's, head upstairs. There's not much any of us can do tonight anyway, so you might as well get some rest."

Trick shifted in the chair. "I would, but I'd just stare at the ceiling. Besides, we still need to talk to Lindsey about tomorrow."

Ben sat on the couch beside the desk. "I figure she's wallowed enough. Whether she likes it or not, she needs to tell us what's going on."

"I was gonna give her a few more minutes, but I don't think I have the patience."

Ben stood. "You and me both. Let's go talk to her."

Glad to have something to do, Trick stood too, but stopped when Lindsey rounded the corner and stopped at the entrance to the office. Her eyes held a haunted look and the darkening circles beneath them told Trick she needed sleep and a serious mental reprieve from whatever plagued her.

Ben remained beside the couch. "Well, my prodigal daughter returns."

She looked at both of them and spoke to Ben. "Did you bring the supply bag?"

"The bag?" he asked.

"With the weapons," she stated.

Ben gestured at the corner. "Over there."

Lindsey glanced over with a frown. "You left them in the bag?"

Ben sighed. "Forgive me. I've had a few other things on my mind. And are you preparing for combat?"

Lindsey went over to a dark nylon gym bag lying on the opposite side of the room. "Aren't you the one who says to always be prepared?" She unzipped the bag.

"Something we should know?" asked Trick.

Lindsey pulled out a small knife secured in a sheath and then a second larger one.

"Any guns in there?" asked Trick.

"Dad doesn't bring guns," said Lindsey.

"Too risky," said Ben.

"I'd sure feel better with one." Trick watched Lindsey pull out another knife. "Why the extra security?"

Lindsey set the small pocketknife aside. "Just being careful."

Trick glanced at Ben, who shook his head. "If you think you're just walking out of here without telling Trick or me squat," said Ben, "you're mistaken."

Holding three knives, Lindsey closed the bag with a huff. "Fine. I'll tell you about tomorrow." She stood and secured the larger sheathed knife to her belt. "But I have to go alone. It's what Proteus wants, and if I don't follow the rules, he'll kill Garret."

"He wants you alone so he can kill you too," said Ben.

"Where's the meet?" asked Trick.

Her knife secured, she crossed her arms. "Tomorrow at noon. At the Olympic."

"Garret's hotel?" asked Ben. "Why there?"

"He told me to wait in the lobby until I get a phone call," said Lindsey. "Then I go where he tells me to."

"Then we can wait outside," said Trick. "And when you leave, Ben and I will follow."

"Don't you think Proteus will expect that?" asked Lindsey. "It's too dangerous."

"What's dangerous is you driving off to wherever the hell he sends you without us knowing," said Ben. "We'll track your car. That way, Trick and I can hang back, and Michael...sorry...Proteus, won't be the wiser."

"It's not the tracking I'm worried about," said Lindsey. "Once I get to wherever I'm going, if you show, Proteus will know. It could be a test to see if I obey, and if I don't, he could kill Garret without a second thought."

"You're not doing this alone," said Trick. "If we have to, we'll stay far enough behind until we know you're with Proteus. And we'll come in quietly."

"Who do you think you're dealing with?" she asked. "This is why I didn't want you involved."

"We're not exactly inexperienced, Lindsey," said Trick. "Ben and I can stay under the radar. We'll be careful. All we need to do is find Garret and get him free."

She groaned. "And what happens when Proteus suspects you're there, and he becomes me or Garret in order to stop one or both of you?"

"If it gets that far," said Trick, "and hopefully it won't, we need safe words. Words that only we know that will protect us."

"It's a good idea," said Ben. He rubbed his chin as if thinking. "My word will be bull-headed, which describes you and Garret perfectly," he said to Lindsey.

"Mine will be Ranger," said Trick. "For obvious reasons."

Lindsey hesitated. "You two honestly think this will work?"

"We don't have a choice," said Ben. "Because you're not doing this by yourself."

Lindsey sighed. "Fine. My name's...freedom, because I desperately want it from both of you."

"Be careful what you ask for," said Trick. He held her gaze until she looked away. "So, Ben and I will go to the hotel, but we'll stay back. We'll track your car, Lindsey, and follow, but not close. Once you meet with Proteus, can you keep him distracted long enough for Ben and me to find Garret?"

Lindsey slid the pocketknife in her back pocket. "That all depends on what Proteus has planned, but if I can distract Proteus, I will."

"I know you, Lin," said Ben. "Don't let him get to you. He'll goad you and expect you to react. This is part of his strategy. To use the anniversary against you, and maybe even kill Garret in front of you. Don't let him play his mind games. If you can give me and Trick enough time to get into position, we can free Garret and stop Proteus." He paused. "The question is, can you wait that long?"

"Garret is all that matters," she said. "I'll do whatever is necessary to protect him."

"Don't forget yourself," added Trick. "We'll all be getting out alive, right?"

"That's the plan," said Lindsey, but without the conviction Trick expected from her.

Something about her body language tugged at Trick. Was she telling him and Ben everything? "Is there anything else we should—"

An alarm sounded from one of the monitors, and Ben quickly sat in the office chair. He studied the cameras and hit a button on his phone, then put it on speaker. It rang and a male voice answered. "It's Trey."

"You seeing what we're seeing?" asked Ben.

"We got someone driving up to the property," said Trey through the speaker. "Camera five. North side at the entrance."

Trick sought the correct square on the monitor that showed the viewpoint of camera five. Lindsey came around the desk and looked, too.

"There," said Ben, pointing at the corner of the screen. "The front drive. A car's pulling up." He hit another button on the keypad and the alarm shut off. "Can you get a license number, Trey?"

Trick studied the grainy image of a car stopping at the front gate.

"Negative," said Trey. "The cameras aren't sharp enough. But there's a man behind the wheel. I'll zoom in as best I can from my end."

Trick leaned closer to the screen and watched as the man reached out his window to press the intercom outside the gate.

"It could be someone who's lost," said Lindsey. "They may be at the wrong house."

"Maybe," said Ben. "But unlikely."

"Could be a delivery," said Trey over the intercom.

Trick narrowed his eyes as Ben magnified the view. The image was still grainy, but Trick could make out an important detail. "Son-of-a..." he said.

"The guy's wearing a cowboy hat and has a mustache," said Trey.

"I'll be damned," said Trick, as the intercom linked to the front driveway buzzed.

Ben answered. "Can I help you?"

A male voice responded. "Mason Redstone to see Trick Monroe."

Lindsey dropped her jaw. "You're kidding." She gaped at Trick. "How the hell did he find us?"

Trick snorted. "Unbelievable." He leaned over to hit the access button to the front gate when Lindsey grabbed his hand.

"How do you know it's really him?" she asked.

"It's a valid question," replied Ben.

Trick paused, tipped his head, and hit the intercom. "Hey, Red. It's Trick. Crazy question, but bear with me. In what bar did I meet Linda Sue Henry?"

There was a moment of quiet, but then came a static-filled response. "You didn't meet Linda in a bar, you idiot. You met her in jail, where you both ended up after a bar fight."

Trick chuckled and sighed. "Those were the days."

Lindsey rolled her eyes and Trick hit the button to open the gate.

Chapter Seventeen

Trick opened the front door as Mason pulled his car up and parked behind Lindsey's rental. He stepped out wearing his usual hat, jeans, boots and long-sleeved shirt. Carrying another cowboy hat, he shut his door and came up the front walk.

"How the hell did you find us?" asked Trick.

Mason held out the hat he carried. "This is yours, I believe." He pointed at Trick's baseball cap. "I'm hoping that's temporary."

"Don't worry. It is." Trick took his cowboy hat from Mason. "You obviously met Danny."

Mason entered the house. "I did. Paid him fifty bucks to find out which mobile home you were in."

Trick shut the door. "I paid him a hundred."

Mason glanced back at him. "Your negotiation skills are rusty."

"Apparently." Trick walked in as Lindsey and Ben greeted Mason.

"It's good to see you, Mason," said Ben, "although surprising."

Lindsey spoke to Trick. "Did you tell him where we were?"

Trick shook his head. "I didn't." He set his hat down on the bar's counter. "I told you forty-eight hours, Red. It's only been thirty-six."

Mason took his own hat off, ruffled his hair and set his hat next to Trick's. "Call it a hunch, and an unexpected but persistent spirit."

Ben frowned. "Persistent spirit?" He walked over to the bar's mini fridge. "You want something to drink? We've got water or juice."

"Water, please," said Mason. "It's been a long drive, plus hunting for you is tiring." He eyed Trick and took the bottle of water from Ben. "Thanks."

"How did you know to look for the mobile home park?" asked Lindsey.

"That was a hint from Trick." Mason cracked open the water. "He suspected where you were and mentioned where his mom used to live when he and I first met, which was an old mobile home in an RV park. When I got into town, Danny's little paradise was the second place I stopped. Once I got inside your mobile home, which wasn't hard, I found Trick's hat."

"You saw my note?" asked Trick.

"I did," said Mason.

"That's why you left your hat behind?" Lindsey asked Trick. "For Mason to find?"

"I had to assume that things might not go according to plan," said Trick.

"That's a safe bet," said Ben. He pulled a bottle of apple juice from the fridge, opened it, and regarded Mason. "What happened after you found Trick's hat?"

"Trick left his current phone number since apparently his personal cell no longer works." Mason drank some water.

Trick leaned his hip against the counter. "It's in San Diego, in some woman's large purse. I didn't want anyone to track me." He thought about the number he'd given Mason. "How come you didn't call the number?"

"I did," said Mason. "You never answered."

Trick pulled his burner from his pocket and frowned. "It's dead, which is strange."

"That's Proteus," said Lindsey. "When he zapped you, it drained the battery."

Mason furrowed his brow. "Zapped you?"

"Long story. I'll fill you in later," said Trick. "What about Novak? I left her name on the note too."

Mason set his water bottle on the bar. "After I left the trailer, I went to the LVPD, but she'd left for the day, and they wouldn't tell me how to reach her."

"So much for leaving clues," said Trick. "How'd you get here, then?"

"That required extra help," said Mason. "I left the police station and sat in my car. I took a second and went to a higher source."

Trick raised his brow. "You mean a ghost?"

Mason stretched his neck. "I do. To be honest, if it wasn't for the ghost, I'd have waited those forty-eight hours. But that spirit gave me a clear message this morning to hit the road. Since it was insistent, I reconnected and asked for some assistance. Thankfully, it gave good directions."

Ben set his juice bottle on the counter. "You mean this spirit told you how to get here?"

"It did," said Mason, "which is rare. They're usually not that cooperative."

"I guess your ghost knew we needed the help," said Ben.

Mason recapped his water bottle. "You might think that, but the message wasn't about you, or Trick."

Trick frowned. "What was it about?"

Mason eyed Lindsey and pointed. "You."

· • • • • • • • • ·

Lindsey widened her eyes. "Me?"

Mason nodded. "Is there a place we can talk? In private?"

Unsure what to think, Lindsey stilled.

Ben pointed to the back of the house. "There's a small bedroom off the hall. You can talk there."

"Thank you," said Mason. He gestured toward the hall. "You up for it?" he asked Lindsey.

Lindsey looked between her dad and Trick. Her heart rate picked up its pace. "I'm not sure."

Ben put his hand on the counter. "Lin, Mason drove to Vegas to deliver a message to you. Don't keep him waiting. Talk to him."

"In my experience," said Trick, "if a spirit is pushy enough to get Mason to drive over three hundred miles and even provide directions, it's important."

Anxious, Lindsey rubbed her arms. After a pause, and seeing she wasn't getting out of this, she turned to head down the hall. "I suppose I don't have a choice."

Mason walked with her, but stopped and turned. "Trick. I brought your gun. It's in the trunk of my car." He pulled out his keys and tossed them to Trick.

Trick caught them and smiled. "I take it that was your idea and not the spirit's?"

"All mine," said Mason. "Oh, and you should know someone is parked down the street, watching this house."

Ben gaped at him. "What?"

"Who the hell is watching the house?" asked Trick.

"I doubled back when I saw the car just to be sure," said Mason. "There's a woman behind the wheel. Attractive with long hair. And she's got a bumper sticker that says, *Cops need love too*. My guess? She's a member of law enforcement."

"We need to check the cameras, Dad," said Lindsey, heading toward the office.

Trick took her arm. "We'll do that. You go talk to Red."

"But—" Lindsey eyed her dad.

"Trick's right," said Ben. "We'll handle this. You go with Mason. If we need you, we know where to reach you."

Lindsey slumped as he and Trick headed into the office.

"You ready?" asked Mason.

Lindsey hesitated. "Does Trick have a self-confidence problem?"

Mason chuckled. "I promise. You're safe with me."

Lindsey sighed. "Fine." She turned and headed down the hall.

"But I can't speak for the spirit. That part is out of my hands."

Before Lindsey could complain, Mason took her elbow and guided her into the bedroom. He closed the door behind him.

Lindsey paced the room. "How exactly do we do this? Do you have to go into a trance or something?"

Mason shook his head. "No. Your spirit is front and center. She's impatient and wants to talk to you."

Lindsey stopped pacing. "She?"

Mason took a second to respond. "It's your mother, Lindsey."

Lindsey froze. For a second, the room spun, and she sat on the edge of the bed.

"You okay?" Mason sat beside her.

Lindsey rubbed her head. "Not really. No."

"Normally, I'd give you some time, but your mother is telling me you've had enough time. You've been shutting her out."

Lindsey set her jaw and tried to breathe. Her heart hammered, and she didn't know what to do.

"To say she's frustrated is an understatement. That's why she came to me. She's not going away without a fight."

That sounded just like her mom. Her memories swirling, Lindsey hugged herself. "I'm not sure I can do this."

"Well, that's the good news because you don't have to do anything but listen."

Lindsey made a low groan. "I'm not sure I want to hear it."

Mason paused. "She says too bad."

Lindsey closed her eyes and, her emotions building, she took a deep breath. "Okay," she said softly.

"Good." Mason straightened and stared off. "First thing, and this is big, she wants you to know that she doesn't blame you. Never has."

Lindsey clenched her eyes tighter, willing herself not to cry.

"What happened wasn't anyone's fault, other than Michael's. He's the one who did this. Not you. She wants you to let yourself off the hook."

The tears swirled despite her attempts to prevent them. "It's not that easy."

Mason stood and returned with a box of tissues. He handed one to Lindsey and set the box on the floor. "She's saying yes, it is. You've been too hard on yourself. She understands why you carry the guilt, but it's been five years. You've done enough penance. It's time to live your life."

Lindsey dropped her head and swiped away a tear that had escaped and slipped down her cheek. "I'll never forgive myself."

Mason paused. "You have to find a way." His voice softened, and he closed his eyes. "I'm fine. So is the family. You're not responsible for anyone's happiness, but your own."

Lindsey fought to get the words out. "I don't deserve happiness."

"Everyone deserves happiness, honey," said Mason. "Especially you."

Lindsey glanced over at Mason, whose eyes remained closed. Was he channeling her mother? Lindsey set her jaw, unable to accept the forgiveness her mother offered. "I miss you."

"If you'd let me in more, you wouldn't miss me so much. I'm right here."

"Everything that happened is because of me. I screwed up. I...I..."

"Honey, you were betrayed by someone who used you. We all trusted him. None of us could have known. You have to start seeing with fresh eyes. And rely on the people who love you. Talk to them. They want the old Lindsey back. So do I."

Lindsey ran her hands through her hair. Her chest hurt and her throat was so tight she could barely speak. "I don't know if I can."

"You can, honey. You came close with that handsome cowboy, Trick. He's good for you, baby. Let him in."

Lindsey clenched her fingers around her neck. "He's not good for me. No one is."

"Nonsense. You're good for him, too. He's there for a reason. I may have nudged both of you in the right direction."

Lindsey bit back a flare of annoyance. "You shouldn't do that."

"Don't tell me what to do. I'm your mother, Lindsey Shay. You've always listened to me. Don't stop now. I let you go too long without hearing me. Now that I have Mason, I'm going to pester you until you beg me to shut up."

Her resistance softening, Lindsey used the tissue to wipe her cheeks. "Dad misses you so much."

"I know he does, honey, but he's doing okay. But he's worried about you. So are Garret, Marcy and Trey. They don't know how to reach you."

Lindsey blew out her cheeks. "I know what losing you did to them. I see it in their eyes every time I look at them."

"They're not looking at you with judgement, Lin. They're looking at you with concern. They love you. Just as much as I do."

Lindsey held her stomach. As much as she wanted to let her mother's words in, her guilt surged. "I...I'm so sorry, Mom." A wave of heat enveloped her as she tried not to sob.

"There's nothing to be sorry for, but if you want forgiveness, you had it the moment it happened. You're my daughter, and your happiness is my priority. But you have to fight for it too. There's nothing your family won't do for you, but you have to let them help. Promise me you'll try."

Lindsey's emotions warred with her, and her head pounded with the pressure. Could she do it? Could she forgive herself? "I don't know."

"Yes, you do. You think it's harder than it is. Fear has never ruled you, Lindsey Shay. Don't let it start now. You're stronger than you think, and you can do this. I insist. And you know how I can be when I insist."

Lindsey couldn't prevent a soft smile. Her mother's presence had worked its way past the hard shell she'd built up around herself and her heart thumped at the warmth that coursed through her.

"Your father always said you took after me. You better prove him right."

Reluctant, Lindsey nodded. "Okay. I'll try."

"Good. And remember. I'm always here. Stop resisting me."

Lindsey wiped away another hot tear. "I'll do my best."

"Small steps, honey. You'll get there. Once you take the first few, I think you'll see it's not as hard as you think."

Lindsey hugged herself harder.

"And don't let Trick slip through your fingers. What a waste that would be."

Lindsey sat up. "Mom...please."

"Don't act like you don't know what I mean."

"I've got other problems to deal with right now."

"And the more help you can get, the better. Open your heart, Lin. It's been frozen for too long. Trick will help thaw some of that ice, if you know what I mean."

Surprised, Lindsey shifted toward Mason, wondering if he was playing games with her, but his eyes were still closed, and he seemed completely detached from his responses.

"I'll go now, honey," said her mom through Mason, "and give you time to absorb what I said and act on it. You better listen, because if you don't..."

"I know," said Lindsey, slumping, "you'll be back."

Mason's shoulders relaxed. "I love you," he said. "Very much."

More tears surfaced, and Lindsey struggled to speak. "I love you too."

It went quiet and several seconds passed before Mason's eyes opened. He blinked and rubbed his neck. "Did you hear what you needed to hear?" he asked, his voice gruff.

Still emotional and trying not to show it, Lindsey wiped at her eyes and sniffed. "Yeah. I think so."

"I hope the channeling didn't throw you. It seemed easier, though, so she could talk to you directly."

Lindsey dabbed her nose with the tissue. "I'm a cryptid hunter. Not much throws me."

"Good point." Mason stretched his shoulders. "You okay?"

She hesitated. "I'm not sure." She looked over at him with watery eyes. "Do you remember what she said?"

"Bits and pieces. But I got the general gist."

Lindsey eyed the floor. "I'm not sure I agree with her."

"That's the whole point. I think it's time to reconsider your perspective."

Her headache flaring, Lindsey pinched the bridge of her nose. "Did she tell you what happened to her?"

"I don't know the details. Your mom doesn't want to revisit the past, or even discuss what you're dealing with right now. This is about you and your mental state."

Lindsey rested her elbows on her knees. "A little information about our current situation would be helpful."

Mason stilled. "I'm not getting anything from her about that. I think she expects you'll know what to do, provided you pull yourself out of the well of darkness you've been wading in for a long time."

"I'm pretty comfortable with that well of darkness." Her chest tightened again, and she fought back tears.

"Lindsey, you've been carrying a staggering amount of guilt, and your mother is telling you to stop. Maybe it's time to listen."

She bit her lip and pushed back her natural inclination to argue. "Mom certainly likes Trick." She sighed. "Does anyone not like him?"

Mason chuckled. "Not many."

"I'm not good for him."

"Why don't you let him be the judge of that?"

"I'll drag him down the well with me."

"Not likely. Trick's a specialist at helping people in need without joining them in their darkness, no matter how ugly it is. He's done it with his mother for years. He did it with me, and if you give him a chance, he'll do it with you."

Lindsey held her head. "I'm not good at being vulnerable."

"Who exactly is?"

Lindsey didn't answer.

"You survived this conversation, didn't you?"

Lindsey thought about her plans for tomorrow. Should she change them? Was she doing the right thing? Her mind spun with her options, but in her gut, she knew she had to face Proteus alone. And no matter what her mother said, until Lindsey dealt with Proteus, she'd never be free of the guilt. She took a long breath to center herself. "Is Mom still here?" she asked.

Mason stilled and appeared to listen. "She's gone, for now."

Lindsey gathered herself and straightened. She blinked and dabbed her wet eyes.

"You need a minute?" asked Mason.

She almost scoffed and said she was fine, but her emotions still swirling, she nodded. "Maybe a few."

Mason patted her knee. "I'll give you some time." He stood and walked to the door. "You want anything?"

"Other than my sanity?" Weary, she looked over at him. "No."

Mason nodded and left the room.

· · · • • • • • · · ·

Mason headed into the office, where several monitors were set up on a large desk. Ben was sitting in the chair, studying them. Mason leaned over and stared at the monitors. "Any luck figuring out who your mystery guest is?"

Ben shook his head. "None. She parked just far enough down the street to not be visible on the cameras."

"Where's Trick?"

"He went out to see if he could identify her. I'm watching the cameras in case he shows, or someone else does." He swiveled in the chair. "How's Lindsey?"

Mason straightened. "She's adjusting."

"I hope her message was a good one."

"It was, but I'm not sure Lindsey sees it that way."

Ben leaned back in the chair. "She's never been one to take the easy road. She's always had to learn the hard way."

"Let's hope she's ready to make some changes."

Ben sighed. "I hope she is. Her safety tomorrow may depend on it."

Curious, Mason was about to ask for an update when Ben sat up and pointed at a square on the monitor. "That's Trick."

Mason saw a grainy black-and-white image of a man walking through the side yard toward the back. "It looks like he's alone."

A few seconds later, the back door that led to the porch opened, and Trick entered the house.

"Well?" asked Ben. "Did you see her?"

Trick nodded. "Sure did." He pulled his gun from the back of his jeans and set it on the desk. "No need to be worried."

"False alarm?" asked Ben.

"No. Mason's right," said Trick. "She's watching the house. But I know who she is."

Mason frowned. "Who?"

"Officer Novak. She must have followed Lindsey and me from the police station."

"She's the one I was supposed to contact?" asked Mason. "Why would she follow you two?"

Trick put his hand on his hip. "Well, Lindsey and I had an argument in the parking lot after what happened with Proteus. If Novak overheard it, it would have aroused suspicion, and my guess is it only added to the questions she must have about us."

"You two argued in the LVPD parking lot about Proteus?" asked Ben, his eyes wide.

"In hindsight," said Trick, "we should have taken our disagreement elsewhere."

"You think?" asked Ben. "Now what do we do? We've got a police officer watching the house."

"Let her watch," said Trick. "She can't hurt anything, and if she gets bored, she'll likely leave. She's a rookie officer and my guess is this is her first stakeout. She's by herself, and even if she makes it through the night, her fatigue or her bladder is going to force her to reconsider. And besides, what does it hurt to have another pair of eyes watching us?"

"He's right," said Mason. "Unless you're expecting something or someone that I'm not aware of."

"Not here, we aren't," said Trick. "But Proteus took Lindsey's brother, and Proteus wants Lindsey to meet him tomorrow, supposedly to get Garret back. Ben and I plan to follow."

Mason sat on the couch. "Then perhaps you ought to get me up to speed and let me know what we're dealing with here."

Trick nodded. "Good idea." He moved around the desk and sat beside Mason. He updated his friend on Proteus and his and Lindsey's day.

Ben filled them both in on his history with Proteus, but didn't go into detail about the events surrounding the anniversary.

"How'd he get loose from the facility?" asked Mason.

"Befriended a guard," said Ben. "When the guard got too close, Proteus took advantage and escaped." He shook his head. "It was gross negligence. That guard should have known better."

"Proteus is smart," said Trick. "He knows how to manipulate. And how he mimics people is astonishing. He even sounded like me. And I collapsed the second he grabbed me." Trick rubbed his forehead. "It makes him formidable."

"How do we stop him?" asked Mason.

"Get to him before he gets to you," said Ben. "And he's weaker after he morphs, which is how we managed to subdue him long enough to restrain him after..." he paused, "...well, after he attacked my wife."

Mason nodded, imagining the horror of that moment. "Anything else we should know about him? Any acquaintances? Family members?"

Ben hesitated.

Trick frowned. "You know something else?"

"We can't be sure," said Ben. "Proteus, like his father, was a loner. We never found a connection to anyone else, but during his captivity, we observed a few things about Proteus."

Mason sat forward. "Like what?"

Ben shrugged. "He would say things that indicated we didn't know everything. That we were overconfident. And when he escaped, we would realize our mistakes. We took it as the ramblings of an angry prisoner and paid little attention." He stared off. "But one day, two years after Proteus was apprehended, Marcy, my daughter, had a strange encounter."

"What's that?" asked Trick.

Ben leaned back in his chair. "I can't go into too much detail since it's need-to-know, but she swore she saw herself during an investigation. She'd been following someone in a grocery store. Nothing dramatic. Just a routine follow-up, when she turned down the spice aisle and saw a woman dressed as her. She took a closer look and realized she was looking at herself. It shocked the hell out of her, and she ran after the woman, but the woman left the aisle and by the time Marcy got to the end of it, the woman had disappeared."

Trick narrowed his eyes. "What did you make of it?"

"We weren't sure," said Ben. "It happened so fast, and it never happened again. Plus, Proteus could never morph into someone without grabbing a hold of them first. So he can get an impression of them, and that weakens the victim, and they usually collapse. That never happened to Marcy. We put it in a report, but nothing ever came of it. I hate to say it, but we assumed maybe Marcy thought the woman had looked like her but was mistaken. But now, I have to wonder."

"You think there's someone else out there who can do what Proteus does?" asked Mason.

Ben sighed. "I don't know. If there were, you'd think there would have been some indication by now, or if they're working with Proteus, they would have come after us, or even helped with his escape. But none of that's happened, which makes me think it's just Proteus we're dealing with, but it can't hurt to stay aware."

"I suppose if someone like Proteus exists, why couldn't someone else?" asked Mason.

"And if that's true, then we need to be extremely careful," added Ben. "You'll need a safe word, too, Mason."

Trying to comprehend the mess they were in, Mason regarded Trick. "I should have stayed in San Diego."

"That's what you get for listening to ghosts, Red," said Trick. He pointed. "That's your safe word. Ghost."

"How original," said Mason.

Trick chuckled. "I'll tell Lindsey."

A door opened and closed, and Mason turned to see Lindsey walk down the hall. She passed the office and grabbed a water bottle from the fridge in the kitchen.

"Lin?" asked Ben. "You all right?"

She opened the bottle and took a long drink of water. After recapping it, she headed toward the stairs, but stopped outside the office. Her eyes were red and weary. "I'm okay. I'm going to head up."

"You want something to eat?" asked Trick. "I can whip up some eggs."

"No. I'm not hungry." She rubbed her eyes. "I just need to sleep."

"You need food too." Trick eyed her with concern. "Tomorrow is a big day."

"I'll eat a big breakfast," she said.

"We should talk about tomorrow," said Ben.

She nodded, and Mason half expected her to burst into tears.

"Can we do it tomorrow?" she asked. "We'll have some time in the morning. I don't have to be at the hotel until noon."

"We can do that," said Ben. "By the way, it's Officer Novak who's casing the house."

She widened her eyes. "It is? How did she find us?"

"My guess is she followed us from the station," said Trick. "She must have overheard our argument. I don't think it'll hurt anything if she hangs around. We're not expecting much to happen here, anyway."

"And if she's still out there tomorrow?" asked Mason.

"We can deal with it then," said Trick. "Who knows? Maybe we can use her help."

"I'd advise against that," said Ben. "The last thing we need is a civilian casualty."

Lindsey yawned. "I'll let you guys figure that out. I'm going to bed."

Trick furrowed his brow, and Ben raised one of his. Mason figured they weren't used to Lindsey not jumping in to offer her opinion.

"You sure you're okay?" asked Ben. "Anything you want to talk about?"

"No, Dad. I'm fine. I'll see you in the morning." She turned toward the stairs. "Good night."

"Good night," said Ben and Mason.

"Night," said Trick, watching her leave. He scratched his head. "What the hell did you say to her, Red?"

"It's not what *I* said," said Mason. "But she's got some things to figure out."

Trick sighed. "Let's hope that happens sooner instead of later."

"For all our sakes," said Ben. "I'm worried about tomorrow. If she decides to take matters into her own hands, there's not much we can do."

Trick walked to the office door and stared toward where Lindsey had gone upstairs. "You think she knows something we don't?"

Ben sat up in his seat. "There's no way to know. Maybe once she gets some sleep and feels better, we can talk to her."

Trick nodded, but his gaze remained on the stairs. "Maybe." He looked back at Mason with concern. "I hope you brought some good luck spirits, Red, because tomorrow, we're going to need them."

Chapter Eighteen

Trick entered the jack-and-jill bathroom that connected his bedroom with Lindsey's. After getting Mason up to speed and eating some scrambled eggs and toast, they'd agreed there was little more they could do until they spoke to Lindsey the next morning. Tired after a long day, Trick had come upstairs, Mason had grabbed his overnight bag from his car and gone to a bedroom downstairs, and Ben had called Marcy and Trey to update them before retiring to the couch in the living room to get some sleep.

After cleaning up and stripping down to his boxers and T-shirt, Trick went to flip off the bathroom lights when he heard a distinct moan from Lindsey's room. He almost ignored it when he heard her yell, "No."

He put his head against the door and heard more moans. Concerned, he quietly opened the door to her bedroom. There was a whimper, and he peered around the frame into the darkness. "Lindsey?" he whispered.

She didn't answer, but as his eyes adjusted, he saw her form move in the bed, and heard another, "No."

He debated what to do. She was obviously having another nightmare, and by the sound of it, a bad one. Should he wake her or leave her alone? A few seconds passed, and she seemed to settle. Trick decided he should stay out of it and started to close the door when Lindsey spoke again. "Please. Don't." She paused. "Mom?" Her breathing came in heavy gasps. "Mom?" she said again, before she moaned again.

Deciding he couldn't just stand there, he entered her bedroom and approached the bed. "Lindsey, honey," he whispered. "It's me. Trick. Wake up."

Her head moved from side to side and her breathing deepened, along with her whimpering.

Trick carefully sat on the side of the bed and touched her shoulder. "Lindsey. Wake up." He spoke a little louder.

"Please," she said again. "Don't."

A soft nightlight in the room provided enough illumination for Trick to see her forehead was slick with perspiration. He'd had some nasty nightmares of his own over the years, and nothing matched the relief of waking up from them. He tried again. "Lindsey." He jostled her shoulder. "It's Trick." He spoke louder. "Wake up."

Her eyes flew open, and she gasped. Her hands gripping the blanket and her bangs stuck to her sweaty face, and she sat up and held her chest.

"Hey," he said softly. "You back?"

Moaning, she stared at the sheets as if unsure where she was.

Worried, he leaned in. "Hey. It's me. You had a bad dream, but you're safe." He touched her shoulder to give her a sense that she was back in reality.

Her face tightened, and she slumped. "Oh, God."

"You're okay."

She shook her head, and her face crumpled. "He killed her."

Trick tried to make eye contact, but she wouldn't look at him. "What?" he asked.

Her eyes closed, she dropped her head into her hands. "He killed her. He killed her. It's my fault." She fought to suck in air.

Seeing her distress, Trick took her wrist and ran his thumb over her skin. "Honey, can you hear me? It was just a dream."

A sob shook her shoulders. "It's all my fault."

Realizing whatever mental hold the past had on her was loosening, Trick scooted closer. "It's okay."

Another sob wracked her body. "It's not okay. I don't deserve forgiveness."

"Yes, you do. Whatever it is, it's not your fault."

She looked up, her expression dark with anger and pain. "It is. I did this." Her voice strained and shook. "I can never undo it." She ran her hands through her hair and sucked in another fractured breath before burying her face in her hands again with another sob. "She can't forgive me. No one should."

Suspecting she didn't need words right now, he moved up next to her and gently pulled her closer. She didn't resist and fell into him, burying her head into his neck.

"Hold on to me," he said, carefully putting his arms around her.

Her fingers curled up into his T-shirt and she let go and sobbed into his shoulder. He let her cry out her anguish, knowing she desperately needed this release she'd denied herself for so long. After a couple of minutes, her sobbing eased, but the crying continued. Hoping she would open up, he rubbed her back. "Feeling better?" he asked.

She didn't look up but still held on to him. "No."

He sighed and considered his next steps. "Stay still." He shifted on the bed so he could face the same way as her, pulled her close and gently lay back against the pillow so she could nestle her head into his neck. She didn't complain and stretched out beside him. He heard her take another shuddered breath and felt the wetness of his shirt where her tears had dampened it. "Talk to me," he said softly. He brought his hand around and stroked her hair.

She made another whimper. "I can't."

"Yes, you can."

There was another hitch in her breath. "You'll hate me."

"I won't. I could never hate you."

"I hate me."

"Then it's time to stop." He rubbed his chin over her forehead. "Tell me."

She paused and clutched his T-shirt. "I...I..." Taking another shuddered breath, she groaned and spoke in a shaky voice. "I...met him in a bar."

"Who?"

She hesitated. "Michael," she whispered.

Trick's heart thumped at the revelation. "You liked him?"

She tensed against him. "He was nice. He...we...laughed a lot."

"What happened?"

Another sob made her tremble. "We dated. I thought...I thought I could trust him."

Trick mentally prepared himself and held her close. "What did he do?"

She turned her face into his shirt. "I couldn't tell him at first...about my family."

Trick nodded. "But you eventually did?"

She groaned and cried some more. "We'd become close, and I...I thought maybe I loved him." Another sob tore through her and she sucked in air and gathered herself. "My family wanted to meet him, but I was scared."

"That's understandable."

"What if I told him and he didn't want any part of it? What if...? What if...he left?"

"But you told him?"

She nodded against his chest. "I wanted him to know." Her chest heaved when she continued to cry. "I wondered if he might want to join us." More tears surfaced. "I was so stupid."

Hating her suffering, Trick rubbed her arm. "What happened?"

Lindsey tensed again, and her grip on his shirt tightened. "I took him..." She took a second to catch her breath. "To the house, where we had our base. Before we went, I told him everything, and he acted excited." She sniffed and covered her face with her hand. "I...I was about to introduce him, and he... he..." Another sob wracked her. "He grabbed me and I...I collapsed. I couldn't move and he...he became me."

She curled inward and Trick tried to pull her closer. "Take your time."

She rambled as the words rushed out of her. "I didn't understand. I didn't know what was happening. He looked like me and I couldn't do anything. I fell to the floor, and he left me there." She took a deep, wrenching breath. "I couldn't stop him."

Trick kissed her head, wanting to do anything to comfort her.

"He walked right in as me." She moaned. "My fam...family. They thought...it was me." She sobbed until she could stop long enough to speak. "My mother." She held her head and cried. "She greeted him, and he...he...oh, god, he stabbed her." Her shoulders convulsed when she couldn't contain her sobs.

His own tears surfacing at the horror of it, Trick turned into her and wrapped his arms around her. "Oh, honey. I'm so, so sorry."

She shook against him and spoke between her sobs. "I woke up, and ran in, and she was...was bleeding, on the ground, and...and I ran to her."

Trick pulled her closer.

"Dad and Garret had Michael, and I grabbed Mom and she...she tried to talk, and she...she said my name...and I held her and begged her to stay, but she died in my arms." Her sobs choked her, and she coughed.

Trick clenched his eyes shut, understanding now the immense burden Lindsey had been carrying for years. "God, sweetheart. I'm so sorry."

Lindsey's sobs came hard and fast. "I killed her. I killed my mother." She held on to Trick like a frightened child clinging to a parent.

Trick tried to breathe slowly. The mere act of witnessing her pain was hard to bear, but he would bear it for her. He couldn't imagine how she'd put up with this guilt for so long without speaking about it to anyone.

Lindsey took a gulp of air. "After, I couldn't function. I couldn't sleep or eat. Dad put me in a mental health facility because he was scared I'd hurt myself. I stayed, but it didn't help. I just learned to say, 'I'm fine,' so people would leave me alone. I checked myself out after two weeks." She hiccupped. "I don't deserve to be alive, or her forgiveness."

Trick deduced Mason's visit had everything to do with her mother. "Was that who had the message for you tonight? Your mother?"

She nodded and whimpered into his shirt.

"She told you she forgave you?"

Lindsey nodded again. "She said she never blamed me."

"Of course she didn't, because it wasn't your fault."

"I brought Michael in. He used me."

"Exactly. He lied to you. He targeted you to get to your family. You had no reason to suspect him. How could you have known?"

She expelled a deep groan. "I should have."

"Why? Did he drop hints? Did you find suspicious texts or messages? Did you catch him in a lie?"

She didn't respond.

"Did you have any reason to suspect him at all? Did you even know he existed and wanted revenge?"

"No." She spoke so softly Trick could barely hear her.

"Michael made you believe he loved you and wanted to be a part of your family, not tear it apart. He's a sociopath, and you were as much a target as your family was, and if Ben and Garret hadn't subdued him, he'd have killed all of you." He trailed his fingers over her back. "That's not on you, Lindsey. That's on him. Your mother knows that. If the situation were reversed, would you blame her?"

She trembled against him. "No."

"Of course you wouldn't. If it had been Garret or Marcy or Trey, would you blame them, or would you blame Michael?"

Her sobbing had slowed enough for her to speak more easily, but her voice still cracked. "But it wasn't them. It was me."

Trick sighed. "Maybe that's a good thing."

She sucked in a breath. "Why?"

"Because you're the only one strong enough to survive it, and it's almost killed you. What do you think any of them would have done if they'd been the targets?"

She moaned. "I wouldn't wish this hell on anyone."

Trick thought back on his Ranger days. "I've seen a lot of things that would make most people's toes curl, and wondered how people survive the most horrific experiences, and you know what's common among the ones who do?"

Her body softened against him, and her crying slowed. "What?"

"Resiliency and acceptance. And becoming stronger despite the circumstances. Those that survive, use their pain for good and often become saviors to others."

She stilled and released a shuddered breath. "You expect me to start group therapy for cryptid hunters?"

He chuckled, happy her tears were slowing, and she could talk without sobbing. "If you want to."

She kept her face buried in his shirt and whispered. "Maybe Mom can forgive me, but I can't forgive myself."

He brushed his fingers against her hair. "That's the hardest thing to do. But I think you should talk to your family. Once you have that conversation and you see they don't blame you either, maybe you'll ease up on yourself." He sighed against her hair. "It takes time, honey, and a lot of communication. But once you let in a little love from the people around you, it can move mountains."

She relaxed a little, her breathing evened out, and her grip on his shirt loosened. "Mom likes you. A lot."

Trick smiled. "Of course she does. I suspect I would have liked her, too."

"Dad says I take after her."

"Then I know I'd like her."

Lindsey's tension eased, and she cuddled up to him with a moan and a long sigh. "I'm so, so tired."

"I know you are. You've barely slept for five years." Trick shifted his head on the pillow. "So sleep now. I'm right here."

Her arms relaxed against his chest, and she settled her head into the nape of his neck. After a few quiet seconds, she whispered, "Thank you."

His heart warmed, and he snuggled against her. "You're welcome," he whispered back.

Within minutes, she was sound asleep against him. Ensuring her comfort, he gave silent thanks that she'd finally opened up, and after closing his eyes and hearing her soft breathing, he fell asleep beside her.

Chapter Nineteen

Novak yawned and stared down the dark street at the quiet house. Since the one car had arrived two hours earlier, nothing had happened other than a downstairs light in the front window had gone out.

Tired, Novak considered her options. When she'd chosen to follow Trick and Lindsey, she had not expected a stake out and was ill-prepared for one. She had no food or water and no access to a bathroom. Her bladder protesting, she shifted in her seat to get comfortable.

She couldn't help but wonder if she'd overreacted. She'd overheard an argument. That was it. Granted, it had revealed that Trick and Lindsey were involved in something much bigger than a missing person or two, but that didn't mean they were breaking any laws. Novak thought back on the conversation, and her gut told her something was definitely going on, but she wasn't going to figure it out sitting on this dark street when everyone around her was going to bed.

Thinking about it and making some decisions, she started the car. She had to go with the odds. It was unlikely anything would happen tonight. If she left now, she'd have time to go home, eat, shower and get a few hours' sleep. Then she could be up early, prepare, and be back out here. She had the day off, so she could sit outside and watch the house all morning if needed. If nothing happened, she'd reevaluate. Believing her plan was solid, and eager to get to a bathroom, she pulled away from the curb and drove off.

· • • • • • • • • ·

Feeling a light touch on his cheek, Trick stirred. Another touch on his jaw woke him, and he opened his eyes. The room was dark, and for a moment, he forgot where he was, until he saw Lindsey lying beside him, her head on her pillow, watching him.

Her earlier sobbing and revelations came back to him, and he turned on his side to face her. "You okay?"

She nodded. "I had another dream."

"Another nightmare?"

"No," she whispered. "But my mom was in it." Her eyes twinkled in the low light. "She brought me flowers and told me she was proud of me."

Trick smiled. "I'm sure she is."

"She told me I could trust you."

"You can." She touched his cheek again, and a shiver ran through him. The way she was looking at him made him want to pull her into his arms. "I have a confession to make, though," he said.

"What's that?"

"I lied to you."

Her eyes widened. "When?"

He reached up and took her hand. "You were never expendable."

Her features softened, and she paused. "You were never expendable, either." She studied him and inched a little closer. "Tell me something."

"What's that?"

Lindsey shifted her head on the pillow. "How can someone like you be such a playboy? You obviously like women. Have you ever stuck with just one?"

It was a direct question, and Trick took a second to answer. It would have been easy to give a flippant response, but after she'd opened up to him, he felt he owed the same to her. "I guess I think it's better if I don't get too serious. Not that I haven't had a few bad breakups, but I'm not sure what I bring to the table is best long term."

"Who told you that nonsense?"

Trick sighed. "If you met my mom, you'd understand. She has her issues, and she's never been a big fan of her son." He held her gaze. "That might have something to do with it."

"So, you think you'll screw it up if you go all in?"

"Something like that."

She traced her thumb over his hand. "You know what my mom would say?"

"What?"

"Horseshit."

Her touch sent another shiver through him. "She would?"

"You're unlike any man I've ever met. You're kind, compassionate, honest, and reliable. And I haven't scared you away. I think that's part of why I've resisted you so much. I was afraid *I'd* screw it up."

"Horseshit." Trick squeezed her fingers. "You have all those same qualities. You've just had other things to deal with."

"You honestly think I'm kind?"

Trick chuckled. "I didn't say you were perfect. But neither am I." He held her gaze. "Since we're being honest, can I ask you something personal?"

She smiled softly. "I sobbed into your shirt earlier and wiped my nose with it. How much more personal can it get?"

He sighed. "What's your real last name?"

Lindsey hesitated. "If I told you, I'd have to kill you."

Trick chuckled. "I'm willing to take the risk." He let go of her hand and ran his fingers down her forearm. "I promise I'll take it to my grave."

Her hand free, she rested it on his cheek and whispered. "It's Donovan."

"Lindsey Donovan," Trick whispered back. "I like it. It's better than Eilish. Do you miss using it?"

She shrugged. "Sometimes. I don't think about it much. Maybe one day, when I'm old and gray, and my CU days are behind me, I'll go back to it."

Her look and closeness made his body warm, and lying next to her in bed without seducing her was tortuous. "Thank you for telling me."

"You're welcome."

"You should go back to sleep," he said. "And I should go back to my room." Not wanting to leave her but believing it was better if he did, he started to get up when she took his shoulder and held it.

"Stay," she whispered.

Her touch sent made his stomach flip, and he stilled. "I really should go."

"Why?"

He fell back against the pillow. "Because right now, I'm having unchivalrous thoughts."

She blinked at him. "So?"

His heart hammering, Trick did his best to think about anything other than Lindsey. "You've been through a lot. You're emotional and vulnerable. You think you want this, but you don't. What you need is time."

She released a slow breath. "I've had enough time." She stroked his cheek with her thumb. "And I'm not emotional anymore."

Her touch almost made him buckle. "God, honey. You're killing me here. Now is not the time for this, although God knows I want you."

Lindsey inched closer to him. "I want you, too."

Groaning, Trick took her hand that was sending chills through him and pulled it away from his face. "The last thing we need is to do something stupid. Today is a big day. It's the anniversary and you're supposed to confront Proteus. The last thing I want is to regret this."

Lindsey interlaced her fingers with his own, and Trick's plan to extricate himself from this situation failed when she guided his hand to her waist. "You won't regret it. I promise." She smiled and ran her fingers up his arm to his shoulder.

Trick held his breath. "I'm sure I won't, but it's you I'm worried about. I don't want you to think—"

Unexpectedly, she pressed him back and rolled on top of him. Her leg slid over his hips and before he could do anything about it, she sat up and straddled him. The only thing between them was the thin fabric of her underwear and Trick's boxers. The sensation was electrifying, and he bit his lip to not react, but it didn't work. His body was quickly overriding all rational thought. "Lindsey, honey—" He grasped her hips to keep her still, but that failed too when she squirmed against him, and he gasped.

"Trick, darling." She leaned down, put her hands on either side of his head, and whispered heavily against his lips. "Shut the hell up." She raised one hand, held his jaw, and lowered her mouth to meet his.

Her kiss turned everything on, and Trick caved. Her warm lips covering his, he eagerly trailed his hands up her torso to her shoulders, where he slid them into her hair. Their kiss quickly escalated to hungry need when she opened her mouth over his, and their tongues met. The fire that raced through Trick shocked him, and he forgot all about potential regrets. All he wanted to do was touch, tease, lick, taste, and arouse her until she begged for release. Wanting to make her forget all her troubles, he pulled her close and ravaged her mouth with his lips and tongue. Their rapid breathing intensified, and she clung to him, returning his passionate kisses with equal fervor.

His mind in a haze, Trick moved against her, and she surprised him when she suddenly pulled away and sat up. Her sexy gaze and pouty lips made him want her more, and he reached for her, but she leaned back, smiled, and pulled her T-shirt off.

Trick gasped and cursed at the sight of her, and when she eagerly tugged on the hem of his own shirt, he sat up and helped her pull it off. She tossed it on the ground, and he wrapped his arms around her. Their lips grazed against each other's, and his heart was thumping so hard he hoped he could stay conscious. "My God," he said against her lips. "You are magnificent."

She wrapped her arms around his neck and kissed him. After a long, languid kissing session, she gently pulled back again. "Why the hell did we wait so long for this?" Her throaty voice and fiery touch thrilled him, and he reveled in her desire.

Trick maintained control despite his desperate need for her. "The best things in life are worth waiting for." He kissed her again and imagined her screaming in satisfaction when he brought her to the height of arousal. His logical brain, though, hadn't completely silenced, and he paused and stared into her hazy eyes. "You're sure?"

She stared back and ran her hands through his hair. "I want this, and I want you, Texas." Her watery eyes sparkled. "I'm tired of being miserable."

He brushed her hair back from her face and couldn't stop thinking about how lucky he was to have this amazing woman in his arms. Giving himself full permission to use all his tools and experience to give her the maximum amount of pleasure, he kissed her passionately, pulled her down and rolled her to her side. Lindsey slid her leg over his and clutched at him, pulling him closer. Taking the initiative, he slid his hand down her body until she arched against him and sucked in a ragged breath. Smiling down at her, he gently nudged his nose against hers as she moaned and wiggled against him. Delighting in pleasuring her, he whispered against her skin. "Then let's make some new memories, honey." Grinning and eager to enact his seductive plan, he captured her lips in another searing kiss.

Chapter Twenty

Novak drove down the road toward the neighborhood she'd left the night before, hopeful she hadn't missed anything. After she'd made it home, she cleaned up, got some sleep and had been up early. She'd made coffee, packed breakfast and a sandwich for lunch and was out of the door before dawn. On her way home the previous night, she'd stopped at a nearby gas station to use the facilities and she stopped at it again on the way in to ensure the fewest number of disruptions. She'd keep her coffee consumption to a minimum, although she would have loved another cup. Telling herself she would take the morning and see what happened before making any other plans, she headed off to the neighborhood. The traffic was increasing as early commuters made their way to work, and Novak slowed and turned onto the street where the house was located. A car going in the opposite direction stopped at the corner and Novak slowed. Looking out the window, she recognized the car she'd followed the previous day and saw Lindsey behind the wheel. Lindsey turned, and making a fast decision, Novak did a quick U-turn, sped up to the corner, and dashed across the street, narrowly missing a car that honked at her.

Curious about where Lindsey was going by herself at such an early hour, Novak caught up to her, and staying a car behind, followed her.

· · · • · • · • · ·

Lindsey pulled up to the curb outside the warehouse facility where Proteus had sent her. Multiple warehouses spanned the block and Lindsey suspected warehouse nineteen would be located toward the back away from prying eyes. Since it was early, Lindsey sat and watched, trying to get a feel for who was coming and going. Workers arrived and others left. Some warehouses showed activity, but others didn't. She guessed warehouse nineteen would be quiet and likely unused, but until she got in and looked around, she couldn't be sure.

Sitting in her car, her mind wouldn't settle. Thoughts of her night with Trick made her heart race and her body warm. Their lovemaking had been more than memorable. Thinking about all they'd done to each other made her squirm in her seat. The first round had been hot and fast; their need for each other outweighing all possibility of going slow, but the second had been mind-blowing. Trick had taken his time with her and brought her to the brink enough times to make her clutch and beg for him until they'd both reached a peak that forced Lindsey to bury her head in a pillow to prevent her cries of pleasure from waking her father.

If it had ended there, it would have been unforgettable, but after a brief respite, they'd reached for each other again. Only the third time, Lindsey had reversed roles, and she'd taken charge. To his credit, Trick had let her take the lead and followed every instruction, and Lindsey had delighted in making him beg with every touch, lick, and stroke. His gasps and curses had brought her immense satisfaction and when they'd reached another peak, she'd covered his mouth with her hands to muffle his cries.

It had been a night like no other and if Trick had been sitting next to her, she'd have been tempted to postpone her meeting with Proteus to pull Trick into her arms so they could ravage each other again.

Not long after the third round, Trick had fallen asleep and Lindsey had dozed in his arms, savoring the feel of lying next to him, and wishing she didn't have to leave. But she knew if she didn't, no one she cared for would ever be safe. So, ensuring Trick slept soundly, she'd slipped out of bed, gathered her things, and tiptoed downstairs. Glad her father was sleeping on the couch, she'd gone into the empty bedroom, showered, and dressed, being as quiet as possible to not wake Mason in the other room. Before leaving, she disarmed the security system and computer, removed the tracker from her car, and left. She'd wondered what she would do if Novak was still surveilling the house, but breathed a sigh of relief when she saw no one on the street. Eager to leave before anyone discovered her missing, she'd turned out of the driveway and driven away.

Now, watching the activity at the facility, she thought of Garret and knew she'd made the right decision to come here alone. Proteus wasn't stupid, and if he spotted anyone other than Lindsey, she'd be risking her brother's life. That wasn't the only reason she wanted to come alone; she and Proteus had a reckoning coming, and it was her job to face him. After her night with Trick, she couldn't risk his life or anyone else's.

Several minutes passed, and seeing nothing suspicious, she checked her watch. She had three hours before her meeting with Proteus. That would give her enough time to check the warehouse and determine her plan. With any luck, she'd have Garret freed and Proteus dead before Trick and her dad even woke up. Something told her she wouldn't be that lucky, though, and she hoped she'd live to see the end of the day, and if she didn't, that Proteus would be dead along with her.

Telling herself not to think the worst, and to stop thinking about Trick, she got out of her car and headed toward the facility.

· · · · • · • · · · ·

Novak sat in her car across the street and watched Lindsey, who'd parked in front of a large warehouse facility and hadn't moved since. Wondering why Lindsey would leave so early to sit in front of a set of buildings and stare at them, Novak considered whether Lindsey had received some sort of tip about her brother and sister's whereabouts. But if she had, why come alone? Or was Trick coming later?

Novak pulled out her phone and debated calling her captain. Imagining how that phone call would go, especially at that hour, when she had nothing to report other than Lindsey leaving her house early to watch a warehouse, Novak tossed her phone into the passenger seat. There was no point in calling until she had more information. If it turned out that Lindsey was waiting on a sofa delivery, Novak would never hear the end of it at the station. She needed more before she could report anything.

She patiently sat in her car, wondering what Lindsey would do next. After several minutes of waiting, Novak was rewarded when she saw Lindsey get out of her car and head toward the facility. Novak didn't hesitate. She got out of her car too, and after crossing the street, she stayed back far enough and followed Lindsey.

• • • • • • • • • •

Sunshine brightened the kitchen as Mason poured himself some coffee and set the pot in the holder. After the long drive yesterday, his talk with Lindsey and the late-night updates from Trick and Ben, he'd slept better and longer than expected. After waking and showering, he'd entered the kitchen, prepared to see the others already strategizing, and was surprised when no one was in the kitchen. He spotted Ben outside on the phone, but Trick and Lindsey were not downstairs. Surprised since Trick tended to be an early riser, Mason pulled out his phone to text him when Ben entered the house.

Mason lowered his phone. "Good morning."

"Morning," said Ben, shutting the door behind him.

Mason sipped some coffee. "It seems we had a quiet night."

"We did. I hope you got some sleep because it won't be a quiet day."

"Slept pretty well, considering." He eyed the blanket and pillow on the couch. "How about you? How was the couch?"

Ben walked into the kitchen and grabbed a coffee mug. "Not bad. I've slept on worse." He helped himself to some coffee. "Any sign of Trick or Lindsey?"

"No," said Mason. "I was about to text Trick to see if he was up."

"It's not like my daughter to sleep in, especially on a day like today." He checked his watch. "Although yesterday was tough on her. I suspect she needs the rest."

Mason recalled his conversation with Lindsey. "I'm sure she does, but if we expect to confront Proteus today, we need to get ready." He started to text Trick when he heard a door open and shut. Mason looked up to see Trick leave the hallway and head down the stairs.

"Look who's up," said Mason. "You must have been tired."

Holding his hat and holstered gun, Trick half-smiled at him. "I was, but not as tired as you'd think."

His partner's cheery attitude made Mason raise a brow. "You must have gotten some sleep."

Trick set his hat and gun on the bar and headed into the kitchen. "Some." He made that half-smile again and found a coffee mug.

Mason studied his partner and knew that grin. It was the expression Trick typically offered after spending a satisfying night with a woman. Mason eyed the stairs, expecting Lindsey to show at any moment with the same grin. He sipped his coffee. "Lindsey get some rest?" He waited to see how Trick would respond.

Trick eyed Ben, and Mason suspected Trick would keep whatever happened between him and Lindsey to himself until he could speak to Mason alone. "Not sure." He poured himself some coffee. "Is she downstairs?"

"Nope," said Ben. "Haven't seen her. She must still be asleep."

Trick stilled and frowned. "She's not down here?"

"No," said Mason.

"I'll go wake her. We've got a lot to do." Ben headed for the stairs.

"She's not up there, Ben," said Trick. He returned the coffeepot to the burner and set his mug down. He walked down the back hall and checked the bedrooms.

Ben stopped and came back into the room. "Then where is she?"

Trick returned and went into the office. "No one's seen her?"

"No," said Ben. His eyes widened. "Hell." He sat at the desk.

"You think she's gone?" asked Mason, walking up next to Ben.

Trick leaned over Ben's shoulder. "Check the cameras."

"It would have alarmed if she left." Ben hit a few buttons. He studied the screen and cursed. "Son-of-a...she turned it off."

"What?" asked Trick.

"The alarm. It's off." He hit another button, and the various camera angles came into view on the monitor. The one facing the entrance was dark.

Trick's expression darkened. "Damn it. She turned off the camera, too?"

Ben cursed again. "I'm going to kill that girl."

Trick ran toward the front door. He flung it open and ran outside.

"Why the hell would she leave?" asked Mason.

Ben eyed the screen, and his face fell. "She lied to us." He swiveled his chair to face Mason. "She's not meeting Proteus at noon."

Trick ran inside. "Her car's gone." He strode into the office. "Where would she go?"

Ben stood. "To meet Proteus." He paused and ran a hand through his hair. "All by herself. I should have suspected she'd do something like this."

"Can we track her?" asked Mason.

"The tracking device," said Ben, his face brightening. "I put it on her car last night." He sat back in the office chair and punched more keys on the keyboard.

"We have to find her, Ben," said Trick. He pulled out his cell and dialed. "I'll call her." He put his phone to his ear and listened. "Answer, damn it."

Ben pulled up a screen and studied it. "Here. This should tell us." He pointed.

"No answer." Trick cursed and put his phone back into his pocket. He leaned over Ben's chair. "Tell me you know where she went."

Ben stared at the screen, and after a few seconds, his shoulders slumped. "I can't."

Mason eyed the monitor. "Why not? Where's the tracker?"

Ben fell back in his chair. "In the front yard. She removed it."

Trick cursed again.

"What about Novak?" asked Mason. "The one watching the house?"

Trick's eyes widened. "Hell. If she followed Lindsey..."

"She'll know where she is," said Ben, swiveling toward Trick.

Mason headed for the door as Trick pulled up Novak's number and dialed. "I'll see if her car is still here." Mason ran out the door, down the driveway, and looked outside the gate. The car he'd seen on his way in was no longer there. He turned and ran back inside. "Nothing. She's not there."

Trick lowered his phone, his face furrowed. "It went to voicemail." He smacked the desktop with the flat of his palm. "What the hell is Lindsey doing?"

Ben blew out a strained breath. "What she thinks is best." He swiveled toward Trick. "She's facing Proteus alone."

Chapter Twenty-One

Lindsey walked down the sidewalk, passing several warehouses, some with activity and others with none. Front loaders beeped as workers loaded and unloaded crates and paid no attention to Lindsey as she walked past them, looking for warehouse nineteen. As she suspected, the farther she walked, the quieter it became. The sounds of workers and machinery faded as she passed warehouse sixteen. She kept an eye on her surroundings, looking to see if anyone was watching her, but she saw no one. At warehouse eighteen, she walked down its width, stopped at the side and peered around it. Warehouse nineteen was just down the long walkway from the main road. She saw no one around, and after a few minutes, she stuck close to warehouse eighteen and crept up to nineteen. Avoiding the front of it, she walked down the side to the back and saw a door and a window. Peering through it, she saw a vast room with a high ceiling. Large and small crates sat inside on the floor but didn't take up the entire space. She tried the door, but it was locked. She tried to open the window too, but it was also locked. Peering through it, she saw another window on the opposite side of the building and worked her way along the back and came up the other side. Seeing another door and the window, she peeked inside and saw more crates and boxes. She tried the door and was surprised when it opened. If it hadn't, she would have had to reevaluate her plan, but since it did, she crept inside. No alarms sounded, but Lindsey guessed Proteus would have done his homework and not picked a place with an active alarm system.

And considering the door had been left unlocked, the facility obviously did not have top-notch security.

She quietly closed the door behind her and stopped and listened. Other than the hum of the air conditioner, it was silent. A few other windows from above provided enough light for her to see and she moved around the crates, staying aware but seeing nothing suspicious. As she'd hoped, she'd beaten Proteus here. Knowing him, she didn't think it was likely he would keep Garret in a place like this and expected they would come here from another location. Looking around, she spotted what looked like a garage door toward the front of the building. If opened, it would provide plenty of space for a car to enter and park inside. If Proteus had a way to open it, he could easily drive into the warehouse with Garret, and shut the door behind him, ensuring plenty of privacy.

Studying the area, Lindsey made a few deductions. She reached into her pockets, removed the two knives she'd taken from the house and detached the large one secured in a sheath at her waist. The smaller switchblade she'd carried with her to Vegas was tucked into the top of the work boots she wore. Trying to think like Proteus, she walked through the facility and hid the knives where she hoped she or Garret might get to them, assuming she could free him before Proteus killed him. All of that would depend on what Proteus had planned and how she reacted.

Once she was done, she stood quietly in the warehouse and prayed her idea would work, and if it didn't, that some other stroke of luck would intervene, because if it didn't, she and Garret would not leave this building alive. Taking one last look around to familiarize herself with the surroundings, her phone buzzed, and she jumped at the sound. She pulled it from her pocket and recognized the number as Trick's burner cell. He was calling her. For a moment, she agonized over answering. One part of her desperately wanted to, the other screamed no. She had to keep him, her dad, and Mason away. Regretfully, she ignored the call and turned off her phone. If she got out of this alive, there would be time to talk to Trick later. And if she didn't survive, then it wouldn't matter.

Gathering her nerves, and checking the time, she slipped out of the warehouse, found a secluded spot tucked behind a set of smaller buildings nearby, and settled down to wait.

· · · · · · · · · ·

Trick paced on the outside porch. He'd tried several times to call Lindsey and Novak without luck. Novak was either ignoring him or didn't have her phone, and Lindsey had obviously turned hers off. Trick kept trying anyway. Ben had spent the morning on the computer and talking to his team, trying to find Lindsey, but he'd had no success. As more time passed, the more scared Trick became. If she faced Proteus alone, she and Garret would likely die, and Trick would never forgive himself. He flashed back to the dumpster behind the apartment complex, where he thought he'd been talking to Lindsey. Proteus had incapacitated him within seconds. If Proteus did that to Lindsey, she wouldn't survive. Trick chastised himself for not anticipating Lindsey's actions and for being so caught up in his night with her that he'd let his guard down. Because of that, he'd slept late, and she'd slipped right past him.

"You need to stop blaming yourself."

Trick turned to see Mason on the porch. He'd been so caught up in his thoughts he'd hadn't heard his friend join him outside. "If this were Mikey, how would you be feeling right now?"

Mason paused, and his eyes narrowed. "Forget what I said. It's all your fault."

Trick sat in the porch chair. "Damn it. I should have seen this coming."

Mason sat beside him. "Lindsey's independent and headstrong. Even if you had, she'd have figured how to get around you."

Trick groaned and leaned back. "I was sleeping next to her, Red. To say I'm an idiot is an understatement."

"If you were sleeping next to her, then you're not an idiot." He rested his elbows on his knees. "What happened between you two?"

Trick stared at the awning above him, thinking about the intimate moments between him and Lindsey, and recalling how'd he woken up earlier and reached for her, eager to touch and kiss her again, but she hadn't been there. "She opened up to me about what happened between her and Proteus, and her mom's death. We talked and fell asleep, and then she woke me, and..."

"Nature took its course."

"It did. I wasn't sure at first, but she knew the buttons to push to break down my defenses."

"I'm sure there weren't many."

Trick sighed. "I don't regret a single second and neither does she. We both needed each other, and it happened when it needed to, but now..."

"Now you're questioning it? You just said there were no regrets."

"There aren't, but she's...she's..."

Mason nodded. "She's wiggled her way into your heart and now you're terrified you're going to lose her."

"I was already worried, but now I can barely think straight." He cursed. "I find the woman I want, and now I may lose her to some psychopath." He rubbed his face and his hands into his hair. "If he hurts her..."

"You can't think like that. You have to remember that Lindsey isn't helpless. She can handle herself. She's not going into this without a plan. She knows Proteus. That will work to her advantage."

"She's also emotional and out for revenge. You know how that works out. The Rangers would have kicked us off the force if we'd responded like that."

"There's a difference between a Ranger and a cryptid hunter. Revenge is a great motivation. You get mad enough, sometimes fate smiles on you."

"That's what scares me. Proteus sees this as his revenge, too. They're both out for blood."

"Based on what you told me, Proteus is mad about what happened to his father. Are you saying his father died under suspicious circumstances?"

Trick scoffed. "That's need-to-know, and apparently, I don't need to know. Either way though, none of it is Lindsey's fault. She was just a means to an end. Now it's more about Proteus being imprisoned for the last five years. And it wasn't your average prison."

"I can imagine." Mason sat back. "No wonder he's pissed, not that it wasn't deserved or necessary."

Trick stood again and resumed pacing. "It's the not knowing part that's killing me. There's no way we can help her." He checked his watch. "Hell, for all we know, she's facing him right now." He stared off. "Or, she's...she's..." He dropped his head. "God. I can't even say it."

Mason stood and patted Trick's shoulder. "She's not dead."

Trick groaned. "You don't know that."

Mason raised a brow at him.

Realizing Mason would likely know, Trick closed his eyes. "Sorry. I guess you'd have some insight."

"Take that as a good sign. And have faith that whatever she's planning will work, and she'll walk through that door with Garret at her side, flashing a victory grin." He poked Trick in the arm. "And she'll be all ready to celebrate with you."

Trick eyed his friend. "If you suspect otherwise, you'll tell me?"

Mason paused. "Yes. Of course I will."

Somber, Trick stared off at the garden.

"Stay positive, Trick," said Mason. "Try not to think the worst."

Trick did his best, but images of Proteus overtaking Lindsey and Lindsey being injured, or worse, wouldn't abate. He set his jaw and headed toward the door. "I'm going to check in with Ben."

Chapter Twenty-Two

After following Lindsey past the various warehouses, Novak squatted behind a dumpster at the rear of warehouse eighteen where she had a decent view of the back of nineteen. She'd almost lost Lindsey when she'd crept up from around warehouse eighteen and hadn't seen her. Being cautious, she'd stayed as far back as possible, but worried she'd stayed too far back. She passed nineteen, but seeing only a tall brick wall beyond it, she returned and watched the area. Intuitively, she didn't think Lindsey had gotten past her, which meant she'd gone inside somewhere. Novak crept up to the back window of nineteen and, peering inside, had abruptly pulled back when she'd seen movement. Careful not to be seen, she peered back in and caught Lindsey looking around the warehouse.

Wondering what she was doing, Novak stepped away and looked for a place where she could watch without being noticed. Behind warehouse nineteen were two buildings which appeared to be empty. Novak didn't want to risk hiding there if someone showed. Spying the dumpster near the adjacent warehouse, she settled herself behind it and waited for Lindsey. If she came back the way she'd arrived, Novak would have to do some fast thinking to stay hidden.

Deciding to take her chances, she stayed put and squatted beside it. She eyed warehouse nineteen, seeing the back but not the far side of it. If Lindsey left from that side and exited out the front of the facility, Novak wouldn't know it. Considering Lindsey's stealthy initial approach, though, Novak guessed Lindsey would leave the back way.

After several minutes passed, Novak worried maybe Lindsey had done the unexpected and Novak was about to leave her hiding spot when Lindsey reappeared. Novak ducked back and was relieved to see Lindsey head toward the empty buildings. She walked in between a set of crates stacked in the small alley where Novak had almost hidden herself. Lindsey crouched low and disappeared from view, and Novak realized Lindsey was hiding too.

Novak leaned against the dumpster and wondered what was going on. What was Lindsey waiting for? Novak checked her watch and considered again whether to call her boss. Something was definitely going down, and likely soon. And if she called, what would she tell them? Conflicted, Novak reached for her phone and cursed when she realized she'd left it in her car. She'd tossed it in the passenger seat, and in her haste to follow Lindsey, had left it behind.

Angry at herself for making a rookie mistake, she debated going back for it, but if she did, she risked missing whatever was about to happen. And something in her gut told her she needed to stay put. Anxious, she remained where she was and waited.

· · ● · ● · ● · · ·

Crouched behind the crates, Lindsey could see the side of the warehouse where the garage door was located. She supposed it was possible Proteus could come in another way, but with Garret, it would be more logical that he would drive up and enter through the garage. Checking her watch, her heart thumped as the clock ticked to nine thirty and then nine thirty-five. She perked up when a small four-door car turned down the side of the warehouse and Lindsey heard and then saw the garage door slide open. The distance and tinted windows made it hard to see who was driving, but she assumed it was Proteus. She didn't see a passenger. Once the door opened, the car drove in, and the garage door reversed course and slid shut with a clang.

Giving Proteus time to settle in, Lindsey waited ten minutes before leaving her hiding space and creeping up to the back window. She looked inside, but the crates and boxes didn't give her a clear view of the center of the warehouse where Proteus would have parked. She could see the back end of the car, though, so he'd turned the car around to face the garage door. There was no sign of Garret or Proteus, and she was due to arrive in ten minutes.

She stepped back from the window and squatted below it. Taking a few seconds, she inhaled and exhaled several times and imagined her plan in her mind, each time with a successful ending. If this was going to work, she needed to believe it could. Stretching her neck, she shook out her hands, took several deep breaths and tried to calm her thumping heart. She forced herself not to think of Trick or her past with Proteus, cleared her mind, straightened, and, ready to face her demons, headed toward the front of the warehouse.

· · • • • • • · · ·

Mason hung up the phone after speaking with Mikey, who'd called him to get an update. Still on the porch, he sat on the chair and thought again about Lindsey and where she might be. He'd tried to tune in to Lindsey's mother, but ever since his talk with Lindsey, her mother had gone quiet. It was as if she knew Lindsey needed to face Proteus and her mother was going to let her do it, despite the consequences.

Putting his phone away, he was about to go inside when he heard a soft thump in the distance. He'd heard it earlier, but had paid little attention while talking to Mikey. Now that he was off the phone, though, he heard it again. It was a distant, muffled thump and Mason wondered if a neighbor was working or gardening in his backyard. Maybe it was hammering or digging. Not thinking much of it, he was about to go inside when the door opened and Trick returned to the porch, looking just as concerned as he had since learning Lindsey was missing.

"I take it there's no change?" asked Mason.

Trick held his head. "None. There's no sign of her." He stopped beside Mason. "You getting anything from..." he waved his hand toward the sky, "you know...out there?" he asked, his tone cautious.

"Nothing." Mason stilled and tried to tune in. "But I sense things are ramping up."

Trick nodded. "Yeah. Me too." He stared out over the yard.

Mason heard the thump again and glanced toward the sound. "You hear that?"

"What?" Trick turned, put a hand on the brick wall of the porch and hung his head. "My worry and fear?"

Mason walked over to the wall. "You've got to have faith. Didn't Pamela ever tell you that?"

Trick frowned at the mention of his mother. "Are you trying to be funny? Because you're failing."

"How is Pamela? Still in rehab?"

Trick shrugged. "I have no idea. I haven't been in touch since I made it to Vegas." He shoved his hands into his pockets. "I saw you on the phone. Were you talking to Mikey?"

"I was."

"How is she?"

"Worried about you and Lindsey."

"I'm surprised she didn't come with you."

"She would have, but she's had a tough week. Plus, she's moving in with Remalla. I told her to stay put, and I'd keep in touch."

Trick nodded. "I hope her week hasn't been as tough as what I'm going through right now."

Mason thought back to Mikey's last few days. "She was almost arrested for murder by an overzealous detective who believed she killed a former friend and cult member."

Trick dropped his jaw. "What?"

Mason patted Trick's arm. "Don't worry. Rem and Daniels sorted it all out, for the most part. Mikey's fine." He declined to go into more detail because he doubted Trick had the capacity for more problems. "I'm sure she'll be happy to fill you in once you're home."

Trick stared for a second and shook his head. "How is it we always find ourselves in these crazy situations?"

"I guess the more you can tolerate, the more you get?" Mason shrugged. "I don't know."

"Lucky us."

"Yeah. Lucky us."

Trick turned and faced the garden. His solemn expression conveyed his worry.

"What's Ben saying?" asked Mason.

"He's in there working the phones and talking to his contacts. It's not doing much good, though."

"We'll find her. Eventually."

"Either dead or alive."

Mason wanted to say something to comfort his partner, but there was nothing to say. Trick was right. If Lindsey was facing Proteus, she might not come home. He took Trick's arm. "Come on. Let's go inside. Maybe Ben's heard something new."

Dejected, Trick sighed and nodded. "This is the longest day of my life." He turned and headed to the door.

Mason walked with him, and as Trick opened the door, Mason heard the distant thump again. He stopped and listened.

"Something wrong?" asked Trick.

"I keep hearing a thump."

Trick eyed the yard. "A thump?"

"Did you hear it?"

Trick shook his head. "No, but I'm a little preoccupied."

Mason waited, but didn't hear it again.

Trick headed into the house. "You coming?"

Mason heard Ben speak from inside. "Trick. Take a look at this."

Trick turned. "I'm coming."

"You go," said Mason. "I'll be right there."

Trick didn't wait and ran into the house.

Mason closed the door, stood on the porch, and listened. After several seconds passed without hearing anything, he reached for the knob when the thump sounded once more.

Mason couldn't determine where the sound was coming from. Curious and, for some strange reason, concerned, he stepped off the porch and headed into the garden.

Chapter Twenty-Three

Wanting to look like she'd just arrived, Lindsey approached the front entry of the warehouse. Bracing herself, she opened the unlocked door and stepped inside. The warehouse was quiet, and she saw the parked car facing the closed garage door. "Hello?" she said, and her voice bounced off the walls in the large space. When there was no response, she took a few steps. The boxes and crates made it hard to see, but when she stepped around one, the interior opened up. Based on her recall, some crates had been moved and she guessed Proteus had moved them. Looking around, she was relieved to see that none of her knives' hiding places had been exposed.

Stepping closer to the car, she walked around a shelf stacked with boxes and stopped short when she saw Garret sitting in a chair. His left eye was black and blue and swollen shut and he was slumped over as if unconscious. His hands and feet were bound, and she rushed over to him.

"Garret." She dropped to her knees and touched his shoulder. "Are you okay? Can you hear me?"

He made a grunting noise and his good eye cracked open. He blinked at her. "Lin?" he said in a croak.

"I'm here." She cupped his face.

He raised his head with a grimace. "Go. Get out of here."

"No," she said. "I'm not leaving without you." She looked around. "Where is he? Where's Proteus?"

"Please," he said. "Just go. He'll kill us both."

She held his gaze with an intensity that conveyed she was not leaving. "I'll get you out of here."

He coughed. "Leave me."

"No."

His face tightened, and he groaned. "You always were a pain in the ass."

"I take after my big brother." He stared back at her, and she debated slipping him her knife from her boot, but suspected Proteus was nearby. "How'd he get you?" she asked.

Garret grimaced. "I saw you in the lobby of my hotel. I watched you, expecting you were him, but you never moved. I didn't think he could stay morphed that long, so I thought it was you." He shook his head. "Stupid."

She patted his dirty hair. "I'm going to get you out of here."

He looked at her with fatigue. "No, you're not. Just leave."

Ignoring Garret, Lindsey looked around but didn't see anyone. She stood and faced the interior of the warehouse. "I know you're here. Come out, you coward."

After a pause, soft footsteps echoed through the building, and Proteus stepped out from an aisle of crates. He showed himself as the man she knew as Michael, and her stomach flipped at the sight of him. Her mind returned to that horrid day five years ago when he'd killed her mother while disguised as her, and that wrenching guilt returned. She fought to push it back.

He stopped at the end of the aisle and smiled at her. "Nice to see you again, Linds."

She swallowed but didn't answer.

"Did you come alone like I asked?"

"I did."

He tipped his head at her. "No Ben? No Trick?"

"No."

"How courageous of you."

She steeled herself. "And if I had brought them?"

"They'd be dead, much like your brother is about to be."

Her heart raced. "What did you do to Garret?"

Proteus chuckled. "It's no surprise that he's stubborn and uncooperative and didn't want to come willingly." He took another step. "I had to show him who's in charge."

"Let him go," said Lindsey. "I'm here now, and this is between you and me."

Proteus chuckled again. "This has never been about you and me. You just got your feelings hurt when I told you I loved you and used you to get to your family. You were just the beginning, and now you will be the ending. But not before I have some fun."

His smile widened, and Lindsey felt the bile rise in her throat. "What do you mean? You plan to kill me in front of him? Or him in front of me?" She eyed the nearest crate, where she'd hidden one of her knives.

Proteus scoffed. "Kill you?" He shook his head. "Not yet. That would spoil everything." He eyed Garret. "But killing him would be very satisfying."

Lindsey stepped in front of Garret. "If you think I'm going to let you do that, you're wrong."

"All I have to do is touch you, and you'll fall like a coconut from a tree." He took another step and Lindsey didn't move. "But there's no joy in that." The side of his lip raised. "I'd much prefer you watch."

"I won't do it. You'll have to put me down first."

"I realize that." He paused and his gaze traveled over her. "I know you're armed. Where's the knife?"

"I'm not armed." She raised her jacket to show him her empty sheath. "You told me no weapons."

He stared at the sheath. "You think I'm that stupid? I know you, kitten. You don't go anywhere without a weapon...and a plan."

Lindsey tensed. "I wouldn't risk my brother's life."

Proteus snorted and took another step. "Where are they?"

"Where are what?" she asked.

"The knives."

She set her jaw. "I told you. I didn't—"

"—bring any," he finished for her. "I heard, but I know you're lying."

Lindsey kept her face flat. "I'm not lying."

He sighed and walked closer. She stepped back, but stuck near Garret. She couldn't let Proteus get too close to her, but that prevented her from helping Garret. Proteus approached her brother, grabbed his hair, and pulled his head back.

Garret grunted and cursed.

"Leave him alone," said Lindsey.

Proteus raised his free hand and touched Garret's arm. He bucked and groaned. "Tell me," said Proteus, "or I'll torture him in front of you." He touched Garret again, and Garret sucked in a harsh breath, grimaced, and groaned again.

"Stop it," yelled Lindsey.

Proteus lowered his hand, but still held Garret by his hair. "One last chance."

"Fine," yelled Lindsey. She ran to the nearest crate and grabbed one of the knives she'd hidden. "Here." She brought it over.

"Toss it. On the ground."

Lindsey dropped the knife in front of Garret, and the knife clanged against the cement floor.

"Good." Proteus let go of Garret, who winced and leaned away from Proteus.

Lindsey eyed the knife and debated her next move. If Proteus came at her or Garret, could she get to the knife fast enough?

Proteus remained near Garret. "Do you honestly think I didn't know you'd come early?" He narrowed his eyes. "You think I'm stupid enough to trust you to follow my directions?"

Lindsey faced him. "Well, you never were that bright when we were together."

His face clouded. "You didn't complain in the bedroom."

"And you think that meant I was satisfied?" She scoffed. "You're right about being stupid enough to trust me, because back then, you did it all the time."

His frown lightened, and he made a satisfied smile. "Says the woman who invited me into her home, allowed me to become her, and then sacrificed her mother. Now who's the fool?"

Lindsey stiffened, and her stomach rolled.

Garret grunted and spoke. "Don't listen to him, Lin."

Lindsey forced the emotions back. If she let Proteus get to her, she'd never survive this. "You killed her. Disguised as me. In front of her children and husband."

Proteus' eyes widened. "Best day of my life."

Lindsey forced herself not to go for the knife.

"Until today, that is," added Proteus.

"That's where you're mistaken," said Lindsey. "Today is a perfect day for you to die."

He laughed out loud. "Oh, I've missed you, Linds. I always liked how you had an opinion and weren't afraid to express it, and your courage. Not much scared you."

"That hasn't changed."

He held her gaze. "Tell me. Does Trick enjoy those things?" He stepped closer to her, and she stepped back. "Does he satisfy you in ways that I couldn't?"

Lindsey set her jaw. She wasn't prepared to talk about Trick. "Leave him out of this. He's got nothing to do with us."

"Oh, but he does. He's an integral part." Proteus made that irritating smile again. "Can you imagine if you walked up to him, and he reached for you, but you pulled a knife and killed him? Like you did with your mother?

Imagine his shock and surprise just before he died." He took a deep breath and blew it out. "I've imagined it several times." He raised the side of his lip. "And doing it today, on the anniversary, would be ideal."

Lindsey felt sick. The thought of that made her want to run from the warehouse and make sure Trick was safe. "That's not going to happen."

"You sure about that?" asked Proteus. He shook his head and pouted. "I know more than you think I do."

Lindsey held her breath. "Care to elaborate?"

"You'll find out soon enough." He took another step toward her. "There's been a lot of assumptions made about me and my time at that prison." He paused. "You thought I'd rot there. That my mind would weaken, and my resolve would diminish. But it did the opposite. It honed my skills, fortified my determination, and burned the need to destroy your family into my blood. You thought you had a problem before you caught me? You have no idea of the problems you have now."

Lindsey caught how he pluralized the word problems, and for the first time, wondered if she'd made a grave error. What didn't she know?

"Lin," moaned Garret, raising his head to look at her. "Get out of here. I can handle Proteus. Find Dad."

Proteus glanced over at Garret. "Talk about delusional." He walked back over to Garret. "Where were we?" he asked. He grabbed Garret's hair again.

Lindsey moved closer. "What are you doing?"

"Where's the next knife?" he asked. "I know you have more than one."

Lindsey stood in shock.

Proteus raised his hand, and Garret shrank back.

Lindsey lifted her hand. "Okay. Don't hurt him. I'll get it." She walked to another crate, shifted it to the side, and reached behind it. She picked up the second knife, returned to Garret, and tossed it next to the other. "There. That's all of them."

Proteus sneered. "I don't believe you. Where's the one that belongs in that sheath?" He nodded toward her.

Lindsey looked down at the empty sheath at her waist. "It's in the car. I didn't bring it."

"What car?"

"I parked on the street. The knife is there."

Proteus eyed Garret and then Lindsey. "Toss your car keys on the floor. Next to the knives."

Confused, Lindsey pulled out her key fob. "Why do you want my—"

"Because you're not going to need them. Just toss them. Now."

Lindsey dropped the fob next to the knives.

Proteus lifted his hand and grabbed Garret's shoulder. Garret lurched, tensed, and cried out.

"Stop it," yelled Lindsey.

Proteus didn't relent, and Garret groaned with pain. "Where's the third knife?" yelled Proteus. He gripped Garret harder, and Garret clenched his jaw shut, and made a constricted, whimpering noise.

Lindsey had no choice. She ran over to the third hiding spot and grabbed the larger knife. "Here," she yelled. "Here it is." She ran over and dropped the knife in front of Proteus. "Let him go. Please."

Proteus lifted his hand, and Garret gasped and slumped forward. He moaned and spat a gob of blood onto the floor. "You better pray I don't get loose," he muttered in a shaky voice.

Proteus frowned at him. "I'll consider myself warned."

Lindsey tried to think. She didn't realize Proteus had the power to inflict pain on someone the way he'd done with Garret. What else didn't she know? "Now you have my weapons," she said. "What happens next?"

Proteus backed away from Garret, checked his watch, and faced Lindsey. "This is almost too easy." He crossed his arms. "I'm a little disappointed I didn't get more pushback. But I guess I shouldn't be surprised I've foiled your little plan to save your big brother."

"I'm sorry I didn't make it more difficult for you." Lindsey eyed Garret, her mind whirling with what to do next. "Is this where you kill him and make me watch?"

"It crossed my mind."

Lindsey steeled herself. "Well, let's make it more interesting, since you're so bored."

Proteus raised his brow. "What'd you have in mind?"

Lindsey glanced at the knives and thought of the one in her shoe. "I get one of those, and you and I have a contest. I win, and Garret and I leave." She nodded toward Garret, who lifted his head to look at her. "I lose, and you can do what you want."

Garret furrowed his brow, but she focused on Proteus.

Proteus studied her. "You want to fight me? And if I win, I can kill him?"

Lindsey took a second and then nodded. "And if I win, he and I both go home. Alive."

Proteus hesitated, but then a slow smile grew on his face. "Now I'm intrigued. You sure you want to do this?"

She eyed her brother, who was offering her an uncertain look. "Lin," he said, "Don't."

"Trust me, Garret," said Lindsey, looking back at Proteus. "This loser won't win. He never was any good in a fight."

Proteus squinted at her with malice. "Deal."

"I have one request though," she said. "Before we start."

"What's that?"

Lindsey softened her tone and face. "Let me say goodbye to Garret. In case I lose."

Proteus' gaze flicked between Lindsey and Garret. "Probably wise, since you aren't going to win."

"Is that a yes?" she asked.

Proteus paused. "You have one minute. Say your goodbyes and make them count."

Lindsey almost sighed in relief. "Thank you." She turned toward Garret, who was gaping at her.

"Lin," he said, "you can't..."

She glanced back at Proteus and squatted next to her brother. "I have to, Garret. It's the only way." She watched as Proteus slid his jacket off and she took that split second to slide the small switchblade out of her boot. "I need to do this." She moved the knife up her leg and slid it into Garret's hands that were tied behind him. She felt him grasp it as his eyes widened.

"He'll kill you," he whispered, taking the knife from her.

"Not before I do some damage of my own." She heard Proteus scoff behind her. She raised her hands and held Garret's face. "No matter what happens, I love you."

"Lin, please," said Garret. "Don't."

She imagined him opening the knife to cut away at his bindings and prayed he'd move fast. "I'm not going to make it easy, I promise." She started to stand.

"Lin, wait."

She stopped and lowered herself again. Garret nodded at her. "I love you too. And I'm sorry I put you in this position."

"It's not your fault."

He paused. "And what happened to mom isn't yours."

Unexpected emotion welled up in her eyes and she bit her lip.

Garret scowled at Proteus. "Hey. Asshole. This needs to be a fair fight. No special powers." He paused. "Unless you're too scared to face her on your own."

Proteus rested his hand on a crate. He eyed Lindsey as if thinking. "If it's a fair fight," he walked over and picked up one of the smaller knives, "then I get one of these."

"You touch her, and she goes down, you lose," said Garret.

"You're lucky I'm bored." Proteus smirked. "I accept those terms."

"So do I," said Lindsey. She spoke to Garret. "Thanks for watching out for me."

"You're welcome." Garret hardened his features. "Now go kick his ass."

Lindsey's heart swelled, and praying she knew what she was doing, she kissed Garret's forehead and straightened.

Proteus stood ready and waved toward the floor. "Take your pick."

She studied the knives and picked up the big one.

Proteus smiled. "Bigger doesn't mean better."

She raised the knife and smiled back at him. "You should know."

His smile fell, and he lowered himself into a defensive position. "Ready when you are."

Holding the knife in front of her, Lindsey prepared for battle.

Chapter Twenty-Four

Lindsey moved to her left, and Proteus did the same. Holding her knife out, she watched his eyes. Her training had taught her they would reveal his next move faster than watching his hands. His face remained impassive, but she sensed his eagerness to strike her down fast. He knew her well enough to know that the longer she prevailed, the greater her chances were of winning.

Taking long, steady breaths, she waved the knife in front of her. Garret watched, but Lindsey sensed he was sawing through his bindings with the knife she'd given him. She moved away from him to keep Proteus centered on her.

Proteus lunged with his knife, but she dodged the blow and shifted to her left again. She made her own jab, but Proteus leaned away and avoided the contact.

"You know," he said, "when I'm done here, I'm going to find your father, where I'll finish what I started." He swiped the knife at her again.

She jumped away from it. "You'll have to get through me first." She waited, expecting his next move, and when he lunged again, she swiveled, knocked his hand away, and swung her knife. The tip caught the edge of his shirt, but he shifted away before she could do any damage.

Breathing faster, he eyed his torn shirt. "Close, but not quite. You must be rusty."

"I'm warming up fast." His next attack was at her midsection, and as she darted to the side, she used his momentum against him and rammed her knee into his stomach.

Proteus grunted and doubled over, and she swiveled back to face him just as he turned to face her, his face slightly paler.

She transferred her weight back and forth to each foot, waving the knife, and staying ready.

Proteus glared at her and straightened. "Not bad."

"Told you I was warming up."

His gaze traveled behind her and before she could wonder what had his attention, he rushed her.

"Lindsey," yelled Garret.

Proteus rammed into her, knocking her into a stack of boxes. Her back hit hard, and she lost her breath with the power of the blow. The boxes remained upright but swayed, and Proteus fought to pull his knife back to plunge it into her. She held onto him, forcing him against her, and tried to raise her knife when the boxes gave way and toppled, sending them both to the floor. Lindsey landed on her side, with Proteus partially on top of her. He raised his knife, and she grabbed his wrist with her hand, preventing him from stabbing her.

Her hand, which held her knife, got caught beneath her and she fought to free it, but Proteus' body was in the way. He raised himself slightly to get more leverage, and his strength was too much for her to slow his knife's descent toward her. When he shifted his position, though, she freed her hand with her weapon and swung it toward Proteus, who pulled back to prevent her from stabbing him.

Lindsey rolled to her feet, as did Proteus. Breathing hard and sweating, she faced Proteus again.

"I think I'm warming up too," said Proteus, smiling. "I forgot how fun combat is."

Lindsey moved in a circle, and Proteus did the same. "We'll see how fun you think it is when my knife is in your gut," said Lindsey.

His eyes gleamed in the light. "Come and get me, my dear." His expression shifted and his grin widened. "I remember so vividly what my knife felt like in your mother's gut."

Lindsey held her breath, and shivers ran through her.

"Don't listen to him, Lindsey," said Garret. "He's goading you."

"She was warm and soft," said Proteus, "much like you were back then." He snickered. "Like mother, like daughter, I suppose." He waved his knife. "Or at least I'm about to find out."

Fury rushed through her. Seeing a crate behind Proteus, she rushed him as he'd rushed her, aiming her knife at his stomach. He swiveled and knocked her hand back, but tripped over the crate and fell backward. Unable to stop her momentum, she fell with him. They both tumbled over the crate and hit the ground again. Her head hit a support post, and the impact stunned her, but she scrambled to get to her feet. Proteus was faster though, and he tackled her and knocked her back to the ground. She swung her knife, but he caught her wrist with his free hand and shoved it down and brought his own knife to her throat.

She stilled, waiting for the final blow, and said a silent apology to her mother for failing.

"Looks like I win," said Proteus, his body pressed against hers and his face mere inches from her own. His breath fanned her face, and she winced. He traced the tip of his knife over her skin. "I could end this right now."

She fought against him, but he pushed the knife harder against her jugular and she stilled again. "Just let Garret go," she whispered.

He shook his head. "That wasn't part of the deal." He leaned closer and smelled her hair.

Lindsey grimaced at his nearness.

"The deal was I could do whatever I want." He leered at her. "And fighting you turns me on."

Her stomach turned at the thought that he wanted more than just her death. "You're crazy."

He moved his nose over her cheek. "Would you do it, my dear? To save your brother's life?"

She closed her eyes and focused. There was no way she was giving herself to this man to save anyone, not even herself. "Go to hell," she muttered, opening her eyes.

His expression softened, and he laughed. "Poor Garret. Now we know how much he means to you." He sighed. "Don't worry. I'm not interested. I just wanted to see if you'd go for it." He raised his head to meet her gaze. "Haven't you figured it out yet that I'm not ready to kill you? I have other plans for the two of us."

She tried to free her hand, but he held tight.

"But Garret's not so lucky. Unfortunately, he's going to have to die."

She cursed at him, and he squeezed the wrist of her hand that held her knife. "Let it go," he said.

"No," she said, clutching the knife harder.

"I said...," Proteus tightened his grip, "...let it go."

The pressure on her wrist increased, and she fought to hold on. Tingles raced up her forearm, elbow, and arm. "You're breaking the rules," she said, feeling a strange lethargy come over her.

"The winner makes the rules, sweetheart. And I'm the winner."

She blinked, fighting to stay conscious. If she went out, Garret would die, and God knows where she'd wake up.

Proteus leaned closer and whispered in her ear. "Nighty night, dear."

Lindsey groaned and made one last effort to fight back when an ear-splitting bellow sounded. Proteus turned toward the sound and rotated off of her just as Garret attacked.

• • • • • • • • • •

Mason wandered down the stony path, passing the pool, flowered shrubs, large cacti, and wispy vegetation. The garage that held the boat trailer was to his right, and he walked over to it, listening. He didn't hear any thump, but he went inside and looked around. The empty trailer sat in the middle of the quiet shop, with shelves of tools and various equipment against the sides of the garage.

Seeing nothing of interest, he left the garage, where he passed a small cabana and sauna and returned to the path. He walked along it and approached the guest house toward the back of the property. He took the steps up to the front door and tried to open it, but it was locked. The blinds at the windows were closed, so he couldn't see inside. When he tried a window and found it locked, too, he stepped off the porch and returned to the path where he followed it to the back fence that surrounded the property. He went to the back gate, which had a simple lock. He undid it and walked out onto a strip of grass that bordered a street that ran behind the house.

He listened again, but heard no thumps. Guessing whatever was causing the noise had stopped, he gave up looking for the source and returned to the backyard. He secured the lock on the back gate and walked back up the path, planning to find Trick and hoping for some news about Lindsey. When he was approaching the pool, the thump came again, and he stopped.

Turning, he felt certain it had come from behind him, and after a pause, he walked back down the path.

· · • · • · • · · ·

Trick studied the monitors in the office while Ben spoke to someone on the phone. When Trick had returned, Ben had told him that Trey, who'd been monitoring the police scanner, had picked up activity from a patrol

in Vegas who'd called in a possible sighting of a missing person matching
Garret's description.

After several tense minutes of Trick waiting and listening as Ben called
a few contacts to get more information, they'd both been disappointed to
learn it was a false alarm. The man the patrol had picked up had not been
Garret.

Ben hung up the phone and sat again in the office chair. "Nothing new.
The patrol apparently picked up a homeless man off his meds."

Trick slumped. "Damn it." He checked his watch. "I don't like this, Ben.
I sense we're out of time."

"I know. I feel the same." He eyed the monitors and tapped on the
screen. "Is that Mason?"

Trick looked closer at one of the screens and saw the small image of his
friend walking through the garden. "Yeah."

"What's he doing?"

"Red?" said Trick. "Probably trying to focus and find his center since
there's nothing else to do."

Ben sighed. "At least someone's finding something around here."

"No kidding."

"I'm going to text Trey and tell him that's Mason in the yard." Ben
picked up his phone, cursed, and lowered it. "Hell. It's dead."

Trick pulled out his. "Here. Use mine if you want."

"Thanks." Ben took it and stood. "I'll get my charger." He typed on
Trick's phone and headed into the living room.

Trick stared at the monitor, praying he'd see Lindsey's car pull up in the
driveway, but she didn't show. His imagination tortured him with horrible
scenarios of what could be happening to her, and he tried to think positive.
Mason was right. Lindsey wasn't a novice. She knew how to take care of
herself, she knew Michael and she'd have a plan, but none of that made
Trick feel any better. She was still on her own against a dangerous adversary
with a grudge, whose abilities gave him the upper hand.

Ben returned to the office and sat again in the chair. He set Trick's phone on the desk. "Thanks. Trey's updated." He plugged in his charger to charge his phone. "Any updates?"

Trick scoffed. "No. Other than Red seems to be enjoying his walk."

Ben studied Mason's image. "Good for him."

The screens flickered, and a few went black. Mason's image froze.

"What the hell?" asked Trick, straightening. "What's wrong?"

The flicker returned, the screens came back to life, and everything resumed normal operation. "Hell," said Ben. "That's the second time it's done that. I think we're straining the Wi-Fi." He hit some buttons and checked something on another screen.

"Great. That's just what we need."

Ben stood. "Hang tight. I have a booster in my car. I'll get it."

"Take your time," said Trick, dejected. "We've got nothing better to do."

"I'm not giving up hope, Trick," said Ben. "We'll find her...," He paused. "...alive." He turned and left the office.

Trick leaned over the desk, set his head in his hands, and whispered to himself. "Where the hell are you, honey?"

· · • • • • • · ·

The tingles dissipated, her strength returned, and now free, she sat up and saw Garret on top of Proteus. He had the knife she'd given him in his hand, and Proteus was holding his wrist, preventing Garret from striking. A second passed, and Garret grunted and dropped the knife. Proteus let him go, and despite his obvious weakness, Garret didn't give up and started swinging with his fists.

Momentarily stunned, Proteus dodged the blows with his arms.

"Garret," yelled Lindsey.

Garret got a good punch into Proteus' midsection, and Proteus grunted with the impact, but just as quickly rebounded. He shoved a hand into

Garret's stomach, and Garret immediately lurched back and fell off of Proteus.

Proteus scrambled to get his feet as Garret crawled away and reached for the remaining knife that was lying next to the key fob Lindsey had tossed to the ground.

Her energy returning, Lindsey hurried to get up but watched in horror as Proteus moved faster. As Garret went for the knife, Proteus rushed at him, swinging his. Garret rolled to avoid the slice of the blade, but wasn't quick enough. The knife caught him across his side below his ribs, and blood spurted from the wound.

"No," Lindsey screamed, grabbing her knife and rushing toward Garret, who held his hand against his wound. Bright red blood ran between his fingers. She ran between him and Proteus, who faced Garret, prepared to strike again. "Stop." Breathing hard, she raised her knife at Proteus.

Proteus looked between her and Garret. "Sorry, dear, but his time is up."

"I won't let you kill him." Lindsey's mind whirled. She had to find a way out of this.

"Oh, but you will." Proteus flexed the fingers of his free hand. "You can't stop me." He shivered, and a ripple traveled over his skin. "But before I finish, let me enjoy one last morph of him, just in case I need it."

Lindsey stared in horror as Proteus' face shifted, his body changed shape, and she stared at Garret. Proteus had morphed himself into a perfect replica of her brother.

Garret cursed from behind her.

Proteus exhaled with satisfaction. "What do you think, Linds? Should I kill Garret as Garret, or maybe..." His skin rippled again, and Lindsey gaped as he morphed into her. "As you?" he grinned. "Just like old times, huh?"

Staring at herself, Lindsey's fury flared. She raised her knife. "I don't care who the hell you are. You're not touching him."

"Lin," said Garret meekly from behind her, "I'm okay. Leave me and get out of here."

"Shut up, Garret," said Lindsey, glaring at Proteus.

Proteus raised his knife. "Time is short. Let's get this over with. But this time, dear, there are no rules." He grinned.

Lindsey steeled herself as Proteus advanced.

A booming female voice rang out through the warehouse, and Lindsey jumped. "Freeze! Police! Don't move!"

Proteus froze, and so did Lindsey. She looked over and dropped her jaw when she saw Officer Novak standing outside a row of crates near the side entrance.

Her hands shaky, she held her gun in a shooting position and yelled again. "Put your hands up and step back, or I'll shoot."

Proteus stared with wide eyes and looked as surprised as Lindsey felt.

"Shoot him," said Garret.

Proteus remained still and spoke in Lindsey's voice. "Who are you going to shoot, officer? Me...," he waved his knife at Lindsey, "...or her?"

Lindsey couldn't imagine what Novak was thinking because she was looking at two Lindseys.

Novak didn't hesitate and straightened her aim at Proteus. "You, you son-of-a-bitch."

Proteus' smile faltered. His skin rippled again and within seconds, he was back to being Proteus. "I hope you're a good shot, officer." He eyed Lindsey. "See you soon." He winked at her and whirled away with lightning quick speed.

Novak yelled again. "Freeze." She ran a few steps forward.

Proteus dove behind some crates, and Lindsey could see where he was going. The front exit was just beyond his car. She ran after him, but he raced into an aisle of shelving and more boxes. She hurried to catch up and tried to bypass and beat him to the exit when he darted from behind a large crate. His knife extended, he lunged at her and a shot rang out. The bullet blasted a chunk of wood out from a crate beside Proteus. The noise deafened Lindsey, and she ducked behind a shelf, not wanting to be hit.

"Stop," yelled Novak.

Proteus exited out the front, with Novak following. Lindsey rushed toward the door and caught up to Novak, who flung the door open and ran into the sunshine. Right behind her, Lindsey squinted in the sun. Holding her knife, she stared out into the narrow road that ran between a row of warehouses. A large truck was parked outside the opposite warehouse and several workers, one using a front loader, were unloading large crates and boxes. The sound of the equipment had likely muffled the sound of the gunshot. Breathing hard, Novak held out her gun, and moved it side to side, looking for Proteus.

Now that it was later in the morning, more workers walked along the far side of the street, and another truck drove by. Lindsey realized Proteus would have morphed again once out of the warehouse and could have been anyone at that point. Chasing him was pointless.

"Where'd he go?" asked Novak, looking pale.

Lindsey put her hand on Novak's hand and lowered her weapon. The last thing they needed was to draw attention from any workers or the police. "He's gone." She took Novak's arm. "Get inside."

Novak sputtered. "But...but...he...he...was you."

"I know," said Lindsey. "C'mon. We have to help Garret." Wondering what to do next and how to explain this to Novak, she pulled Novak back into the warehouse.

Chapter Twenty-Five

Novak, still reeling from what she'd seen, let Lindsey guide her back inside. Part of her wanted to chase after the man named Proteus, but another part wanted to stay as far away from him as possible.

When she'd seen Lindsey approach the warehouse and disappear down the side of it, Novak had inched out enough to watch her walk toward the front and turn the corner. Novak didn't think Lindsey was leaving, so she crept up to the back window and peered inside. It surprised her to see a parked car, which hadn't been there before. Squatting low, she debated what to do. The car had obviously entered through the garage door, which Novak hadn't seen from her vantage point. She guessed the car's arrival must have been Lindsey's cue to go in and meet whoever had arrived. But who was she meeting? The man Lindsey and Trick had been arguing about in the parking lot? Or someone else?

Confident something was up, Novak straightened and peered inside again and quickly ducked back down when she saw the back of Lindsey's head near the center of the warehouse

Cautious, Novak slowly raised herself again. She saw Lindsey talking, and Novak shifted to the other side of the window to see better. A man sitting in a chair came into view. She couldn't see all of him, but based on his body language, he appeared to be injured or unconscious. Novak couldn't tell if it was Garret, the man Lindsey and Trick had reported missing. Needing a better vantage point, Novak left the back window and moved around to the side. There was another window and door there, but shelves and stacked boxes blocked her view. Eyeing the door, she had to decide. Go inside or wait?

Her father had always told her that a big part of being a detective was learning to trust your gut despite what anyone else said or even what appeared logical. Her heart thumping, Novak tuned in, trying to figure out what her gut was saying. Part of her wondered if she should find the nearest phone and call for a patrol, but she still didn't know enough to report anything. It wasn't against the law for Lindsey to meet someone in a warehouse, and Novak hadn't see the injured man well enough to say it was Garret. She needed to get inside.

Guessing that was her answer, she moved to the door. Hoping it was unlocked, she sighed with gratitude when the knob turned. Saying a prayer she wouldn't be heard, she opened it. Holding her breath, she slowly pulled it wide enough to slip inside and carefully closed it. She took a second to catch her breath and allow her heart rate to slow, but hearing voices, she edged up the aisle. Not ready to risk a peek, she sat still and listened, but pulled her weapon in case she needed it. The voices were hard to make out, but they sounded strained. When she heard a man yell Lindsey's name and a crash, she jumped up and ran to the end of the aisle. She saw the front end of the car and ducked low to get around a set of crates. She heard more talking and then a bellow and another crash. Staying low, she raced over to the end of another aisle where she could see better but also use it for cover if needed.

She peered out and saw Lindsey holding a knife and facing an angry man, who also held a knife, and another man on the ground, clutching his bloody side. Getting a look at him, Novak recognized him as the missing brother, Garret.

Novak raised her weapon but froze in shock when the man suddenly changed form and transformed into Garret. Novak blinked, wondering if something was wrong with her, when the man suddenly changed his appearance again, and became the exact match of Lindsey. Novak couldn't believe what she was seeing. Was she delusional? Had she been drugged?

The person who'd become Lindsey waved the knife and sneered at Lindsey and Novak's gut told her now was the time to act. Screaming at them to freeze and not move, her hands shook, and her voice trembled. Nothing in her training had ever prepared her for this. After a pause, the bizarre man sneered at her, and Novak sensed he was picking up on her uncertainty. He shifted back to his original self and ran, and, breaking out of her frozen state, she ran after him and fired when he'd lunged at Lindsey with his weapon, but he'd been too fast and had escaped out of the building.

Now, following Lindsey back into the warehouse, she tried to come to terms with what she'd seen, but she couldn't. None of it made sense. What the hell was going on?

Lindsey ran to Garret's side. "Garret." She got to her knees beside him. "How bad is it?" She tried to move Garret's hand, but he winced and clutched his wound harder.

"I'm okay," said Garret. "Go find Proteus."

"You aren't okay," said Lindsey. "You need help."

Garret regarded Novak, who holstered her gun and squatted next to Lindsey.

"Who the hell are you?" asked Garret. His forehead was slick with sweat and his voice shook.

"This is Officer Novak. And be nice. She saved our asses." Lindsey looked back at Novak. "You obviously followed me?"

"I did," said Novak. "I saw you leaving the neighborhood."

"She followed you?" asked Garret. "And you didn't notice, Lin? That's a rookie move."

"You must be Garret," said Novak. She spoke to Lindey. "Your missing brother?"

"How the hell does she know my name?" asked Garret.

Lindsey tried to check the wound, but Garret resisted. "Because there's a missing person report out on you, and Novak wrote the report."

Garret narrowed his eyes at Novak. "How much does she know?"

"She saw Proteus morph into you, and then into me. I'd say she knows a lot." Lindsey looked around. "We need something to staunch the blood."

Novak didn't understand any of this, but she knew what to do next. "Either of you have a phone? I need to call this in. And we'll get you an ambulance."

"No," said Garret and Lindsey at the same time. "You can't," said Lindsey.

Novak frowned at them. "What are you talking about? That crazy man was going to kill you both, and," she waved a hand at Garret, "you've been reported missing and you're hurt. We need to get you to a hospital."

"You call this in and you're putting other lives at risk," said Lindsey. She took her large knife and slid it into the sheath at her belt. "This has to stay quiet."

"I can't do that," said Novak.

"What are you going to tell them?" asked Garret. "That a man changed and shapeshifted in front of you? Twice? And then took off as someone else?" Garret grimaced and held his side.

Novak hesitated. That part of the story wouldn't go over well. "Who was that guy? What did I see?"

Lindsey didn't answer.

"He was no one," said Garret. "Forget you ever saw him. Go home and pretend this never happened."

Novak gaped at him. "Are you serious?"

Garret set his jaw. "Do I look like I'm kidding?"

"His name is Proteus," said Lindsey.

"Lin, don't," said Garret. "It's need-to-know."

"She saw him morph," said Lindsey. "I'd say she needs to know. He's dangerous. He—" She froze.

Garret's face fell. "What's wrong?"

Lindsey stared off, her eyes widening. "He wants to kill us."

"I got that much," replied Novak.

Lindsey sucked in a breath. "He said he didn't want to kill me yet. That he had a plan, and that he'd see me soon." She paused. "And he said I didn't know everything."

"You think he's coming back?" asked Novak, looking back toward the entrance.

"No," said Lindsey. She looked at Garret. "He knew."

"He knew what?" asked Garret.

Lindsey held her stomach. "That I was armed, that I came early, and alone. He never checked to see if anyone else was with me. That's how Novak didn't get caught."

Novak didn't understand what she was talking about.

"I don't think it's a big stretch to assume you were armed," replied Garret. "Or came early."

Lindsey suddenly straightened and started looking around. "Where is my key fob?"

"Your what?" asked Novak.

"On the ground," said Garret. "You tossed it with the knives."

Lindsey searched for it and shook her head. "It's not here. He took it." She ran to Garret's side. "He knows where the house is. He knows where Dad and Trick are. That's where he's going."

Garret stilled. "Shit." He struggled to get up. "Help me. We'll take his car. He left the keys in the console." He grimaced and more blood ran through his fingers.

Lindsey glanced toward the car in the warehouse. "I have to go. Right now. Proteus can walk right into that house as me, and none of them will know."

"You can't go alone," said Garret. "Take me."

"I can't. You're injured and you need a doctor." She looked at Novak. "Get him to a hospital. Just don't involve the cops." She jumped up.

"Lindsey, you need help," yelled Garret.

"I can't wait, Garret." Lindsey ran past the car and to the garage door, where she hit a button. The door began to roll open. "We're running out of time." She ran back to the car. "Take care of my brother, Novak."

"Wait," said Novak. "You're going to the house? Let me call this in. I can have a patrol head that way."

"You do that, and you'll risk their lives, too," said Lindsey. "No cops."

"Lindsey, dammit." Garret struggled to get up and partially succeeded until he fell back on his side. "Don't do this without me. He'll kill you. This is what he wants. That's why he left the keys. He wants you to follow."

Lindsey ignored him and jumped into the car. The engine turned over, and the tires squealed as Lindsey gunned it out of the warehouse.

Chapter Twenty-Six

Mason walked down the path toward the guesthouse, waiting for another thump so he could follow it. It had sounded close but not loud enough to pinpoint. He stopped midway down the trail and waited. A minute passed. He heard a car drive by, and it was quiet. Turning, he looked around, searching for any potential source.

Thump. He swiveled and eyed the small house at the rear of the property. The sound had come from that direction. Heading toward it, he looked around the area but saw nothing out of place. He returned up the steps and tried the doors and windows again, but they remained locked. He checked the front mat and potted plants for a key but didn't find one. Putting his ear against the door, he listened. Could someone be inside? He went to the window. The blinds were down, but he could see a sliver of the inside through a partial opening between the slats, but all he saw was the edge of a bed. Nothing appeared disturbed.

Frustrated, he backed off the stairs and stared at the building. Maybe it was an electrical problem, or the air conditioning?

Thump. Mason stilled. The sound was definitely coming from the guest house. Determined, he left the walkway and followed the grass to the back. There wasn't much there other than landscaping, but he shoved past two large shrubs and stopped when he saw a narrow stairwell leading down to another door. The guest house had a basement.

Heading down the stairs, he heard a louder thump and knew then he'd located the source. It was coming from the other side of the door. He approached it and listened. Not hearing anything, he knocked. "Hello? Anybody in there?"

After a pause, he heard *thump, thump, thump.*

Mason put his hand on the door, certain someone had just responded to him. He tried the door, but it was locked. He knocked again. "Is someone there? Can you unlock the door?"

Thump. Thump.

Mason searched outside, but there wasn't a mat or potted plant to hide a key in. He jogged back up the steps and saw a cactus planted in a decorative bucket. Hopeful, he checked beneath it and was thankful to see a key. He picked it up, returned to the door, and was relieved when the key slid in and turned with ease. Opening the door, he stepped inside and listened for more thumps. The small room contained a twin bed, a tiny bathroom, and two interior doors. He opened one door and saw a narrow stairwell that led to the upper floor of the guesthouse. Before going up, he turned and opened the other door, which he guessed was a closet.

A rolled-up carpet spilled out, almost knocking him down. He fell back on the bed and, staring at the carpet, he dropped his jaw when it moved.

Shocked, he kneeled beside it. "Hold on," he said. "I'll get you out."

He reached for the edge, prepared to unroll it, when something touched his arm. Before he could turn his head to look, tingles raced through him and a strange lethargy ran up his shoulder, neck, and into his body. His heart raced, his strength vanished, and unable to even look behind him, he collapsed onto the floor.

· · · • · • · · ·

Trick sat on the sofa in the office and stared at the ceiling. It had taken every ounce of his sanity not to jump in a car and search for Lindsey. If he'd thought it would do any good, he would have left the second he'd realized

she was gone. But driving around in circles might keep him busy, but little
more. All he could do was wait and pray she got away from Proteus alive.

For the millionth time, he thought of their night together. It had been
memorable for several reasons beyond their sexual compatibility. Lindsey's
vulnerability and his honesty had changed everything. It was rare for him
to discuss his past and especially his mother with anyone, but he'd been
willing to do it with Lindsey. And he'd done it with ease.

Trick had enjoyed plenty of relationships and endured a few heartbreaks,
but nothing measured up to the intensity and emotional connection he'd
experienced with Lindsey, and he prayed to God he wouldn't have to lose
it mere hours after finding it.

Needing to move, he stood and paced. He took his phone from the desk,
planning to call her again. At some point, if she survived, she'd answer. He
cursed though when he realized the battery was dead and prayed Lindsey
hadn't been trying to reach him. Eyeing Ben's phone, he almost reached
for it when he realized Ben was taking a lot of time to retrieve the Wi-Fi
booster. Tucking his phone into his pocket, Trick left the office, went to
the front, and headed outside. Ben's car was in the driveway, but Trick
didn't see Ben. He looked around. "Ben?" he called, but didn't get an
answer.

Trick returned inside, wondering if Ben had walked around to the backyard. Trick checked the cameras but didn't see him, and didn't see Mason
either. Frowning, he suspected Ben may have headed into the garage to
look for a tool or something he needed, and Mason may have met up with
him there. Trick went to the back door and opened it. He walked out onto
the porch and saw the raised garage door, and expected to see Ben and Red
talking outside of camera range, but didn't.

"Ben? Red?"

No answer.

He stepped down into the yard but paused. Standing there, Trick got
the uncomfortable feeling that something wasn't right. Based on Ben's

thoroughness, Trick had relied on the equipment to tell him if something was amiss, but now he questioned whether he'd assumed correctly. Could Proteus have slipped by their security?

"Red?" he yelled again. "Ben?"

Neither responded.

Staring out at the yard, a sliver of anxiety crept up Trick's spine. His gun was inside, and he debated whether to get it or look for Red and Ben instead. Not liking the eerie quiet, he turned and jogged back inside.

· · · · ● · ● · ● · · ·

After Lindsey tore out of the warehouse, Novak debated her next move. Listen to Lindsey? Don't call anyone and get Garret to the hospital? Or ignore her and bring in reinforcements? Her training told her that, despite the risk, Lindsey and Garret needed help. "Stay put. I'm going to find a phone and call this in."

Garret grabbed her arm. "The hell you will."

Novak widened her eyes. "What are you talking about? Your sister has gone off on some personal crusade. I don't know what the hell is going on here, but if this Proteus is going after more people, despite what you two say, I have to contact the police." She tried to stand, but Garret wouldn't let go of her. "And you need an ambulance."

In a surprising show of strength, Garret yanked on her. "You're not calling anyone."

Novak widened her eyes. "Is your brain damaged, too?"

Garret grimaced. "You're right about one thing, Officer Novak. My sister needs help." Still holding his bloody side, he pushed up into a sitting position. "But no police patrol is going to provide it. You'll only put them in danger and risk Lindsey's life when she ends up trying to save them."

Novak pulled her arm free. "Then what do you propose we do?"

Garret took a shaky breath. "Over your right shoulder, there's a shelf of supplies. Grab the duct tape."

Novak glanced behind her. "Why?"

"We don't have time to discuss why. Just get it."

After a pause, Novak stood, grabbed the tape and handed it to him. "I can run to the front office. Use the phone there."

Garret scooted backwards until he reached the wall and leaned against it. "No front office. And no calls. Where's your car?" He pulled on the edge of the duct tape and yanked off a strip from the roll.

Novak watched him secure the free end to his bloody shirt and wrap the tape around his midsection. "What are you doing?"

"What's it look like? Creating a tourniquet. The cut's deep but not fatal. I'll live. Now where's your car?"

Novak shook her head. "My car?"

Garret cursed. "Hell. How'd you get on the police force? Yes. Your car. Where are you parked?"

Novak watched as he wrapped the duct tape several times around his waist. "Close to Lindsey's."

"Go. Now." Garret stopped briefly to hold his side. "Drive it here and pick me up." He resumed wrapping his abdomen with his bloody hands.

Novak dropped her jaw. "That's your brilliant plan? For me to take you to the house?"

"That's the only plan," said Garret. He cut the tape with his teeth and secured the other end to the tape around his middle. "You and I are the only two who can help Lindsey and my dad, and apparently that half-wit, Monroe, who my sister appears to like. Normally, I'd leave you behind, but you've seen too much, and, obviously, it's best I don't drive."

Novak scoffed. "Look at you. You can barely stand, and one eye is swollen shut. How are you supposed to help anyone?"

"I'll manage." He held his stomach and winced. "By the time you get back, I'll be by the door. I'll jump in and we'll go."

Novak shook her head. "This is—"

Garret glared at her. "Dammit, Novak. We are running out of time. Lindsey's going to walk in on God knows what, and if we don't do something, she and the rest of the people in that house are going to die. You send cops, and you could have a bloodbath on your hands. If you're prepared to live with that on your conscience, then run to the office to call your superiors. But if you really want to help Lindsey and stop Proteus, then go get your car and come and get me!"

Novak studied his pale face and saw the fear behind his eyes. Recalling Proteus changing shape not once but twice, she understood the risk if she sent in officers. But if she didn't, she had no idea how she would explain this to anyone. It could risk her career and her future. Uncertain, she stilled when her father's voice spoke in her ear. *Trust your gut.*

"Please," said Garret. "I know you don't know shit about me, but you have to trust me. This is the only way."

Following her dad's advice, Novak made up her mind and prayed it was the right decision. "Be ready to go in five minutes."

Garret relaxed against the wall. "Thank you." He reached for the chair, pulled it closer, and grabbed onto it with a bloody hand to help pull himself up. "I'll be ready."

Novak turned and ran out of the warehouse.

· · ● ● ● ● ● ● · ·

Tearing out of the facility's parking lot, Lindsey pulled out her phone and turned it on. As soon as it came to life, notifications popped up with all of Trick's attempted phone calls. Cursing at herself, she quickly dialed his number. A car honked at her as she zoomed through a light and listened to his phone ring. No one answered.

"Damn it," she yelled. She took a fast corner, and her tires protested, but she didn't slow.

Her hands shaking, she dialed her father's number and listened as it went to voicemail without ringing, as if his cell was turned off.

Knowing her dad would never turn off his cell in the middle of a crisis and that Trick would have been waiting on her call, Lindsey's hair rose. Had Proteus already arrived at the house? Had he killed Trick and her father? The timing didn't make sense, though. Proteus would only be a few minutes ahead of her, and if he got the chance, he'd want her to watch.

Lindsey wished she had Mason's number, but she had SCOPE's, the agency that Mason ran in San Diego. Running out of options, she dialed SCOPE's number. Lindsey knew Mason's sister Mikey, and when she answered, Lindsey didn't waste time.

"Mikey? This is Lindsey. I need your help. Can you call Mason? It's urgent." She zipped through another light, narrowly missing a passenger van.

"Lindsey?" asked Mikey. "What's wrong? Where's Mason?"

"That's what I'm trying to find out. I called Trick and Dad, and they're not answering, but I don't have Mason's cell. Please call him and tell him that Proteus is on his way."

"Proteus? The man chasing you and your brother?"

"Yes," said Lindsey. "Hurry. They're in trouble. I'm on my way, but Proteus has a head start."

"Hold on." Mikey clicked off the line.

Lindsey turned another corner with a screech and prayed Mason would answer. She raced by several vehicles, soared through a stop sign, and almost hit a van when she was forced to stop at a red light. As soon as the intersection was clear, she sped through it.

Mikey came back on the line. "He's not answering, Lindsey."

Lindsey cursed again.

"Has Proteus hurt them?" asked Mikey, sounding anxious.

"I don't know. It's too soon for him to be there. Plus, with all the security, he'd have been seen. There has to be something else going on."

"Where's he going?"

"Our safe house, where Dad arranged for us to stay. He, Trick and Mason are all there. Dad set up security."

"How does Proteus know where to go?"

"He must have—" Lindsey thought about it. How did Proteus know where to go? Had he done the same as Novak and followed her and Trick the previous day? But even if he had, the security at the house would have stopped him. Something tugged at Lindsey. Why had he acted so smug and certain at the warehouse? How had he known about the weapons Lindsey had brought with her?

She gripped the steering wheel. The knives. He'd known she'd brought three knives.

"Lindsey? You there?"

Lindsey's mind whirled as pieces of information clicked into place and her heart, already racing, raced faster. "Shit." She punched the accelerator to the floor. "Shit. Shit. Shit." If what she suspected was true, she understood why no one at the house was answering their phones.

"Lindsey," said Mikey. "You're scaring me. What's wrong?"

"They're in trouble, Mikey. I've got to go. I'll call you as soon as I know something."

"Lindsey, don't—"

Lindsey hung up and drove faster.

Chapter Twenty-Seven

Trick entered the house. Eyeing his gun still in its holster and laying on the counter of the bar, he headed over to it.

"Trick."

Trick stopped and swiveled to see Ben sitting at the office desk.

"Ben?" asked Trick. "Where were you? I didn't see you out front or back."

"I ran around to the side to adjust a camera."

"What about Mason?"

Ben glanced at the cameras. "He must be in a blind spot."

"I just went out there. He didn't answer me."

Ben's phone vibrated. He picked it up, eyed the display, and his eyes widened. "It's a text from Lindsey."

Trick ran into the office. "What? Where is she?"

Ben texted back. "Here. She's at the gate." He hit a button on the keyboard. "I'm letting her in."

Trick eyed the camera on the driveway and saw Lindsey's car at the entrance. The gate slowly opened. "She's okay?"

Ben stood. "Yes. Said she'd fill us in."

Trick's heart hammered as he watched Lindsey pull into the driveway. Ben jogged to the door and opened it. Lindsey got out and ran up to the door.

Ben pulled her into a hug. "Are you okay?"

She nodded against his shoulder. "I'm fine."

Trick walked into the living room. Lindsey stood with her father, looking relaxed and unharmed.

Ben shut the door. "Where the hell did you go? Did you face Proteus?"

Lindsey entered the house and saw Trick. She stilled. "Hey."

"Hey," said Trick. "You all right?"

"I am." She held his look.

Trick wanted to run into her arms, but something stopped him. "Why the hell did you sneak out?"

Ben walked over to Trick. "You shouldn't have done that, Lindsey. Where's Proteus? Where's Garret?"

She glanced between the two of them. "Garret's okay. Novak is taking him to the hospital."

Trick frowned. "Novak? How's she involved?"

"She followed me to my meeting with Proteus," said Lindsey. "She saved my ass. But Proteus escaped. I told her to get Garret to a doctor, and I drove here because I was worried Proteus would come to the house. Are you guys okay?" She watched Trick.

"We're okay. Does Proteus know we're here?" asked Ben.

"He implied he did." Lindsey stepped farther into the room. "And if he does, we have to be on alert."

Trick thought of Mason. "We need to find Red. Get him inside."

"I'll go check the cameras." Ben turned back toward the office.

Trick turned to follow him.

"Trick. Wait," said Lindsey.

Trick held back. Uncertain of how to respond to her in front of Ben and because of the fear she'd caused him, he waited to see what she'd say.

She took a step toward him. "I'm sorry I left without telling you. I wanted to, but I had to go on my own."

Angry that she'd left without telling anyone, and hadn't answered his calls, Trick took a calming breath. "I've been scared shitless. I've been calling you all morning. Why didn't you answer?"

"Because I knew what you'd say." She took another step. "You'd be angry, demand to know where I was, and insist I come back."

"You're damn right. What you did was impetuous and risky. What if Novak hadn't been there?"

"You're right. It was risky. But this is between me and Proteus."

Trick's frustration spilled over. "When are you going to realize that you don't have to take on the world by yourself? And that it's okay to ask for help? Proteus has scarred everyone in your family. Not just you."

"I did what I had to do. Just like I'm sure you've done a million times when you were a Ranger."

"I never went off on my own. I have a partner. That's what they're for. And I thought that's what we were. Especially after..."

She moved closer. "...after last night?"

Memories of her moving against him and moaning his name made him clench his jaw. "Yes."

"I know. And I'm sorry I frightened you. But you know who I am, and why I had to do what I did. Please don't hate me for it."

"I don't hate you. But if you ever do that again, I..." He stared off.

"You'll what?" She stood in front of him.

He shook his head. "I don't know." He put his hands on his hips. "I don't know how to feel right now." He swiveled toward the office. "I have to find Mason."

"Wait." She took his arm. He stopped and looked back at her. "Tell me we're okay," she said.

Holding her gaze, that familiar longing returned, and he wished he could pick her up and carry her upstairs. "We're okay. We'll talk more later once we know we're safe."

"Okay." Still holding his wrist, she pulled him closer. "Come here."

Hesitating, he wondered how much PDA was called for, but he wanted to hold her. He leaned in and she reached for him when the front door banged open.

Trick jumped back in shock when he saw a second Lindsey staring back at him. Breathing hard, she stared at the first Lindsey, who stepped away from Trick and pulled out her knife.

"Get away from him," yelled the second Lindsey. She stepped inside and pulled her own knife. "Trick. That's not me. That's Proteus."

Ben appeared at the door to the office and looked between the two women with wide eyes. "What the...Lindsey?"

Trick studied both women, who were identical.

"It's me, Trick," said Lindsey Two. "Don't listen to him." She eyed the first Lindsey.

Lindsey One waved her knife. "I'm not Proteus. She is." She jabbed her knife at Lindsey Two. "Get back. He'll kill you both."

Lindsey Two glared. "Proteus almost killed Garret. And me. Novak showed, and Proteus took my car and drove here to kill you. I raced to catch up."

Trick didn't know what to think. One of these women was the actual Lindsey, and the other was a killer. His logical mind raced. Both women knew things, and he took a second to collect himself. He eyed his gun on the counter, but even if he had it, he wouldn't know who to use it against.

The first Lindsey spoke to him. "You and I shared a passionate and unforgettable night together. We were just talking about it. You know it's me." She glanced at Ben. "Ben. I'm your daughter. You know that."

"You are not Lindsey," said the second Lindsey.

Trick thought of the keywords. "What are the keywords?" he asked.

"You're Ranger," said Lindsey One. "Mine is freedom. And dad's is bull-headed." She eyed Lindsey Two with a look of triumph.

Lindsey Two narrowed her eyes. "The keywords don't matter because Proteus knows them."

Trick stared in surprise. "How could he know them?"

"Because you've been compromised." Lindsey Two glanced toward her dad. "There's another Proteus. Or one like him. Someone who can do what Proteus does, that slipped under our radar."

"What are you talking about?" asked Ben.

Lindsey One scoffed. "Nice try. You're justifying why you don't know the keywords." She waved at Lindsey Two. "That's Proteus. I swear it."

"Where's Mason?" asked Lindsey Two. "It could be him."

Trick straightened. "You think this second Proteus became Mason?"

"Someone got into this house and knows things." Lindsey Two faced her counterpart. "They knew I was coming to the meeting alone and when. They knew about the weapons I brought with me, but didn't know about my hidden switchblade."

"It can't be Mason." Trick recalled their talk on the patio. He was certain he'd been talking to his friend. But Mason had disappeared into the garden. Was it because he was Proteus' accomplice, and if so, where was the real Mason? Had the accomplice subdued him?

"This is nonsense," said Lindsey One. "It's all a smokescreen. If you believe her, you'll die." She spoke to Trick. "You know it's me. If it wasn't, I would have killed you the moment I stepped into the house."

"You didn't kill him because you were waiting for me," said Lindsey One. "You want to kill him as me while I watch."

"No," said Lindsey One. "That's what you want to do."

Worried about Mason, but needing to figure this out, Trick used the one thing he knew the real Lindsey would have knowledge of. He looked between them. "Tell me what I said last night."

Both Lindseys looked over at him.

He thought back to their conversation. "What were the two things I told you that were common among those who've survived horrific experiences?"

Lindsey Two paused, and Lindsey One smiled. "Resiliency and acceptance."

Lindsey Two widened her eyes, dropped her jaw, and her face went pale.

Chapter Twenty-Eight

Lindsey stared in shock at the woman who claimed to be her. How the hell did Proteus know what Trick had said to her? The only way would be if the accomplice had been listening at their door. And if that was true, what else did the accomplice overhear?

Trick studied her, and she could see his doubt. "Trick," she said. "The imposter overheard us."

"Or, there is no accomplice," said Trick. "And you're Proteus."

Ben stepped closer. "That makes the most sense." He raised his hand. "Put the knife down, Proteus. You can't kill us all."

The fake Lindsey grinned at her. "We all know it's you. Give up while you still have a chance."

Forcing back panic, Lindsey realized Trick and her father were quickly turning against her. They weren't buying the accomplice theory, so Lindsey resorted to all she had left. The accomplice may have eavesdropped on her and Trick, but couldn't have seen them. "Trick," she said, "I know things nobody else does." Her memories of the previous night swirled, and she recalled kissing his stomach. "I touched you in one place you didn't like."

"There weren't many of those," replied Trick.

"But there was one." She thought back on their trip to the Sierra Madres, which wasn't that long ago, and used it. "Remember the chase through the cave? In the mountains? Remember what chased us?"

The other Lindsey's face tightened.

"I do," said Trick. "Do you?"

She nodded.

Trick eyed Proteus. "Do you?"

The fake Lindsey smiled. "I do. The Dogman."

Lindsey couldn't fathom how Proteus knew so much, but he couldn't know everything.

"Yes," said Lindsey. "The Dogman." She spoke to Trick. "And I know what the Dogman did."

Trick glanced at the fake Lindsey, who didn't respond. He looked back at Lindsey.

Lindsey pressed forward. "He attacked you and took you, and you were wounded." She glanced over at the other Lindsey. "And I know where."

Trick tensed, and she suspected he recalled the sensitive spot she'd touched the previous night. The Dogman had slashed him across his stomach and although it was mostly healed, the scar was still tender in spots. Trick eyed the false Lindsey. "Care to elaborate?"

The false Lindsey sneered.

"The scar on your stomach," said Lindsey. "It's still sensitive."

Trick stared at her. "And where did I touch you? That made you giggle?"

Relief flooded through her. "You—"

"Wait," said Trick. He looked at the other Lindsey. "You first."

"I giggled when you nibbled my neck," said the fake Lindsey. "That's what I recall."

Lindsey's heart skipped when Trick looked her way, and she answered. "You licked me behind my knee."

Trick's expression softened toward her, but just as fast, his demeanor shifted, and he faced the other Lindsey. "Looks like we have a winner...Proteus."

The fake Lindsey's sneer turned into a grin. "Well," she said with a sigh, "it was worth a shot." She put a hand on her hip. "I had you going there for a second, didn't I?" The surface of her skin rippled, her face morphed, and her form shifted into the Proteus Lindsey knew well. He looked at her. "But we're not done."

Lindsey's relief flipped back into fear when she realized Proteus was right. They weren't done. They may have discovered the real Proteus, but that meant there was an accomplice. She watched Trick's face shift when he came to the same realization. "Then who...?" His brow furrowed.

Ben pulled a knife from his belt. "Get on the ground, Proteus. You're going back to prison."

Proteus smiled again. "I am?" He held up his hands. "Who's going to take me in?"

Lindsey looked between her father and Proteus. She'd been in such a hurry, it had been hard to put all the pieces together. She recalled Garret telling her that the Lindsey he'd seen at his hotel had stayed morphed much longer than he'd thought possible. Had that been the accomplice? If it wasn't Mason, could someone else have been hiding in this house without them realizing it? She thought back and certain events confirmed her worst fears. Making eye contact with Trick, she saw something in his expression that told her he was coming to a similar conclusion.

His gaze steely, Ben raised the knife and pointed at the floor. "Get on your knees, Proteus. Now."

· · · · ● · ● · · · ·

Mason stirred on the floor, trying to remember where he was. He felt the carpet beneath his cheek and electric tingles traveled down his limbs. Slowly regaining awareness, he blinked, and everything came back in a sudden shock of recall. He'd found a small room in the basement of the guest house. He'd gone inside when he'd heard the thump, and opened the closet. Something spilled out...it was a rolled-up carpet...but before he could find out what was in it, someone had come up behind him.

Mason blinked again, trying to remember the rest, but it was a blank. Realizing he'd blacked out, he attempted to move, but his body protested. The tingles subsided and, feeling stronger, Mason pushed up and saw the carpet. It was lying on the ground in front of him. Getting his feet under him, he tried to remember what had knocked him out, but all he could recall was being touched, and then everything had gone fuzzy.

Another memory sparked of the carpet moving. He crawled closer and reached for it. Pushing on it, he waited to see if it would move, but it didn't. He tried again with no response.

Knowing he wasn't losing his mind, and that the carpet had moved before someone had attacked him, Mason moved around to the other side of the rug. He found the edge and tried to unroll it, but it was heavy. The tingles had dissipated, and gathering his strength, he pulled hard. The carpet partially unfurled and, using his hands to push it open the rest of the way, he sat back in shock when a man, bound, gagged and unconscious, appeared.

Looking closely at him, Mason gasped when he realized it was Lindsey's father, Ben.

• • • • • • • • •

Lindsey's eyes told Trick everything. She knew who the accomplice was, and since it wasn't Mason, there was only one person left.

Ben took a step toward Proteus.

"It's you," said Lindsey.

Ben stopped. "What?"

Lindsey kept her eyes on Proteus but faced Ben. "You're not my father."

"What are you talking about?" asked Ben. "Of course I'm your father."

Lindsey shook her head. "No. You're not."

Trick's mind assembled the various pieces required for Lindsey's theory to work. Ben had disappeared when he'd gone to his car, and Mason had disappeared soon after. Trick's phone had been drained right after Ben had borrowed it. Ben had been in charge of security and had been supposedly talking to other contacts, but Trick couldn't verify any of that. And he could have fooled Marcy and Trey just as he'd fooled him and Lindsey. And because Ben had been in the house, he knew their keywords and could have overheard him and Lindsey the previous night. "Who are you?" he asked Ben.

Ben sputtered. "I don't know what either of you are talking about? I'm your father, Linds."

Trick stiffened at the nickname.

Lindsey hardened her gaze. "I should have known. The signs were there, but I was too preoccupied to catch them. The supply bag. My father always pulls out the weapons and arranges them. He never leaves them in the bag."

Ben gaped at her. "That's your evidence? The damn supply bag?"

"And the apple juice," she said.

Ben widened his eyes. "I can't drink apple juice?"

Lindsey tightened the grip on her knife. "Two years ago, Dad got sick and puked after drinking a bottle of apple juice. He hasn't touched it since."

"Maybe I'm over it," said Ben.

"Maybe you're not," added Lindsey.

"You just called her Linds," said Trick. "Even I know Ben would never call Lindsey by that name." He eyed Proteus, who watched the exchange with interest. "Right, Proteus?"

Proteus chuckled and spoke to Ben. "I think your cover is blown."

Ben sighed and slumped. "Too bad. I was getting used to him." A shimmer rippled over his skin and Lindsey tried not to scream when her father morphed into a tall, slender pale woman with reddish blonde hair, dark eyes, and thin lips. She shivered and shook out her hands. "But it is good to be back." She smiled at Proteus. "Isn't it, Michael?"

Trick took a step back. He eyed his gun on the counter. "Who the hell are you?" he asked.

The woman smiled at him. "My name is Gail."

"Gail is a long-lost cousin," said Proteus. "Imagine my surprise when I met her not long after you murdered my father." He smirked at Lindsey. "She showed promise, and when her family disowned her for spending time with me, I took her under my wing, and to my surprise, her skills outweigh mine. She can morph into anyone without touching them, has excellent sensory skills, and can stay morphed for long periods with no effect on her physically." He paused. "I hate to admit it, but I'm jealous."

"You listened at our door last night?" Lindsey asked Gail.

Gail's smile grew. "Information is key. I have excellent hearing, though, and you two weren't exactly...quiet."

"Gail has been my eyes and ears while I was imprisoned," added Proteus. "She's been watching you and your family, Linds, since your mother's funeral, and preparing for this moment. Just like I have." He met Gail's gaze. "After I escaped, Gail filled me in. I know all about your last five years without me." His smile fell, and he frowned at Lindsey. "I've been looking forward to this anniversary."

"Where's my father?" asked Lindsey, clutching her stomach with her free hand. "Is he alive?"

Gail snickered. "He's not far away, and assuming he hasn't smothered to death, he lives at Michael's request. Killing your father in front of you is on his bucket list."

Trick's stomach turned. "Where's Red?"

"Your nosy friend was snooping around," said Gail, "so I took care of him."

Trick went rigid. He eyed Lindsey, who eyed him back, her expression communicating everything.

"Looks like we have a standoff," said Proteus. "How fun."

Trick glanced again at his gun and noticed Gail do the same. "You want your weapon, don't you?" she asked, raising her knife. "Let's see who can get to it first."

Trick didn't move, but Proteus faced Lindsey. "What do you say, Linds? One last battle before Gail and I destroy you and everything you love?"

Lindsey faced him in return, her glare as intense as the moment she'd faced the Dogman. "You aren't leaving this house alive," she answered, gripping her knife.

Trick steeled himself, and glancing again at the gun, he watched as Gail did the same, and praying he and Lindsey would survive this, he took his shot and lunged for his weapon.

Chapter Twenty-Nine

Novak drove down the street. Garret sat in her passenger seat, his face tight, his clothes bloody, and clutching his stomach. After she'd made it back to her car, Novak returned to the warehouse to find Garret waiting for her as he'd planned. He'd almost collapsed before getting into her car, but he'd slid in and told her to drive. She'd been doubting herself ever since.

"Are you okay?" she asked. She debated again whether she should turn the car around and head to the police station.

"I'm fine. Drive faster." He grimaced and tightened his hold on his belly.

"You're going to bleed to death." She stopped behind a car at a red light.

"The bleeding's slowed." He waved. "Run the light."

"I'm behind someone."

"Then go around them."

"We can't help your sister or anyone else if we die in a car accident on the way there."

"By the time we get there, they'll be dead, anyway."

Novak pulled around the car, slowed at the light, and ran it when no one else was crossing the intersection. "I hope you know what you're doing."

"How much farther?" he asked.

"Ten minutes."

Groaning when she swerved around a car, he gripped the door handle with his bloody fingers. "Make it five."

• • • • • • • • •

The second Trick made his move, Proteus rushed at Lindsey. Lindsey dodged to her left and let his momentum carry him past her. She swiped out with her knife, but narrowly missed him when he shifted away from her. He turned swiftly though and faced her again.

Lindsey could hear the scuffle between Trick and Gail, who'd knocked him to the ground when he went for his gun, but Lindsey had to focus on Proteus, who risked a glance at his protégé. "I told her if it came to this, not to kill him yet," he said. "Not until I can subdue you and you can watch us take his life. And then we'll find your dad."

Lindsey gritted her teeth, determined not to let him win. "You're at a disadvantage. You've morphed several times. I know what that does to you."

Proteus raised the side of his lip. "Gail's shown me a few things. I've learned to protect my energy. I'm not as weak as you think."

She swiped out with her knife, and he swiped with his, but they both avoided the other's blade. They circled each other, gauging when to strike. Proteus took a step forward, and she darted back and bumped against the wall near the dining room. Proteus came at her again and she knocked his hand with the knife away and brought hers to his stomach, but he grabbed her arm and deflected her swing. Tingles shot through her at his touch, and she twisted away before he could incapacitate her. Breathing hard, she stepped back into the living room. She heard a crash behind her, but Lindsey kept her sights on Proteus, who followed her into the living room. Lindsey backed up to the glass coffee table just as Proteus lunged again. She moved to her right and used his balance against him as she pivoted away. Proteus, unable to slow his momentum, fell forward onto the coffee table. The glass shattered under his weight, and he landed on the floor. A small crystal vase on the table fell on the rug and rolled away.

Seeing her advantage, she came at him with her knife, but he rotated to his side, swinging out with his blade, and caught her across the meat of her shoulder. Blood sprayed, and she fell back with a gasp. Proteus was on his feet in a lightning quick move, and glass crunching beneath his feet, he faced her again.

• • • • • • • • • •

Knocked to the floor by Gail before he could reach his gun, Trick grabbed for her knife, but she fought to keep it and gripped his neck with her free hand. His vision swam, and he had to roll away from her before her touch took his strength. The moment he moved back, and her hand left his throat, his vision cleared. She jumped to her feet, but he caught one of her ankles and she fell forward onto a side table beside the couch. The table toppled and the lamp on the tabletop slid off. It hit the tiled section of the floor and the base shattered. Still holding her ankle and not feeling any tingles, Trick tried to pull her toward him, but Gail slashed at him with her knife. He cursed and released her again, barely avoiding the swipe of her blade. Free, she scrambled to her feet along with Trick. He heard a loud crash and saw Proteus fall backward onto the coffee table.

Facing Gail, Trick saw his holstered gun on the bar's counter. He raced to get it, and Gail did the same. He grabbed the weapon just as Gail did and she swung her knife with her free hand. Trick grabbed a hold of her wrist to keep her from stabbing him. Those strange tingles returned, but as they fought for the gun, he squeezed her wrist until she winced and let go of the knife, which clattered to the floor. Feeling the effects of her touch intensify, he yanked the gun from her other hand, but it flew from his grasp. Pulling back, he slipped when he stepped on a piece of the broken lamp and fell backward on his butt. Seeing her knife on the tile, he reached for it, but she tackled him. The unexpected move caught him off guard, and he fought to shove her off as more tingles raced through him. Gathering his fading strength, he pushed her away.

Gail fell back, and weakened, he did too. But the tingles stopped, and his strength returned. Seeing the knife, he grabbed it just as she reached for it, but instead of going for the weapon, she gripped his shoulder. Something sizzled through him like an electric current and his body jolted with the shock. He dropped the knife and rolled away from her, hoping to avoid another jolt.

When she didn't touch him again, he pushed up to see her holding the knife and racing out the back door that led into the yard. Trick searched for his gun, but not seeing it, he made a split-second decision to follow Gail before she could find and kill Ben and Mason. He jumped up and followed her out of the house.

• • • • • • • • • •

Lindsey ignored the flaring pain in her shoulder. Breathing fast and sweating, she faced Proteus, who sneered at her. "Had enough?" he asked.

She sneered back. "Not until you're dead."

"You're injured, Linds."

"You just shattered a glass table with your body. I suspect you are, too."

His sneer became a smile. "Gail just lured Trick outside. It's only a matter of time now before she kills him and your father."

Lindsey refused to think of that. "If she's as overconfident as you, my money's on Trick."

Proteus chuckled. "I can't wait until you're begging me to spare his, and your father's, life."

"You'll have to kill me first."

He narrowed his eyes. "Be careful what you wish for." He swung out at her, and she jumped back. He came again, and before she could dodge him, he anticipated her move and swung again. Lindsey barely avoided his swing, and she swiped out at him, but caught off balance, she missed. He took advantage and shoved her backwards. She hit the wall with force. Grinning, he aimed his knife at her gut, but she shifted away just before his blade hit the wall instead.

Trying to avoid his touch, Lindsey swiveled away, arced her blade, and caught him across his tricep. His jacket tore and blood spurted from the wound. Before he could yank his knife out of the wall, she saw her advantage and swiped again. Trying to avoid her blow, he yanked his knife out, jumped back, but the tip of her knife caught his wrist, and he dropped his weapon.

Her anger flaring after all the trauma he'd caused her, Lindsey kicked him hard in the knee, and he cried out and buckled to the floor with a grunt. He tried to roll to avoid her, but she reared her foot back and kicked him again in the midsection. He curled up with another grunt, but that didn't stop her, and she lashed out again. All the pain and rage she'd held onto for so long erupted and she wanted to pulverize him. She kicked him over and over, wanting to make him suffer for all the damage he'd done. He remained in the fetal position, holding his stomach and lowering his head, trying to protect himself from her blows.

Her rage cooling and ready to end his reign of terror, she raised her knife to strike the fatal blow when he reached out and grabbed her ankle. In mid-swing, she tried to stay on her feet, but he yanked hard, and she fell backward. Her head hit the tiled floor with a thud, and she saw stars. Tingles raced up her legs, and she fought to sit up and swing with her knife, but he was on her too fast. He grabbed her wrist, slammed it to the ground, and she lost her hold on her knife. His other hand came up and gripped her throat and she clutched it with her free hand, trying to find air.

Leaning over her, he brought his face close to hers. "Now who's the overconfident one?"

His ragged breath fanned her face, and she grimaced. She struggled to get away, but the tingles raced through her.

"I'm going to kill you, dear," he said. "But not before your loved ones die first. I suspect Gail will bring them here soon." He chuckled. "Why don't we wait?"

Lindsey grunted and fought to push him off. If she didn't do something soon, she'd end up dying at his hands, and she couldn't allow that. Proteus couldn't win again.

"Just relax, kitten," he said. "It will all be over soon."

His grip on her neck lightened enough for her to breathe, but not without effort. Forcing herself to relax, she let go of his wrist. Before her strength vanished, she reached out with her hand, looking for anything on the floor to use as a weapon against him. As the tingles raced through her, she saw spots and knew her time was short.

"Just like old times, isn't it?" he whispered in her ear.

Disgust rippled through her and she moved her hand over the ground until it touched something. She grabbed onto it, feeling the long and slender hilt of a knife. It had to be the one Proteus dropped.

Gathering what little strength she had left, she took the deepest breath she could and wrapped her fingers around the weapon. She held his gaze, narrowed her eyes, and spoke in a harsh whisper. "When you get to hell, say hello to your dad for me."

His eyes clouded in confusion, and using everything she had, she swung the knife and buried it into his ribs.

Chapter Thirty

Trick raced into the yard, but didn't see Gail. Stopping to catch his breath, he listened. Not hearing anything, he debated his options. The stony path led into the garden, where there were plenty of spots to hide. But to his left was the garage, and at the back of the property was the guest house. Wondering where Gail might go, he headed toward the garage. If he didn't find her there, he might find a weapon instead. He bypassed the garden path, and staying alert, he jumped over a row of cacti and stopped at the entrance to the open garage. He peered inside, but only saw the boat trailer, lawn equipment, and various shelves of supplies.

Trying to slow his breathing, he quietly crept inside, staying low. He ran up behind the trailer and looked deeper into the garage. Nothing moved, and he didn't see her. He moved up along the trailer and farther into the building. Seeing a shelf full of tools, he stopped and grabbed a hammer. Glad to have a weapon, he silently stepped to the rear of the garage, listening and looking for anything that might indicate that Gail was there, but saw and heard nothing. Cautious, he stopped when he saw a partially open door. He inched over to it, used his fingers to slowly open it wider, and looked outside. He saw a stretch of grass that grew along the perimeter of the property near the back fence. The back gate leading to the street was partially open. Eyeing his surroundings, he ran out of the garage and up to the gate. Not seeing anyone, he peered outside the gate, pulled it open, and darted through it.

· · · · ● · ● · ● · · ·

Proteus' eyes widened, and his hold on Lindsey's neck relaxed when her knife slammed into him. He made a pained grunt and released a gust of air, just as Lindsey took a deep breath. Her strength almost gone, Lindsey fought to get out from under him. The blood from his wound pooled on the floor and air bubbled up at the injury, telling her she'd pierced his lung. With any luck, she'd damaged his heart as well. Proteus fought to hold on to her, but as the tingles coursing through her slowly subsided, she shoved him off of her. His blood covered her shirt and, leaving the knife inside him, she scooted over to the wall. She saw and grabbed the small crystal vase that had fallen from the coffee table to use if he came at her again.

Hearing his labored breathing and watching his eyes, she knew the wound was fatal. Copious amounts of his blood spread out over the floor, and her heart thumped as he took his last breaths, but it didn't stop him from his threats.

"She'll kill them," he whispered.

Lindsey's rage flared again. "At least you'll go first."

Proteus forced in another breath and blinked. "She'll kill you too."

"You said you'd kill me, but you were wrong." She paused as his eyelids drooped. "Goodbye, Michael."

With one last gasp, his face twisted, and he cursed her. Watching him die, Lindsey's head pounded, her body ached, and her vision briefly blurred before returning to normal. Proteus stilled, the light faded from his eyes, his shallow breathing stopped, and his stare went flat.

Pangs of relief that her nemesis was dead flooded through her, but she also felt dread, because it wasn't over. Gail was still out there and had to be stopped. Rousing herself, Lindsey attempted to get to her feet, but the aftereffects of her battle with Proteus and his last attack made it hard to stand. Her body trembled, her arm ached, and she was covered in her, and Proteus', blood.

Getting to her feet, her legs wobbled, and she gave herself a few seconds to gather herself. She left the vase on the floor and looked for her knife, which was lying nearby. Feeling stronger, she picked it up with a grimace and, after one last look at Proteus, she raced out of the living room and out the back door.

· · · ● · ● · ● · ·

Mason untied Ben and removed the gag from his mouth. "Ben. Can you hear me?" He jostled Ben's shoulder.

Ben didn't move, but uttered a low moan.

"Ben?"

Ben's eyelids fluttered.

Mason didn't see any outward signs of damage, but that didn't mean Ben didn't have internal injuries. "It's Mason, Ben." He tried again to rouse him.

Ben blinked and opened his eyes. He didn't focus on anything, though, and didn't appear to know what was happening.

Mason leaned closer. "Can you see me?" He waved his hands in front of Ben's face.

Ben grunted and blinked again. He tried to talk. "Wh...where...?"

"We're in a guesthouse. It's in the backyard of the home you found for Trick and Lindsey. In Las Vegas." He hoped he was making sense. "Does that ring any bells?"

Ben blinked again and still looked confused.

"We're searching for Proteus. He took Garret and Lindsey went after him."

Ben's brow furrowed. "Pro...Proteus."

"Yes," said Mason. "Can you sit up?" Mason got his hands under Ben's shoulders and attempted to lift him.

Ben's awareness appeared to be improving and with another groan, he moved and, with Mason's help, lifted his torso. Mason grabbed pillows from the bed and propped Ben up against the wall.

Seeing Ben was more coherent, Mason sat beside him, where he could see the door and stairwell, and no one could come up behind him. "What happened? How long have you been down here?" As his own brain fog began to clear, Mason thought of Trick and put the pieces together. If this was Ben, then whoever was in the house with Trick wasn't. He searched for his phone.

Ben grimaced and moved his head. "I...I...was checking the house."

Mason found his phone, but it was dead. He searched for his gun, which had been in a holster on his belt, but it was no longer there.

Ben raised his arm and rubbed the back of his head. "I came out here. To...to walk the grounds." He clenched his eyes shut and gripped his temples. "Something hit me."

"You've been out here since yesterday?" asked Mason, incredulous. That meant the man he and Trick had been interacting with since arriving had not been Ben. "Hell."

Ben blew out a long, unsteady breath. "I woke up out here. I was in the bed but tied up." He paused and blinked several times. "Someone came out last night. A woman. She gave me water, let me use the bathroom, and then...something hit me again."

"How'd you get in the closet?"

"I'm not sure. I woke up in there. I was wrapped up and could barely breathe." He held his stomach. "The only thing I could move was my foot. So I started kicking."

Mason stretched his neck. "That was the thump I heard."

"What are you doing here?"

Mason looked around the room. "I came to help you, Trick, and Lindsey, but I'm not doing very well."

Ben held his head, and his eyes widened. "Lindsey. Garret. Where are they?" He tried to stand, but didn't have the strength.

"Take it easy," said Mason.

"Where are my kids? Where's Proteus?" He sat up and moaned. "Everything hurts."

"I bet. Whoever knocked you and me out packs a punch."

Ben shot a look at Mason. "Proteus. It has to be Proteus."

Mason thought about it. "I'm not too sure about that."

"How'd you get down here?"

"I investigated when I heard you kicking. Apparently, whoever knocked you out, knocked me out too, after I found you. My guess is it was the fake Ben."

Ben dropped his jaw. "The fake Ben?"

"Trick and I, and Lindsey, met you at this house yesterday and spent the evening and this morning with you."

"This whole time? You thought it was me?"

"The whole time. And as far as I know, the false Ben has been talking to Trey and Marcy, too."

"That's impossible."

"Apparently not."

"It's unheard of, staying morphed that long." Ben tried again to stand. "We've got to get out of here."

"Hold on." Mason stood and went to the door. It surprised him when it opened. Peering up the outside steps, he didn't see anyone. He had no idea how long he'd been out, but he hoped it wasn't long. His worst fears would be to return to the house to find Trick, and possibly Lindsey, dead. He left the door open and returned to Ben's side. "Can you walk?"

"I can try." Ben hooked an arm over Mason's neck.

Mason lifted Ben with a groan, but Ben struggled to stay on his feet.

Before Ben could fall, Mason lowered him to the bed.

Pale, Ben sat heavily on the mattress. "Leave me. You go."

Still a little wobbly, Mason took a second to catch his breath. "Hell, no. I'm not leaving you behind for someone to return and finish the job. If I go, you go."

His face beaded with sweat, Ben nodded. "If this is Proteus, we'll be no match for him."

Mason eyed the door. "Well, I don't intend to sit around and wait."

Ben rubbed his legs and stretched. "Neither do I." He laid his arm over Mason's shoulders. "C'mon. Let's try again."

· · • • • • • • • · ·

Doing his best to focus and ignore the fire in his gut, Garret gritted his teeth as Novak pulled into the driveway of an impressive home on a large lot. At some point, there had been a gate at the entrance, but it was bent and sitting at an odd angle to the side, as if someone had hit it with a car. He wondered if it had been Lindsey.

Novak pulled in behind Proteus' vehicle. "That's Lindsey's car," she said, pointing to another car in the driveway. "She and Proteus are here." She opened her door and got out.

Garret opened his door and slid out a foot.

Novak raced around to help him stand. "Why don't you stay here?" she asked. "Let me go in."

"No," said Garret, getting out. "I'm coming with you." He put his bloody hand on the car's roof to stabilize himself.

"You can barely move."

"I'll manage." He steeled himself against the pain. "Just be careful."

Novak scoffed. "Me be careful? At least I'm uninjured and have a gun."

"I don't suppose you have another?"

"No. This is it." She pulled her weapon from her holster. "Just stick near me."

Garret straightened and centered himself. "Don't let him get close. If he touches you, it's over."

"I'll be careful."

"And watch where you're shooting that thing." Garret eyed the entrance to the house. "If he morphs, you may have to shoot Lindsey or me, or my dad."

Novak stilled. "What?"

Garret shut his door. "It may come to that. This is going to take nerves of steel, Novak. This is not your average citizen. Maybe *you* should stick close to *me*."

Novak eyed the house with uncertainty.

"If you're not sure, give the gun to me."

"I can't. I'd get fired."

"Better than getting dead."

"No." Novak held his gaze. "I'm going in."

Garret admired her courage. "Just be sure to trust your gut. You hesitate, and you won't survive. If you know it's Proteus, even if it doesn't look like him, shoot."

"I understand."

Garret took a deep breath, and forcing the pain out of his mind with monumental will, he pushed away from the car and walked toward the house. "Then let's go."

· · · · ● · ● · · ·

Not seeing anyone in the backyard, Lindsey stepped off the porch. She didn't want to yell for anyone because it would give away her position, so she tiptoed down the path and into the garden. The high grass and tall shrubs provided some cover and, staying low, she crept down the stepping-stones, still listening. Stopping behind a decorative boulder placed among the flowering plants and cacti, she squatted. Still a little shaky, she waited for a sudden dizzy spell to pass. After a few seconds, she felt stronger and, moving out from the boulder, she continued down the path. She passed another large rock and a swing that hung from a low tree branch. Moving out of the garden, the guesthouse came into view, and she stooped again behind a cacti cluster, careful not to touch them.

Deciding that the guesthouse would be a likely place to hide her father, she stepped back into the yard, planning to come up the side to stay out of view, when she heard a rustle among the shrubs. She turned and froze when Trick walked out of them and stepped out onto the path behind her.

He grinned at her. "Hey, honey. Nice of you to join me."

"Trick?" she said, relief flooding her. "You're okay?"

"I'm doing great." He stepped toward her.

At that moment, she realized her stupidity. It wasn't Trick. She'd been so relieved to see him, it had clouded her judgement. Lindsey arced her knife, but her reactions time was too slow. Trick easily deflected the attack and grabbed her arm. Lindsey instantly froze. Her legs gave way, and she collapsed to the ground. Trick took her knife, grabbed her wrist and as he dragged her into the tall grass, his shape shifted, and he morphed into Gail.

Fighting to stay conscious, Lindsey tried to pull away but couldn't summon any strength.

Gail stopped, dropped Lindsey's arm and Lindsey moaned, trying to talk, but couldn't form words. Proteus had been right. Gail was far more powerful.

Gail stared down at her. "Is Proteus dead?"

Lindsey could only blink at her.

Gail studied Lindsey with an unreadable expression. "I'm going to go get your lover now." She leaned closer. "And then I'll get your dad and Mason. And then you." Her eyes glimmered in the sunlight, and she held the tip of the knife to Lindsey's neck. "Proteus wanted you to suffer, so I'll leave you here while you think about what I'm going to do to each of them. In a few minutes, your strength will return. You'll hope it's enough time to save Trick, but it won't be." Her eyes narrowed, and she straightened. "Proteus would be proud."

Lindsey could only whimper as Gail walked away.

Chapter Thirty-One

Garret entered the silent house. The door had been open, and cautious, he listened for any activity but didn't hear anything. Novak came in behind him, her gun in her hand and aimed at the floor.

"Anything?" she whispered.

Garret noticed the broken lamp and shattered coffee table. "Somebody put up a fight."

"Garret." Novak took quick steps into the living room and stopped in the dining area. That's when Garret saw the body of a man, blood pooled beneath him, lying on his side.

Novak cursed and squatted next to the body. She put her hand on the man's neck and held it there. "He's dead." She leaned closer to look. "It's Proteus."

Garret studied the scene and cursed.

Novak straightened. "If he's dead, then where's Lindsey? Where's Trick?"

Garret thought back over his time in captivity. In between bouts of Proteus beating and torturing him, Garret had remained conscious enough to pay attention to Proteus' activity. He'd heard him on the phone several times. Not well enough to hear everything that was being said, but enough to know that whoever Proteus was talking to had integral knowledge of Proteus' plans. Garret recalled Lindsey's words before she'd left the warehouse. She'd said that Proteus knew about her weapons and that she'd arrived early and alone.

Eyeing the damage, he had to assume that Proteus wasn't working by himself. Someone else had knowledge of Trick and Lindsey's plans, and if that were true...

"Search the back rooms," he said. He held onto the wall when a wave of pain raced through his gut.

"You okay?"

He set his jaw. "Go. Hurry. And be careful."

She raced out of the living area and headed down the hall.

Another lance of pain caused him to buckle to his knees. He landed on all fours as blood dripped from his taped abdomen to the floor. Cursing at himself, he grabbed his stomach, took several deep breaths, and forced the pain back again. Feeling stronger, he crawled to the bar and reached for the counter to pull himself up when he saw something lodged underneath the sofa. He let go of the counter, scooted over and almost cried in relief when he saw it was a gun. He pulled it from its holster, tucked it into the back of his jeans with a wince, and, using the back of the couch for support, carefully pulled himself back up.

Novak returned from the hall. "It's clear. No one's here."

Garret headed to the back door. "They're here, Novak. We just have to find them." He opened the door and stepped out, seeing a large backyard with a pool and sauna, an impressive garden and trail, a guesthouse in the rear, and a garage behind the house.

Novak joined him. "How do you want to do this?"

Garret studied the too-quiet yard. "You take that side and come up to the back of that guesthouse. I'll take this side." He pointed toward the garage. "Stick to the perimeter and stay hidden, but watch yourself. There are too many hiding places around here. I'll meet you at the guest house and we'll check it together."

Novak nodded. "You up for this?" she whispered.

"Stop worrying about me. Worry about yourself first. And remember. Watch who you fire at. Don't kill my family."

Novak frowned. "But Proteus is dead."

"I know."

She stilled, and her jaw clenched. "Are you saying there's more than one Proteus?"

"I don't know what I'm saying, but it's best to be prepared."

"How am I supposed to know who is who?"

Garret wondered the same. "Do what I do. Trust your gut."

Novak held his gaze with a furrowed brow. "See you at the guest house."

"See you."

Novak headed one way, and pulling out his gun, Garret headed the other.

• • • • • • • • •

Trick walked up and down the greenbelt along the street that backed up to the rear fence line of the home. He had to consider whether Gail could have left the property and vanished. If she had, then Lindsey and her family would never be safe. He also had to wonder where the real Ben was. Had he been taken out of the back gate and driven off? Could Mason have been taken too? Trick looked for any signs of a struggle or blood, but saw nothing alarming.

Thinking of Lindsey and Mason, he returned to the gate, slipped through it, and closed it behind him. He studied the backyard, but it remained eerily quiet. To his left was the garage and to his right was the guest house. The main house showed no activity and Trick worried about Lindsey. Was she okay? Was she still battling Proteus? He thought of Mason, too. The logical conclusion was Gail had overpowered him, and he was in the guesthouse.

Debating his options, he decided to check the guesthouse first because it was closer and Lindsey was well equipped to take care of herself, although his heart urged him to rush inside the home to be sure she was okay. Staying aware, he walked toward the guest house and stealthily walked up the front steps. He tried the door, but it was locked, and the drawn blinds blocked his view through the windows. He almost busted out a window with his hammer, but decided to go around to the back first to see if there was another entry or any sign of Ben or Mason.

Cautious, he stepped off the porch, but a rustle made him stop. It sounded like it came from the garden. He faced it and held still, listening.

The rustle came again, and clutching the hammer, Trick took a step toward the garden trail when Mason, his torso covered in blood, suddenly stepped out of it.

Shocked, Trick froze.

Clutching his stomach with bloody hands, Mason stumbled to the ground. "Trick," he said. "Help." Blood seeped through his fingers and dripped onto the grass. "Please."

Horror-stricken, Trick broke free from his frozen state. "Red." He ran over. "Oh, my god."

Mason fell to his side and rolled onto his back.

Trick dropped beside him. "Red?" He let go of his hammer. "What happened?" He put his hands over Mason's wound.

Mason moaned and gripped Trick's hands. "Help me."

Trick eyed his partner's injury. "Let me see. How bad is it?" He tried to check the wound, but Mason wouldn't let him go.

Mason groaned again. "It's bad."

"Who did this?" asked Trick, frantic to help his friend.

Mason moaned. "Ben. Ben did it."

Trick stared in shock at the blood Mason was losing. "You need a hospital."

"No," said Mason, his face clenched and pale. "It's too late for me."

Trick shook his head in disbelief. He couldn't fathom losing his partner and best friend. "You are not going to die. Do you hear me? You can't."

"Trick..." Mason let go of Trick and uncurled in the dirt. His eyes opened and closed. "There's nothing you can do."

Terrified, Trick leaned over his friend. "You can't die, Red." He pressed his hands against Mason's wound. "Please don't die."

Gasping, Mason's hands fell to his sides. "You sure you don't want me to die?"

Trick, oblivious to anything happening around him, frowned. "What kind of stupid question is that?" Obviously, Mason wasn't thinking clearly. "No. I don't want you to die."

Moaning, Mason laid his head back and slid his hand behind him.

"We've got to get you to a hospital," said Trick, wondering how to call nine-one-one since he didn't have a phone.

"Trick!" Trick heard a familiar voice shout his name and, confused, he turned to see Mason, supporting Ben, appear around the side of the guest house.

Mason stopped when his gaze flicked to the man lying on the ground, and his eyes widened. "Trick," he said. "No. That's not—"

"Trick!" Lindsey screamed and shot out of the garden. Seeing Trick and Mason, her eyes rounded. "No!"

Clarity pierced Trick's confusion, and he realized he'd been duped. The injured man wasn't Mason.

Time seemed to still as the injured Mason pulled a knife from behind him and raised up. Defenseless against a deadly assassin, Trick reached for his hammer. Time slowed further when he realized he wouldn't be fast enough. Gail would slice him in two before he could bring the hammer down or even try to get away.

Bracing for the impact, Trick shut his eyes, hating that he'd failed. Lindsey and his best friend would have to witness his stupidity and death and would forever be haunted by it. In his mind, he apologized, and preparing himself, he opened his eyes. It shocked him to see that it was no longer Mason in front of him, but Lindsey.

Her midsection soaked with blood and holding the knife, she grinned at him. "Sorry, Texas."

Trick grabbed the hammer as the knife arced toward his gut. He braced for the impact, but jumped when two gunshots rang out instead.

The Lindsey from the garden screamed again, and the fake Lindsey jolted. Her expression went flat, her arm dropped, and the knife fell from her grasp. Two spots on her chest filled with blood and her head fell back with a thud. Her body went still, and the life went out of her eyes.

Stunned, Trick fell back and turned to see a tall man with a bruised face standing at the side of the garage. It was Garret. Covered in blood, he was aiming a gun.

Novak ran out from the side of the guest house and over to Trick. "Are you Trick?" She held her gun on him, but her hand shook.

Lindsey raced over. "Don't shoot."

Trick raised his hands. "It's me, Novak."

"It's him," said Mason.

Gripping his stomach, which appeared to have duct tape wrapped around it, Garret somehow managed to walk closer. "It's okay, Novak."

Dead Lindsey slowly morphed into Gail. "That's Gail," said Lindsey, pointing. "She's Proteus' accomplice."

"Holy hell," said Novak. "What is happening here?"

"Put your gun down, Novak," said Garret.

Staring at Gail's body, Novak slowly lowered her weapon.

"Dad?" asked Lindsey, holding her shoulder. "Are you okay?"

Mason walked Ben over and sat him on a bench in front of the guesthouse.

"I'm okay," said Ben. "Just a little weak, but getting stronger."

Garret collapsed to his knees. "Garret," yelled Novak, who ran over to him.

"I'm okay," said Garret, clutching his belly.

Lindsey ran to Garret's side. "I can't believe you're here. How are you walking?" She checked his injury. "You should be at the hospital."

"He wouldn't let me take him," said Novak, helping Garret stand.

"It's a good thing he isn't at the hospital." Trick, still a little shaken, slowly got to his feet. "You saved my life, Garret."

Holding on to Novak, Garret looked at Trick. "You should have left Vegas when I told you to," he said with a scowl.

"Red will tell you I'm lousy at taking advice." Trick went over to Garret's other side. He took what he realized was his gun from Garret, slid it into the back of his jeans, and helped Novak bring him over to the bench where Ben was sitting with Mason. He sat Garret down and eyed Mason. "You okay, Red?"

Mason rubbed his neck. "I'll live." He paused. "How are you?"

"Pretty good for a man who almost died," said Trick. "That was a little too close of a call."

"Too close for my taste," said Mason.

"Well, seeing you on the verge of death wasn't great either." Trick shivered at the memory.

"You should have known that wasn't me," said Mason. "I'm way better looking."

Trick smiled, appreciating the much-needed light-hearted moment.

"Lindsey," said Ben. "You're hurt, too."

Trick straightened and turned to see Lindsey. Blood ran down her arm and was all over her shirt. There were leaves in her messy hair, her face was pale, and she stared at him with wide eyes. His relief that she was alive raced through him, and he took a step toward her. "You all right? Where's Proteus?"

"Dead," said Garret. "In the house."

Lindsey's weariness and exhaustion were evident. All Trick wanted to do was take her in his arms when she suddenly ran toward him. He met her halfway, and she wrapped herself around him. She buried her face in his neck, and he felt her trembling against him. "Are you sure you're okay?" he said into her hair. He pulled her as close to him as he could.

"I thought...I thought..." Her shoulders shook, and she cried into his shirt.

"I'm here," he said, imagining what she'd felt when she'd seen him with Gail. "I'm all right." He held her while her tears fell. "It's all over." The joy of holding her and knowing she was safe brought tears to his own eyes.

They clutched each other, and her tears slowed. When she sucked in a breath, he pulled back and saw his clothes stained with her blood. His fear returned. "Hell. Where did he get you?"

Lindsey, her eyes red, held her arm. "Most of it's Proteus' blood."

"But not all of it?" he asked.

She shook her head and slumped against him. "He got my shoulder."

"Whoa. Hold on to me." Trick got his arm under her knees and lifted her. "We'll get you checked out." Settling against him, she rested her head in the hollow of his neck.

Mason stood. "Let's get everyone checked out."

"I'll call nine-one-one," said Novak, pulling out her phone.

Ben straightened. "No. You won't." His voice sounded stronger.

"What do you mean?" asked Novak. "You've got two dead people here, plus several injured ones."

Ben slowly stood with Mason's help. "I realize that," said Ben, "but this isn't a job for law enforcement."

Novak dropped her jaw. "I am law enforcement."

Ben stared in surprise.

"This is Officer Samantha Novak, Ben," said Trick. "A rookie with the LVPD."

Ben lifted an eyebrow. "Is that so?"

"It's so, Dad," said Garret. "But for a rookie, she handles herself well." He eyed Novak. "Better than I expected."

Ben looked Novak over. "That may come in handy."

Novak dropped her jaw. "Would someone please tell me what the hell is going on here?"

Ben, with Mason's help, stabilized himself. He let go of Mason and walked over to Novak. "I know this is a lot to take in, Officer, but I'll tell you what I can. My name is Ben, and this is my son, Garret and my daughter, Lindsey." He gestured toward Lindsey. "We are members of the cryptid unit, or what we call the CU. We hunt cryptids. And you just helped us hunt down two of the most dangerous ones. Shapeshifting assassins who planned to kill my entire family."

Novak stared at him with wide eyes. "Do you expect me to believe that?"

"It's all true," said Garret. "You saw it with your own eyes."

Novak shook her head. "But I...I...certainly there's another explanation."

"There's isn't," said Mason.

"Ben's telling the truth, Novak," added Trick.

"So, Officer Novak," said Ben, "if you call in the cavalry and try to explain all of this to them, your peers will look at you like you're crazy. If you let me handle it, I'll call in my people, who are more than capable of cleaning up this mess, and you can go home like nothing ever happened."

Novak gaped at him. "I can't do that."

"You don't have a choice, Novak," said Garret. "This never happened."

"We can't tell people who we are," said Ben. "For obvious reasons."

"But what about the bodies?" asked Novak.

"We'll take care of it," said Ben. "They need to be studied anyway, for research. To figure out how they do what they do. Especially Gail. Her abilities far exceeded those of Proteus." He eyed Gail's body. "Hopefully, they're the last of their kind, but in case they're not, we have to learn how to handle them."

"But the gunshots," said Novak. "What if someone heard and called the police?"

"If that happens, I'll meet them at the door and handle it," said Ben. "We've dealt with worse."

"But this is Vegas," said Mason. "I doubt anyone's called the cops."

Carrying Lindsey, who was holding on to him, Trick spoke to Novak. "This is the only way, Novak. Unless you want to explain this to your fellow officers."

"But you're all here," she said. "You can back me up."

"Sorry, but no," said Ben. "We can't. We have to protect our identities and our organization."

"But I fired my weapon," said Novak. "I have to account for that." She looked at Garret. "And what about what happened at the warehouse?"

"We can handle all of it," said Ben. He took Novak's phone from her. "You're officially off duty, officer."

Novak's confusion was obvious, but she stopped objecting and rubbed her forehead. "I'm baffled by all of this. I don't know what to think." She lowered her hand. "Did you say the cryptid unit?"

"I can explain more later," said Ben, "but right now I need to call in a medical team to have my kids looked at. Plus, I need to contact Marcy and Trey. Let them know we're okay."

"I'll help Garret," said Mason. "You need to be checked too, Ben." Mason helped Garret to stand.

Novak shook her head. "This whole thing is crazy."

"It's not that crazy." Garret took a step with a gasp. "You'd be a good addition to the team."

"Team?" asked Novak.

"She was good under pressure, Dad," said Garret, who was holding onto Mason with a grimace. "We need a civilian like that." He frowned at Trick. "Like him, only less obnoxious."

Trick rested his chin on Lindsey's head. "Your sister likes me."

"She likes toe socks too," said Garret, taking slow steps with Mason's help. "That should tell you something about her taste."

Lindsey lifted her head. "Shut up, Garret."

Ben smiled. "Seems like we're back." He waved at Novak. "C'mon, Novak. Help me up to the house and let's talk about the future." He put his arm around her, and they walked toward the house.

Mason, supporting Garret, followed them.

Holding Lindsey, Trick walked behind Mason. Lindsey rested her forehead against Trick's neck and curled her fingers into his shirt. "I guess you think this means you and I are a couple?" she whispered.

Smiling, Trick kissed her forehead. "You're damn right it does, honey. Toe socks or not."

She curled in closer and spoke softly. "Good."

His heart full, and grateful, Trick carried her into the house.

Chapter Thirty-Two

Trick ran his lips up the soft skin between Lindsey's breasts, peppering light kisses all the way to her collarbone, where he poked his head out from beneath the sheet that covered them both. She sighed with pleasure and cupped his jaw, guiding his face up to her lips, where she kissed him softly but eagerly.

Thoroughly satisfied, Trick leaned back and admired her features.

"What?" she said.

He traced his fingertip down the side of her cheek. "We've been in this bed for three days and I still can't get enough of you." He stroked his thumb over her jaw. "How is that possible?"

Lindsey smiled, and his heart pounded. "It's a unique gift." She turned toward him and rested her head on the pillow. "You have it too, you know." She ran her hand down his chest. "It's some sort of animal magnetism."

Trick pursed his lips. "Maybe we're cryptids, too. You think your dad would want to study us?"

"I think he's got his hands full right now."

"I suspect he does." Trick thought back on the day of Proteus' and Gail's deaths. After returning to the house, Ben had contacted his people and within an hour, a large white van had pulled up with the logo *Las Vegas Air Conditioning* emblazoned on the side panels. Three men had gotten out and entered the house. One helped Garret and Lindsey into the back of the van, and the other two began the arduous task of removing the bodies and cleaning the house.

Trick and Mason had sat back in astonishment at the work that was being done. Novak seemed shocked as well, but Ben walked her through the process, and, once the bodies were removed and plans were in place to return the house to its previous state, it was obvious Novak was enthralled. Mason guessed she'd be on the team before Ben left town and he'd been correct. Ben had successfully recruited Novak, and she'd accepted a civilian position with the CU. For now, she would remain on the LVPD, but in her new role, she'd work with the unit to keep an eye out for cryptid activity in Las Vegas, which was no small feat, considering the people in Sin City. She could be the eyes and ears the unit needed and could use her position as a law enforcement officer to determine threat levels and assist with apprehension if needed.

Once in the van, which was set up to provide medical treatment, Lindsey received several stitches in her arm. Garret had been examined and transported to another facility, but had since been released and was already home with Ben. Mason had returned to San Diego the day after the attacks to allay Mikey's fears. After receiving her stitches, Lindsey had called Mikey to apologize for hanging up on her and scaring her to death.

Lindsey had planned to return with her father, but he'd told her no. It had been clear to everyone that Trick and Lindsey were together, and Ben told her to stay in Vegas to recuperate, enjoy her new freedom, and spend some time with Trick.

Neither she nor Trick had argued. As soon as they were free, they'd headed straight to the mobile home, stopping only for some basic groceries and to speak to Danny to extend their stay. They'd barely made it through the door before their desire took over. Kissing and touching, they'd stripped down, and eager for each other, they'd fallen into the bed. They hadn't left it since, other than for food or bathroom breaks.

Looking into Lindsey's eyes, Trick marveled at his good fortune. "How's your arm?" he touched her bandage. "Still hurt?"

"A little. Not bad, though."

"Good." He paused. "How'd you sleep last night?" he asked her. "Any more bad dreams?"

"No," she said. "But considering I didn't sleep much, that might have been a factor."

Recalling their amorous night, his body warmed. "You'll tell me if you do?"

She nodded. "I will." She stretched. "But to be honest, I haven't felt this good in a long time, so maybe my dreams are done."

Trick hoped that was true. "That would be great, but trauma has a way of sneaking up on you."

She stilled. "I know. What happened with Proteus will never go away. I think about it every day, but now that he's gone and, well, me and my family are talking and healing, I think I'm better equipped to handle it." She touched the tip of his jaw. "And I have you."

He took her hand. "You do. And you can talk to me about anything, no matter how dark it may seem." He kissed her palm.

"Same goes for you."

"As long as we don't have to face any more shapeshifters, animal or human, I'm good."

She interlaced her fingers with his. "I think we're done for a while."

He relaxed against the pillow. "Good."

"Let's just hope we don't have to confront the Mogollon Monster or Batsquatch. They're way worse."

Trick raised his head. "The what and who?"

Lindsey chuckled. "I'm kidding."

"God." Trick sighed and lowered his head. "I thought you were serious."

"I am, but not about the danger part. They're both actually quite docile, unless you piss them off."

Trick grunted. "Aren't there any pleasant cryptids?"

"Most of them are, actually. They just prefer to keep to themselves, and we help with that. It's the nasty ones that take most of our time and attention."

"Your work seems similar to mine. Most of it is mundane."

"Until it isn't."

Trick brushed back a lock of her hair. "Yeah. Until it isn't." He smiled and shifted closer to her. "I guess we're still planning on going home tomorrow?"

Lindsey sighed. "We should. You've missed plenty of work and so have I. We need to rejoin the world."

"Does that mean putting our clothes on?"

She pouted. "I hate the thought, but I'm sure Mason, Mikey, and your clients would appreciate it. So would my dad."

"I was afraid you were going to say that." Trick rolled onto his back. "I think Danny's going to miss us, though."

Lindsey snuggled up to him and he put his arm around her. "The only thing Danny's going to miss is the rent we're paying him."

"You'd think, but he didn't seem too thrilled when we rented the room for an extra few days."

"Maybe he'd rented it to someone else."

Trick scoffed. "I don't think this place owns a *No Rooms Available* sign."

Lindsey rested her head on Trick's chest and traced a fingertip through his chest hair. "Maybe he doesn't like tenants. It means more work."

"It's an odd way to run a business. He didn't even act annoyed when I told him you and I weren't siblings and there was no inheritance from the fake father I made up."

"Maybe we should tell Novak." She rested her chin on Trick's shoulder. "She can monitor him. Report back any suspicious activity."

Trick chuckled. "I still can't believe she's helping the CU. I never saw that coming."

"Doesn't surprise me at all," said Lindsey. "Who wouldn't want to hunt cryptids?"

"And Garret even supported her involvement. I thought he was anti-civilian."

"He is, but that's because of you, and has more to do with him protecting me."

"I guess that makes sense. It's still surprising he took to Novak so fast."

"You don't see it, Mr. Ranger?" Lindsey moved her foot against Trick's. "He likes her."

Trick widened his eyes. "You're serious? He's attracted to her?"

"What's not to like? She's beautiful, calm in a crisis, intelligent, brave. Novak's just like me." She grinned and ran her toes over the arch of Trick's foot.

Chills ran through Trick at her touch. He trailed his fingers over her soft skin, wondering if there was an inch of her body that he hadn't already touched that he could explore. "You do have some redeeming qualities." He rolled to face her. "You are exquisite." He brought his face close to hers. "Extremely smart, and wicked brave."

She frowned. "What about calm?"

"In a crisis, yes, but in bed..." He leaned in and kissed her. "You're not calm at all."

She kissed him back, and their passion escalated. "Yet another redeeming quality."

Trick cupped her face and his heart racing, he wished they'd never have to leave their bed. "Definitely." He slanted his lips over hers, kissing her hungrily.

Her hand trailed over his chest, and she moved it under the sheet and slid it lower. Feeling her touch, he gasped into her mouth.

Smiling seductively while she drove him crazy with her fingers, she whispered against his lips. "Then let's not waste any more of our remaining trailer time."

Loving her ability to drive him wild, he groaned with need. "Oh, God, honey. Let's not." He slid his other hand down to her buttock. Squeezing it, he could barely breathe as he pulled her close and silenced her moans with a fiery kiss.

· · • • · • • · ·

The next day, Trick reluctantly tossed his duffel bag and Lindsey's backpack in the trunk of her rental car and closed it. "You ready, honey?"

Lindsey closed the trailer door and locked it. "I am." She stepped off the porch and stared back at the mobile home. "Who knew a place like this could hold so many unforgettable memories?" She sighed. "When I checked in, I certainly didn't expect this."

He came up behind her and put his arms around her. "Fate has a way of surprising you." He kissed her neck.

She held his hands. "It certainly does." She giggled when he kissed her behind her ear. "Don't start, Texas. We have to hit the road."

Trick nipped her ear. "Any rest stops along the way?"

She turned in his arms. "Are you suggesting we have sex at a rest stop?"

He widened his eyes. "What? Is that wrong?"

Lindsey narrowed her eyes. "I'm afraid to ask." She pulled away. "Let's go check out with Danny before we end up back in the trailer."

Trick followed her as she headed to the office. "Would that be so bad?" He watched her walk and considered picking her up and carrying her back to bed.

She glanced back at him with a grin. "Don't tempt me."

Trick pulled on his shirt. "I'm still trying to get used to these clothes."

She rolled her eyes at him and took his hand. They walked down the narrow road and headed up the steps to the trailer that was Danny's office. "C'mon, handsome. Let's cut the cord."

Trick held the door open for her. "Tough love sucks."

Lindsey entered Danny's trailer, walked up to the desk, and rang the bell.

Trick looked around the small room. The TV was off, and Danny was absent, but Trick could smell the lingering cigarette smoke. "What if he's not here?"

Lindsey rang the bell again. "I'm sure he is."

Trick leaned over and whispered in her ear. "If he's not, then we can…" he told her what he'd do to her if got her back into bed.

Lindsey blushed.

"I'm here." Danny walked through a door leading to the back.

Lindsey jumped, and Trick straightened and sighed. "Too bad."

Danny's face fell. "Huh?"

"Nothing," said Lindsey. "We need to check out and pay, Danny."

Danny nodded. "Oh, yeah. Okay." He went around the counter and opened his laptop. "You two have a nice stay?"

"Very," said Trick.

"It was great," said Lindsey, still blushing.

Danny typed fast. "It'll just be a sec." He cursed and retyped something.

Trick noticed his hands were shaking. "You okay?" asked Trick. "You seem nervous."

Danny's eyes rounded, and he chuckled. "I do? Sorry. It's nothing. My mom's visiting. It always throws me." He hit a button, and the printer whirred to life. "I used the card on file. Is that okay?" he asked Lindsey.

Lindsey nodded. "That's fine. Thanks."

Trick noticed the sheen of sweat on Danny's forehead. "Mom's will do that to you. I have some experience of my own."

Danny yanked the paper from the printer and set it on the counter. "Just sign here."

Lindsey signed and handed the paper to Danny. He pulled off a receipt and handed it to her. "Thanks for coming."

"Thanks, Danny," said Lindsey. "Nice meeting you." She turned to leave.

"Take care, Danny," said Trick. "Good luck with your mom."

"Wait," said Danny.

Lindsey and Trick stopped.

"I forgot." Danny leaned over and picked up something from under the counter.

"What is it?" asked Lindsey.

Danny set two plastic bags on the counter, each filled with what looked like salt. "These are for you. For...for your stay."

Trick eyed the bags. "What's that?" He picked one up and studied it.

"It's bath salt," said Danny. "My mom makes spa stuff and sells it on the internet."

Trick saw a label on the other side of the bag. It said *Momma's Spa* and had a website listed beneath it. "You give it away? That's odd."

Lindsey frowned at him and picked up the other bag. "That's actually very nice. Thanks, Danny."

Danny shifted on his feet. "Mom, um, insists on giving her salt to guests when they leave." He waved his hand. "So, there you go."

"That makes more sense," said Trick, holding his bag. "Don't make Mom mad, right?"

Danny nodded. "Right. You guys have a nice day." He walked around the counter and disappeared into the back room.

Lindsey shook her head. "He is a little odd, isn't he?"

Trick wondered what Danny's hurry was. "A bit. Let's go."

They left the office and returned to the car. Lindsey held out her bag to Trick. "Here. You take it. I'm not much of a bath person."

"And I am?" asked Trick.

"Give it to Mikey. I bet she'd like it."

Trick considered that. "Good idea. I'll give mine to Mason."

"Mason likes baths?"

"He's in touch with his feminine side. He once confided in me that he likes a good bubble bath with a candle."

Lindsey chuckled. "A nice bubble bath and candle wouldn't hurt you either."

Trick grinned. "Care to join me?"

She grinned back at him. "After these last few days, I think you know I like my showers."

Trick groaned, recalling their shower together that morning. "I am very aware."

She leaned up and kissed him. "C'mon, handsome. We go now and we might have time to detour at a rest stop." She wiggled her eyebrows.

A shiver of anticipation shot through him. "Don't tease me."

Smiling, Lindsey got in the driver's seat. "I'll take the first leg."

· · • • • • • · ·

Inside the office, Danny watched Lindsey drive the car out of the trailer's lot and head down the street. Relieved they were gone, he took a deep breath and relaxed. Still nervous though, he walked behind the counter, grabbed a shot glass, poured himself a shot of bourbon, and tossed it back. His nerves a little calmer, he went to the couch and flipped on the TV. He found a baseball game and, telling himself he'd done nothing wrong, he settled in, prepared to spend the rest of the afternoon watching sports.

His phone buzzed, and he jumped. His anxiety returning, he pulled out his phone and read the text message.

Is it done? They have the bags?

His hands shaking, he typed back.

It's done. They have them.

His phone buzzed with a response.

Any problems?

Danny typed back.

No problems. They just left.

Another buzz.

Good.

The texts stopped and Danny set his phone down, praying that was all he'd have to do with the woman who'd come in four days earlier. At first glance, she'd looked much like his usual patrons—broke and unkempt with long, frizzy hair and dirty clothes. He'd thought little of it until she'd started asking about his tenants in trailer #22. He'd been reluctant to discuss them, but her tone and threats convinced him she meant business. Scared, he'd told her when they'd arrived and planned to check out. She'd left the office, returned with the two bags of salt and asked him to give them to Lindsey and Trick when they departed. She'd given him a card too, with a number on it but no name. Danny had conveyed his reluctance, but she'd smiled, and told him if he wanted his mother to live to the end of the week, he'd do as requested. The woman then pulled out a photo of his mother doing yard work in her garden, a place where Danny had spent many hours weeding.

Frightened, Danny didn't argue and agreed. When Lindsey and Trick had extended their stay, he didn't know whether to call the number or ignore it, but he'd received a text that day requesting an update, and he'd replied with their new departure date. He'd been sweating it ever since. But now that Lindsey and Trick were gone, he tried not to overthink it. It was just two bags of bath salt. How bad could they be?

Convincing himself the threat was over, and he and his mom were safe, he tossed his phone on the couch and resumed watching the game. As he relaxed, he heard a hissing sound. Frowning, he sat up and listened. The sound became louder, and smelling gas, he stood. Alarmed, he started to investigate when there was an ear-splitting boom, and, as his last baseball game played on the TV, Danny was hurled into the air when his trailer exploded.

What's Next?

As I plan what's next for the Redstones, get ready for *Vendetta*, the next book in the crossover series with the Redstones, *Detectives Daniels and Remalla*. After the events of *Illusions*, Daniels and Rem battle a secret society whose motives are unclear, but their grudge against the detectives isn't. When an ally is targeted, an assassin comes out into the open, and the society's dangerous roots are revealed, Daniels and Rem will have to fight to find the truth before it tears them apart. Enjoy an excerpt below.

Order *Illusions* on Amazon.

Want more from J. T. Bishop?

Subscribe to J.T. Bishop's newsletter at jtbishopauthor.com to get two Daniels and Remalla prequel novellas, *The Girl and the Gunshot and The Magic of Murder,* for free, in addition to extra content, plus opportunities for more free books.

Follow J.T. on Amazon to be notified when new books are released.

I hope you will take a moment to leave a review for *Lost Love.* Your opinion is always appreciated.

New to Detectives Daniels and Remalla?

Check out these books.

The Family or Foe Saga with Detectives Daniels and Remalla - this four-book series introduces Detectives Daniels and Remalla. A killer with powerful abilities is out for revenge against those he believes wronged him. Can he be caught before he kills again?

Detectives Daniels and Remalla—Our detectives get their own series. Their search for murderers will lead them down unexpected roads filled with odd encounters, supernatural experiences, and deadly consequences. And when evil has the upper hand, their only hope is to rely on each other.

Murder Unveiled, a prequel to *Haunted River*, book one in the series, is a great place to start.

New to the Redstones?

Then get started with *Lost Souls*, book one in the series, and see how it all got started.

Note: Because the Daniels and Remalla books and The Redstone Chronicles are a spinoff and crossover series, they share an overarching story, and the characters from each are mentioned or appear in all the books, so reading both is ideal. The books published alternate between both series. A list of books in chronological order follows below and is available at jtbishopauthor.com.

Do you like stories with light sci-fi, urban fantasy and paranormal romance?

Then check out Bishop's first series, *The Red-Line Trilogy*. One woman holds the key to unlocking a secret that will ensure the existence of a secret community. One man, assigned to protect her, will risk everything to keep her alive, but when he falls for her, will their destiny be enough to save them both?

And the Red-Line series continues with the sister series to the trilogy, *The Fletcher Family Saga*. A distant but deadly threat risks the lives of three unique siblings, but life can't stop because of who they are. They'll endure love, loss and a dangerous enemy determined to destroy them.

Either the trilogy or sister series can be read first. Take your pick. Boxed sets are available, too!

A Note From J. T.

After I finished *Lost Time*, I was ready to address the simmering attraction between Trick and Lindsey. They were a romance on the brink, and I just needed the right setting and characters to bring it to life. Enter Las Vegas, a deadly cryptid assassin, and Lindsey's heartbreaking back story. It was the perfect way to bring Trick in to help and force Lindsey to confront her past.

I also wanted to see more of Lindsey's family. You get to learn about Garret and Ben and the complicated relationships they share with Lindsey. Lindsey has always been fiercely independent and reluctant to talk about herself and her past, and she's not one to be vulnerable, especially with Trick. Based on what we now know about her, we can see why she was hesitant to form any deep attachment to anyone outside of her family, and she even held them at arm's length.

If you're familiar with my work, you know I love to dive deep into the emotional side of things. My characters eventually must deal with their heartbreak, and they rely on the deep bonds of friendship and love to do it. Lindsey and Trick are no exception. We saw a lot of that with Trick in *Lost Time* as he dealt with his mother, and now we can see him offer the same understanding to Lindsey. It's so delicious to convey these scenes. I loved watching them come together as a couple through a dangerous situation. They are a love story that will continue for a while. (As long as the bags of bath salt Danny gave to them don't put a kink in things. We'll see where that leads.)

And since this is a Redstone book, I had to include Mason. I liked the idea of having him show up out of nowhere with a message for Lindsey from her mother. Plus, he provided another character for Proteus and Gail to potentially morph into, which was helpful for the story line. He's also fun to write, plus the Mason/Trick bond is hard to pass up. Like Daniels and Remalla, they're good together. I gave Mikey some time off in this one, but she played a prominent role in *Illusions* and she'll show up in *Vendetta*, so there's more to come from her.

Novak was a great character, too. I wanted to add a civilian into the mix, and by the end of the book, I realized she'd be a perfect addition to the CU and would be a logical love interest for Garret. He needs a good woman in his life, don't you think?

Not sure where I'll take the CU from here. They'll pop up in future *Redstone Chronicle* stories, I'm sure. First, I have to figure out what happens next for the Redstones and the woman who wanted Trick and Lindsey to take the bath salt. Who is she? What does she want and who is her target? Those are all mysteries to solve in the next book. I hope you'll continue to join me on the journey to find out the answers.

Now that *Lost Love* is complete, I'd love to hear your feedback. Reviews are a huge plus and big help for an author and potential readers. I would love it if you could please take a couple of minutes to leave a quick review for *Lost Love*. And if you'd like, please leave a few comments, too.

As always, thank you for your time and readership. It is deeply valued and appreciated.

Now, on to the next book!

Books in Chronological Order

In case you like to read in order...

Prelude to The Shift, a short story (subscribers only)
Red-Line: The Shift
Red-Line: Mirrors
Red-Line: Trust Destiny
Curse Breaker
High Child
Spark
Forged Lines
**

The Girl and the Gunshot, a novella (subscribers only)
A Hamburger Christmas, a novella
The Magic of Murder, a novella (subscribers only)
First Cut
Second Slice
Third Blow
Fourth Strike
Murder Unveiled
Haunted River
Of Breath and Blood
Lost Souls
Of Body and Bone

Lost Dreams
Of Mind and Madness
Lost Chances
Of Power and Pain
Lost Hope
Of Love and Loss
Lost Lives
Dominion
Lost Time
Illusions
Lost Love
Vendetta

About the Author

A ward-winning author, J.T. Bishop, is a writer of mystery thrillers with a paranormal edge. Growing up, she read Stephen King, Mary Higgins Clark, and Dean Koontz, devoured every episode of the X-files and watched plenty of TV shows with great partnerships that leave you wanting more. She loves tangled relationships, unexpected twists and turns, heart-stopping love stories and the complications that come with all the above. Throw in a little supernatural fun and she's hooked. Her evil plan is to hook you, too.

She's the author of The Red-Line Trilogy and its sister series, The Fletcher Family Saga, which features touches of urban fantasy, light sci-fi, and paranormal romance. She's also happily writing mystery thrillers featuring two charismatic detectives who may occasionally encounter a supernatural villain or two, and a crossover series which follows the exploits of a gifted, but troubled, paranormal P.I. and his spunky sister.

All the above keeps her busy, but in her spare time, she loves good movies, tasty food, an unfortunate sugar addiction, and traveling.

Acknowledgements

Another book is complete, and again, I have many to thank. This doesn't happen alone, and I am indebted to family and friends for their help, support, and encouragement. It is truly appreciated.

I also want to thank my Beta and ARC teams, and everyone who helps proof my books. You guys keep me on my toes, ensure I write a great story, catch plenty of typos, and help with early reviews. Thank you for being honest and offering your guidance.

I love writing about the bonds between loving family, deep friendships, and the ties that hold them together. Plus, my fascination with the unknown thrown into the mix makes for a satisfying story and hopefully, adds a little more thrill for my readers. Thank you to those who continue to come back for more. Hearing from you and knowing that you're enjoying my books makes all the hard work worthwhile. None of this would matter without your tremendous support. If I can help you escape from this crazy world for a short period each day, then I've done my job.

Here's to more stories, more fun, and more time for yourself. If you can have a little of that each day, you're on the right track.

Enjoy an Excerpt from Vendetta, Book Nine in Detectives Daniels and Remalla

Jerry Lee tried not to stare. The pretty redhead standing beside the older gentleman who was checking in to the hotel ran her hand down the man's chest to his abdomen and lower, but the high counter prevented Jerry from seeing how much lower. The man sucked in a breath, though, and the pen in his hand jerked as he signed the paper Donald, Jerry's boss at the front desk, had given him. The woman grinned, chewed some gum, made eye contact with Jerry Lee, and winked at him.

Jerry Lee blushed and looked away. He'd just returned to the front after delivering a guest's bags to a room and hoped the man checking in with the sexy redhead also had bags Jerry could deliver. The redhead was the best-looking woman to enter the lobby all day, and probably all week.

Curious, Jerry glanced over Donald's shoulder and saw the man's name was Reginald Durning. He didn't recognize him, but it looked like Reginald was only staying the night, and glancing at the redhead again, Jerry Lee could assume why. He spied a wedding ring on Reginald's finger but not one on the redhead's. Jerry Lee had worked at the hotel long enough not to be surprised. It happened frequently.

Donald took the signed form. "Thank you, Mr. Durning. Do you have any bags you need help with?" He gestured toward Jerry Lee. "Jerry here can help you with them."

Hopeful, Jerry Lee waited. He guessed Mr. Durning might be a good tipper, and ogling the redhead a bit more would be an added bonus.

Reginald smiled at the redhead. "No bags, Donald. Thank you."

Jerry Lee deflated.

Reginald put his arm around the redhead. "C'mon, beautiful."

The redhead giggled and put her arm around his waist. "I can't wait to get you into bed."

Jerry Lee widened his eyes, and Donald glared at him. "Why don't you go to the kitchen, Jerry Lee?" asked Donald. "See if room service needs any help."

Jerry Lee sighed. It was definitely one of those nights. Check-ins had been light, and Jerry had struggled to stay busy. He still preferred working at the front desk, although room service wasn't bad. He just didn't like Marty, the man who ran the kitchen. He was short-tempered, stressed, and hard to please. Once he'd found out who Jerry Lee was related to, Marty had called him "Little Mobster" ever since. Jerry Lee hated the name, but didn't dare tell Marty. "Sure thing, Donald."

Reginald stopped on his way to the elevator and looked over his shoulder while the redhead clung to him. "Room service," he said. "That's a great idea." He smiled at Jerry. "How about you bring some champagne to our room, kid?"

Jerry eyed the redhead, who still clung to Reginald. "That's a great idea, baby." She spoke to Jerry Lee. "Something expensive."

"The nicest bottle you got," said Reginald. "Room 302. Charge the card on file."

"Of course, Mr. Durning," said Donald. "Jerry Lee will bring it up right away, sir."

Reginald pulled the redhead closer, and she giggled again and glanced back at Jerry. "Thank you, Jerry Lee." She narrowed her eyes and almost cooed. "See you soon." They headed to the elevators and Reginald hit the "Up" button.

Donald smacked Jerry Lee's shoulder and whispered. "Would you stop drooling? You're embarrassing yourself."

The elevator dinged and opened. Reginald and the redhead stepped on and disappeared when the doors closed.

Jerry Lee closed his mouth, which had been hanging open. "Man, she's pretty. Did you see that outfit she was wearing?" He couldn't stop thinking about the woman's short skirt, which had revealed her long shapely legs, and her snug short top, which had exposed plenty of cleavage and her toned midriff. He didn't care much for all the heavy makeup she wore and the ostentatious jewelry. He guessed she'd be much prettier without it.

"What our guests wear is none of your business." Donald went back to the computer. "But yes. I saw. It was hard to miss." He typed something. "I've requested the order. Now go get the champagne. And don't act stupid when you deliver it." He rolled his eyes. "Marty won't be happy if you look foolish."

"How's Marty going to know?" asked Jerry. "He doesn't have eyes and ears everywhere."

Donald arched an eyebrow at him. "How do you think Courtney got fired?"

Jerry Lee recalled Courtney Givens getting the boot after flirting when she delivered a steak dinner to a celebrity from a reality show the previous week. "Seriously?" asked Jerry. "That was Marty?"

"That was Marty, so behave yourself. Now go."

Jerry nodded, turned and headed toward the kitchen, wondering how Marty could have known about Courtney. Jerry could only guess that the celebrity had complained. Courtney had been forward with the staff and apparently the guests, too.

Walking down the hall, Jerry Lee thought of the redhead and wondered if he'd ever check in to a nice hotel with a sexy woman on his arm. At the rate he was going, it wouldn't be soon. Although if his grandfather had any say in it, Jerry would have gorgeous women on his arm day and night. But his mother had insisted that Jerry limit his time with his grandfather and with good reason. His grandfather was Sammy Caruso, the well-known senator from Illinois, whose powerful connections had almost gotten him into the White House. When one of those connections turned out to be the mob, and one of Sam Caruso's opponents had been shot at, the presidency had slipped away, but it didn't make Sam Caruso any less powerful.

Jerry Lee barely knew his dad, but he'd been a big Jerry Lee Lewis fan. After his mom had given birth, his dad hadn't stayed long, and his mom had moved back to Chicago. Jerry Lee had been raised among the influential men who'd sworn loyalty to his grandfather, and the women who'd raised the children and kept the homes of those men. His mother, who'd never wanted Jerry Lee to join the ranks of their political family, had done her best to shield Jerry Lee from the activities surrounding his grandfather, but Jerry Lee had seen some things, and had grown up fast. No matter how much his mother had tried to protect him, his grandfather wanted the opposite, until his grandfather had been indicted for racketeering and tax evasion two years earlier. By then, Jerry Lee was graduating from high school, and his mother had endured enough. She packed her and Jerry Lee's bags, and they'd moved to San Diego.

The transition had been difficult at first, but Jerry had enrolled at a community college and his mother had found a good job that paid the bills and a decent boyfriend that treated Jerry well. Jerry made friends and had come to love the California lifestyle. His mother liked the change, too, and they'd settled into their new life, although his grandfather frequently requested they come home, but with the trial looming, the unrelenting press coverage, and his political future in limbo, his mom refused until her father's issues were settled.

Jerry Lee entered the hotel kitchen and saw a nice champagne bottle in a bucket of ice with two champagne flutes beside it sitting on the counter. Jerry moved them to a tablecloth covered cart and pushed them toward the door.

"Watch yourself, Little Mobster."

Jerry turned to see Marty staring at him from the other side of the kitchen, where Jerry hadn't seen him. His dark curly hair, angular cheekbones and jaw, and beady brown eyes reminded Jerry of some of the men who worked for his grandfather. "Remember what happened to Courtney." He sneered at Jerry and walked away.

Wondering if Marty had ESP or maybe secret spies in the lobby, Jerry pushed the cart through a set of double doors and headed toward the service elevator. He hit the button, and the doors opened. As the doors closed, he hit the button marked "3", and the elevator ascended. After reaching the third floor, he pushed the cart to door 302 and knocked. "Room service," he said.

The door swung open, and Jerry Lee saw Reginald. His tie was undone and his shirt unbuttoned. "Bring it on in." He opened the door wider. Jerry pushed the cart into the room and set the champagne and glasses on the table beside the bed and tried to hide his disappointment when he didn't see the redhead.

He heard a high-pitched voice from the bathroom. "Is that the champagne, baby?"

"It is," said Reginald. "Better get out here and drink some with me."

"On my way," she said with a giggle.

"Thanks, Jerry." Reginald pulled some cash from his wallet, paused, eyed the tray, and glanced at the bathroom door. "You know what? Let's surprise her." He grabbed some more cash. "Go get some strawberries and whipped cream, too." He handed Jerry Lee the money with a grin. "And make it fast."

Jerry took the cash. "Yes, sir." He put the money in his pocket and pushed the empty cart toward the door.

Reginald walked with him. "And if you knock and we don't answer," he raised the side of his lip, "just leave it outside."

Jerry nodded. "Yes, sir."

"See you, kid." He closed the door.

Pulling out the money, Jerry headed toward the elevator with the cart. The elevator was still on the floor, and after entering it, he counted the money and whistled when he realized it was a hundred bucks. Not believing his luck, he returned to the kitchen, told the staff what he needed, what room it was for, and to hurry. The strawberries didn't take long to prepare, but apparently, the whipped cream was. No one could find it until Marty appeared, yelled at the staff, told them they were idiots, and found the whipped cream himself. He spooned some out in a bowl, and without calling Jerry any names, stormed away, still yelling. Glad not to be the object of his hostility, Jerry pushed the cart with the strawberries and cream back to the elevator and rode it up to the third floor. Hoping he might get another hefty tip, he pushed it to the door of 302 and knocked again. "Room service, Mr. Durning."

There was no answer. Guessing Reginald was getting lucky, he pushed the cart against the wall and knocked softly again. "Strawberries and cream are outside, sir, when you're ready."

He started to walk away when a distinct odor made him stop. It smelled like something was burning. He returned to the door and sniffed. The smell was definitely stronger near the door. Uncertain of what to do, he recalled his training. Fire was a major concern at a hotel. Was something on fire inside Reginald's room?

Jerry Lee recalled entering the room earlier with the champagne. A candle had been lit beside the bed. The hotel didn't provide candles, so it must have belonged to Reginald or the redhead. Had the candle caught the bed sheets on fire? The odor grew stronger, and it had an unpleasant tinge to it—something Jerry had not smelled before, but it made him wince. The acrid smell worried him, and he knocked again softly. "Mr. Durning? Is everything okay?"

There was no answer.

His worry grew, and he imagined unpleasant scenarios. What if the room was aflame and Reginald and the redhead had succumbed to the smoke?

Or had Reginald and the redhead accidentally set the fire and now they were trying to put it out without getting into trouble? Jerry eyed the fire alarm on the wall across from him. Should he pull it?

About to knock again, Jerry heard a thump in the room, and knew someone was inside, but no one had answered. Thinking he had better check, he pulled out his key card, which gave him access to the rooms. He suspected Donald would disapprove, but he'd rather be yelled at than have a guest injured or risk a fire. He spoke as he waved the card in front of the reader. "Mr. Durning? I can smell something burning. I'm coming in to be sure you're okay."

The light flicked to green on the reader, and he pushed on the handle. The door opened, and he spoke before looking. "Mr. Durning? Ma'am? It's Jerry." The smell was much stronger, and he almost gagged. Something was definitely wrong. "Sir?" He poked his head inside and dropped his jaw when he saw Reginald, partially clothed, lying on the floor beside the bed. His eyes were partially open and there was a wound in his chest. Blood ran from the wound to the carpet. Looking closer, Jerry saw what looked like a star burned into Reginald's thigh. Shocked into silence, he started to enter when the redhead stepped out of the shadows. She held a weapon in her hand, and she pointed it at Jerry.

"Hi, handsome," she said. Her top was open, and Jerry caught sight of her lacy black bra. Her short skirt was pulled slightly down, exposing a tattoo on her hip. "You really should have left the strawberries outside."

Jerry froze, but the gun in her hand told him she meant to kill him, and thinking of his grandfather, he darted backwards and raced through the door just as he heard a thunk and a piece of the wall near his ear exploded into shards. Shrieking, he raced out of the room, pulled the fire alarm, and as the sirens wailed, he made it to the stairwell and sprinted down the stairs to the garage. Terrified, he passed the parked cars, ran out into the street and sprinted away from the hotel.